Praise for *T[ ]*
Book I:
Book

"...a fantastical journey..."—*The Globe and Mail*

"... an imaginative, action-packed narrative.... Children who love reading will adore this book."—*The United Church Observer*

"... J. C. Mills has crafted an intriguing fantasy... an engaging adventure.... Altogether a delightful read-aloud."—Martha Scott, Canadian Children's Book Centre

"A new, young hero is about to emerge in children's literature, from the imagination of author J. C. Mills."—*Books for Everyone*

"Certain books keep our attention to the point that we have difficulty putting them down. But these are books intended for adults. It comes, therefore, as a surprise when a children's novel has the same don't-put-me-aside impact on an adult reader.... *The Sacred Seal*... is one of those books."—*Lancette*

"Action-packed and fast-paced... this trilogy offers intricate plotting, enjoyably touching inter-species friendships, and a sense that young people have an important role to play in the workings of our world."—*Resource Links*

"This imaginative fantasy novel for middle readers... owes much to Kenneth Grahame and that older, slower-paced tradition of English children's fiction."—*The New Brunswick Reader*

***

Book I: The Sacred Seal:
Shortlisted for the 2003 Red Maple award
Winner of The Canadian Toy Testing Council's
Great Books for Children 2002 award
Chosen as one of the "Best Books for the Fall" by CBC Radio
"This Morning" Children's Book Panel, November 2001

Praise from readers

"Thank you for writing the fantastic novels, *The Goodfellow Chronicles*. Your books are really exciting because they are full of suspense and action. We've been reading your books in our classroom and they really keep us on the edge of our seats.... When is the third Goodfellow book coming out?"—*Class 6B from Gordon Price School, Hamilton, Ontario*

"...my name is Shawna and I am 12 years old and I love your books. I don't think I will ever outgrow them!"—*Shawna, 12*

"I'm loving your new book, *The Sacred Seal*, and I'm going to read your second book, *The Messengers*. I thought you would be a man since you know what boys thought.... Thanks, from the kid who loves your books a lot!!!"—*Dane, 11, Saskatchewan*

"My 8-year-old son received *The Sacred Seal* last year for Christmas.... What a wonderful story! We could hardly wait to see what they would get up to next! Hope to hear from Jolly and the gang again soon...."—*Tanis and Shane Wiersma, British Columbia*

"Me and my friend have read both Goodfellow books and were wondering when the last book will come out. We'll go crazy if it doesn't come out soon."—*Vicki and Michelle*

"I just read your book called *The Goodfellow Chronicles* and loved it! When are the next books coming out, because I really want to read them soon. I wanted to keep reading the book, but unfortunately, I finished it. I did not want it to end."—*Valerie Christine, 13*

"I am typing to tell you how much I love your books! I kept re-reading them over and over again. I love Sam and the whole crew, but I have two favorite characters: India Jaffrey and Edgar Goodfellow!... Thank you for being the best author in the world."—*Shirley Poon, 13*

THE GOODFELLOW

CHRONICLES

THE GOODFELLOW CHRONICLES

BOOK III

THE BOOK OF THE SAGE

J.C. MILLS

KEY PORTER BOOKS

National Library of Canada Cataloguing in Publication Data

Mills, Judith
    The book of the sage / J.C. Mills.

(The Goodfellow chronicles ; bk. 3)
ISBN 1-55263-559-7

I. Title. II. Series: Mills, Judith Goodfellow chronicles ; bk. 3.

PS8576.I571B66 2004   jC813'.54   C2004-901807-8

The publisher gratefully acknowledges the support of the Canada Council for the Arts and the Ontario Arts Council for its publishing program. We acknowledge the support of the Government of Ontario through the Ontario Media Development Corporation's Ontario Book Initiative.

We acknowledge the financial support of the Government of Canada through the Book Publishing Industry Development Program (BPIDP) for our publishing activities.

Key Porter Books Limited
70 The Esplanade
Toronto, Ontario
Canada M5E 1R2

www.keyporter.com

Design: Peter Maher
Electronic formatting: Jean Lightfoot Peters

Printed and bound in Canada

04 05 06 07 08 09 6 5 4 3 2 1

To the loyal band of Goodfellow readers
whose encouragement and enthusiasm has been a
treasure—far greater than I could ever
have imagined.

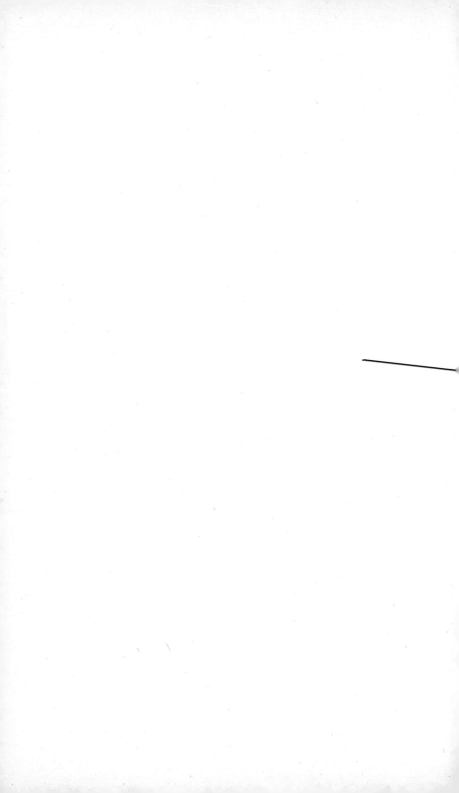

"Dare to be right! Dare to be true!
You have a work that no other can do;
Do it so bravely, so kindly, so well,
Angels will hasten the story to tell."

Anonymous

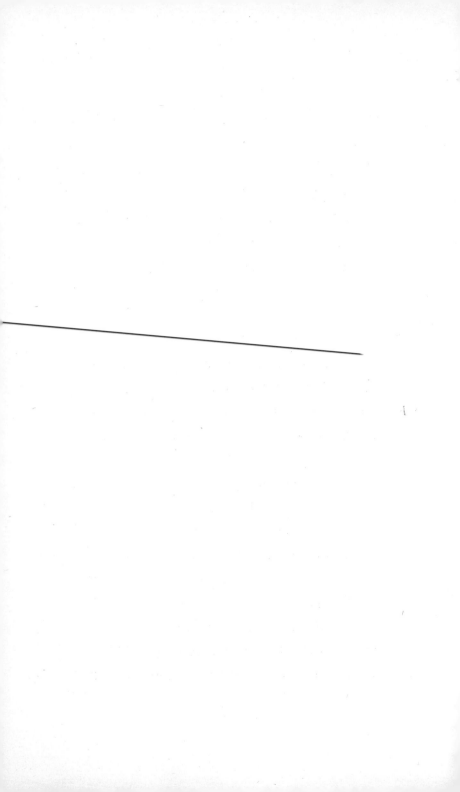

CONTENTS

1

RED SKY AT NIGHT, SAILOR'S DELIGHT

Sam Middleton couldn't have imagined a more beautiful morning. The weather report the previous day had warned of poor conditions, but the wind had picked up at suppertime and blown the stormfront out to sea, leaving a rose-colored sunset sky and an ocean of gentle swells.

Dawn was just beginning to break when Sam cleared the end of the harbor pier. He turned his wooden sailboat into the wind and began to raise the mainsail. He pulled hard on the halyard, sending the huge sail to the top of the mast. He wound a line around the metal winch in front of him and began to spin the crank as quickly as he could, pulling the billowing white canvas tighter and tighter with every turn. When Sam shut off the engine's power, the air became still, the silence broken only by the lapping sound of water against wood and the shrill cry of a herring gull. He closed his eyes, briefly enjoying the solitude of the moment, before he reached forward to let out the jib. Sails set, Sam nestled his back into the stern of the boat, gripping the steering tiller in his hand as the wind rushed across the canvas and propelled the boat forward.

In this tranquil place of wind and water and weather, it seemed to Sam that time moved in a different rhythm. It didn't stand still, or move at a faster or slower pace, but shifted and swirled from past to present and back again. As he sailed his small boat past the rocky Maine shoreline, Sam felt a special kinship with those who had come before. In this very same place, over 400 years earlier, Captain John Smith had been welcomed by dozens of leaping porpoises as he and his men searched for a sheltering harbor. Sailing their dragon ships across the waters of the harsh North Atlantic, Leif Eriksson and his band of Viking explorers had arrived 700 years earlier still. And throughout it all, generations of indigenous peoples—the Red Paint Tribe, the Oyster Shell Men and then the Abenaki Nation, the "People of the Dawn"—had hunted, fished, farmed and lived out their lives along the same shores. Mr. Goodfellow believed that the sea had a way of soaking right into you, of leaving a special mark on a person's soul, and Sam couldn't agree more.

A half a mile or so out, Sam spied the fluke of a right whale as it broke the surface of the sea. A second or two later, the animal breached, throwing itself out of the water before it fell backward with a thundering splash. Closer to him, just off the port bow, a group of harbor seals appeared; their sleek, gray heads bobbing up and down in the waves as the sailboat sliced through the water toward them. Out of the corner of his eye, Sam noticed a head that was slightly smaller than the rest. As the boat passed, the seal broke away from its companions and began to follow it, watching with curiosity, but disappearing under the waves whenever Sam turned his head. Again and again, Sam tried to steal a closer look, but the creature was too quick. Amused, Sam finally leaned over the side and trailed his hand through the water. The magnifying glass that he wore on a string around his neck slapped noisily against the boat's hull. The longer chain and the tiny piece of silver metal that was hooked into it dangled in and out of the water a few times before Sam scooped it up into his fist and shoved it safely down the front of his shirt. As he removed his hand, it brushed against a bulge in the inside breast pocket of his jacket—a letter that he had reached for many times over the past week but couldn't quite bring himself to open. Sam's hand trembled as he cautiously pushed the pocket flap aside with the tips of his fingers. Making contact with the edge of the envelope released a flood of bittersweet memories. But the harbor seal suddenly appeared again, this time fixing his round, black eyes straight on Sam and shifting his thoughts elsewhere. After a puzzling moment of communion, the creature finally dove under the water and disappeared.

Perplexed, Sam settled his back against the stern. He stared into the crystal-clear sky above, fully illuminated now by the bright rays of the morning sun. He had been relieved to take his fingers away from the letter and was now absently moving them along the chain around his neck. When he reached the tiny piece of silver—his Scandinavian Sea Mouse Knife, given to him for bravery at sea and for saving the life of another— the memory of that day came back to him. Sam always felt a surge of pride, but never without remembering those who had saved *his* life. And as he thought now of the little seal, he couldn't shake the feeling that he had stared into those deep, dark eyes somewhere before.

Taking hold of the boat's tiller again, Sam tore open the left side of his life vest with his free hand, reached inside the jacket and pulled at the front pocket of his flannel shirt.

"Are you *ever* coming out?" he exclaimed with exaspera-

tion. "You're missing everything! And I'm not giving up, you know. I'll make a sailor of you yet!"

There was a loud groan and a rustle as a small figure, no more than four inches high, dressed in a meticulously hand-crafted mouse costume, grasped the sides of Sam's vest with a determined grip, then slowly pulled itself out of the pocket and into the light of day.

Edgar Goodfellow, struggling under the bulk of his mouse suit, a safety harness and the two life preservers that were dangling around his neck, began an awkward descent down the front of Sam's vest and onto the wooden bench below.

"I'll never get the hang of it," he panted. "Never! Not if I live to be 2000!"

"It's all in your mind, Edgar! Just fix your eyes at something on the horizon, okay? You'll feel better soon. I promise."

Unable to hide his irritation, Edgar snapped back, "Uncle Jolly used to say that, too. And what were you doing back there anyway, leaning way over the boat like that? I almost fell out, you know!"

"A really strange thing happened—" Sam began, but he was interrupted by a cry of panic.

Struggling to keep his balance, Edgar staggered forward and fell to his knees. He grasped the side of the bench with a grim expression, rushing to tether his harness onto the boat as a powerful wave suddenly rolled it from side to side. Sam turned in his seat and pointed across the water.

"Look! See that lobster boat that's just passed on our starboard side? Keep your eye on it."

Unfamiliar with nautical lingo, Edgar immediately looked in the wrong direction. Another wave from the lobster boat's wake slapped against the side of Sam's boat, sending a huge spray of seawater over the side and drenching Edgar from the top of his mouse ears to the tip of his tail. Sam winced. As the smell of wet fur wafted up to him, he pulled a wad of crumpled tissues from his pants pocket and started to blot up the water that was dripping from Edgar's nose mask. What incredibly bad luck, he thought. Maybe Edgar's aversion to watercraft (and airplanes, and trains) wasn't totally unwarranted after all. It was quite perplexing, but Edgar Goodfellow really did seem to invite misfortune whenever he attempted to travel.

The lobsterman who'd overtaken them a moment before had stopped up ahead to haul his traps. Sam waved cheerily at him as he gaffed a colorful bobbing buoy with his hook and passed the trapline over the automatic hauler. When the wooden trap had been hoisted far enough out of the water, the lobsterman leaned forward and pulled it onto the boat. A young man joined him at the rail and they emptied the trap together. The older man turned toward Sam and grinned, raising both arms high above his head as he waved two huge lobsters in the air.

"Do you see that, Edgar?" exclaimed Sam. "Look at the size of them! There's not been lobsters like that around here for years!"

As soon as they'd heard the wailing of the trapline on the hauler, a noisy squabble of seagulls began to gather. They were circling directly over the lobster boat now, knowing from experience that the trap was about to be cleared of old bait. Screeching loudly, they fluttered above the waves, diving down to the water's surface to retrieve the bits and pieces of old fish as soon as they were tossed.

Edgar, who had taken Sam's advice and fixed his eyes on the scene in front of him, was starting to feel less groggy. He had even grown confident enough to untether his harness and sit closer to the outer edge of the boat where the warm rays of the morning sun could dry his damp parts. With the light dancing playfully on the water, the gentle sound of the wind in the sails and the caress of a cool ocean breeze, Edgar Goodfellow almost forgot where he was. Filling his lungs with fresh, clean air, Edgar closed his eyes, turned his face toward the sun, and began to feel a great surge of contentment. This welcome feeling lasted right up until the moment a swooping gull carelessly opened his beak too far and dropped a smelly morsel of lobster bait right onto Edgar's face, sending him into a fit of dizziness and nausea. Sam removed the offending article as quickly as possible, set Edgar back on his feet again and mumbled the sincerest apology he could.

"It's not your fault," Edgar sighed, as he delicately picked the last piece of rotting fish scale out of his fur. "I've grown quite accustomed to all of this, I'm afraid. You're a good friend, Sam, and I know you mean well, and I really do consider it an honor that you thought to invite me on your maiden voyage," Edgar looked up at his friend and smiled weakly, "but, all things considered, maybe I should just stay home next time. She's a cracker of a boat, though, isn't she?"

Sam nodded and smiled back. "Designed and built from scratch, just the way they used to do it. It may have been a bit of an ambitious project, but I think it was worth all the—"

Sam suddenly stood up, sending Edgar scrambling to retether his harness.

"Hey! What's going on?" Edgar protested.

"Over there! Look! It's him again!" Sam pointed into the wind.

"Who?"

"That harbor seal! There's something very different about him."

Edgar leaned as far forward as his tether would allow, and strained his eyes to get a better look.

"Curious fellow, isn't he?" Edgar remarked. "Rather a strange pattern of stripes running down his back."

"You see them, too!" Sam exclaimed excitedly. "He's not like the rest of them, is he?"

Mr. Goodfellow's words began to echo in Sam's thoughts. *"Animals are ancient spirits, older than even The Sage. They return to Earth again and again, throughout Time, in many different forms."*

"Do you know what I'm thinking, Edgar?" Sam whispered. "It may sound crazy, but I can't seem to get old Figgy off my mind today. He was different, too, just like this little fellow."

"He's unique, I'll give you that," replied Edgar, staring intently at the seal. "And by the way he's looking at us, I'd swear he knows you. But the odds of *that* happening here and now, Sam, with all of the millions and millions of miles of earth and sea and the multitude of creatures that have come and gone since—"

"But it's not impossible, is it?" interrupted Sam.

"No, I suppose not," Edgar smiled knowingly at his friend. "Not for someone like you, anyway."

"Or you, either."

Sam shielded his eyes from the bright sun and stared out to sea. The little seal had slipped away from the boat and joined the rest of his companions.

"The oddest coincidences always seem to come looking for us, don't they?" Sam said quietly. "Something's going on, Edgar. I can feel it. Maybe the Fates have something interesting in store for us again."

Sam took the tiller and began to change direction. For the next few minutes, neither he nor Edgar spoke a word. A large flock of black cormorants passed in front of the boat, the tips of their wings skimming the surface of the sea.

"Have you opened the letter, yet?" Edgar asked, with a little hesitation, as he unclipped his harness again.

Sam shuffled about uncomfortably and stared straight ahead. "No," he replied, clearing his throat awkwardly. "I just haven't gotten around to it, I guess." He slipped his hand into the inside breast pocket of his jacket again and ran his fingers along the top of the long and crumpled envelope.

"But you've had it for over a week now!" exclaimed Edgar. "Aren't you curious? It's not every day that a person receives a letter on NASA stationery with the words 'Strictly Confidential' scribbled across the front."

"I know. But I've always had this thing about opening letters, Edgar. Remember? Sometimes they tell you things you'd rather not know. And anyway, I already know who it's from. I recognize the handwriting. He probably left it for me, with instructions to forward it in the event of his—well, you know. I figure it can only mean one thing."

"You can't be sure of that, Sam."

"Why not? Think about it, Edgar! NASA was obligated to fulfill a promise they made to Fletcher, maybe years and years ago, and now they've made the delivery. Wait and see. It'll be announced on the news any day now that the mission has been officially declared lost. They've stopped looking for them. I just know it."

Sam slowly pulled the letter out of his jacket pocket and stared at it. The wind rattled at the edges of the envelope, brown and brittle with age—like the hands that were holding it. And as those hands began to tremble, Edgar reached out one of his paws and placed it on top of Sam's thumb.

"Come on. You know you can't put it off forever," Edgar

said gently. "I'll help you open it, if you want. It's what old friends are for, right?"

Sam looked at Edgar with eyes that had pooled with tears— eyes that Edgar Goodfellow had known for more than seventy-five years—and slowly nodded his head. And even though the face that framed them had weathered and wrinkled with the passage of time, Sam's eyes still held the same light that they always had. It was the light that Mr. Goodfellow had seen in his nephew's eyes, too; the light that had bound the two friends in a Sacred Seal that had almost spanned a lifetime.

While Sam held it tightly on his knee, Edgar dug one of his claws under the edge of the envelope and began to tear open the long flap. Sam slipped his trembling fingers through the jagged opening and pulled the letter from inside. He actually closed his eyes while he unfolded the paper, as thoughts of what might be written there filled his mind. An uplifting poem perhaps. Fletcher was good at those. Or, even better, a joke. Sam hoped that it wasn't something gloomy and serious like "The Last Will and Testament of Fletcher Jaffrey." Sam shook that thought right from his head. That wouldn't be like Fletcher at all.

"There's nothing on it, Sam," said Edgar quietly.

"Huh?" Sam opened his eyes and stared. The blank piece of paper fluttered in his hands. Something small and shiny slipped onto his knee, then fell to the wooden floorboard below with a soft ping.

Sam reached down, moving his hands over the wet wooden slats until he felt something smooth and hard. He lifted the object with the tips of his fingers and rolled it into his palm.

"What's this, then?"

"It's a key, Sam."

"Well, I know it's a key, Edgar. But the key to what?" Sam sighed. It was *just* like Fletcher to do something like this; to leave some kind of annoying puzzle to solve while everyone was grieving his loss.

"But it was left specifically for you, Sam. Fletcher must have been sure that you would know..."

"But I've never seen it before!" Sam exclaimed impatiently. "Or I don't remember it, at least. By the looks of that envelope, this thing could have been sitting around at NASA for the last fifty years. My memory was a lot sharper then. I *am* 86, you know!"

Edgar opened his mouth to speak, but Sam jumped in.

"And don't tell me you're 270! You don't look a day over twenty!"

"Actually," piped Edgar, "I was just going to say that the key appears to have some initials scratched into it at the top. An 'S' and a 'J,' I believe."

"Oh," mumbled Sam. He looked up and offered an apologetic smile. "This whole thing has got me a little on edge."

"Quite understandably," Edgar replied.

Sam's eyes suddenly flew wide open. He grinned and slapped his knee. "Sanjid Jaffrey," he announced with conviction. Edgar looked up. "Fletcher's father?"

"S.J.! That's it, Edgar!" Sam rubbed his hands together with satisfaction. "And I remember that key now, too! It used to open a little box in—" Sam stopped speaking and looked down at his wristwatch. "Good grief! Is that the time? I've lost all track of it out here! Charlotte will be wondering what's become of you, Edgar. I won't have her thinking that I've lost her young husband at sea. We really shouldn't be leaving her alone too long in her condition, either. And I promised Alice I would pick her up!"

Sam gripped the tiller and turned for home. The sailboat heeled on its side as it sped across the waves. Edgar sighed and retethered his harness. In all the years that they had been friends, Edgar had never known Sam to break a promise.

2

An Englishman's Home
Is His Castle

At the shoreline, behind the crescent-shaped strip of sand that ran south of the river mouth, other creatures were also welcoming the dawn.

Struggling into his bathrobe, Mr. Goodfellow opened the front door of his house, hopped down three stone porch steps and sank into a mound of soft sand. He hurried along the pebble pathway that led to the edge of the dunes, letting out a frustrated sigh as he turned back to retrieve a bedroom slipper that had snagged on a thorn. When a short-tailed shrew popped his head out from a clump of beachgrass, Mr. Goodfellow sent him a quick but friendly wave, and a hastier "Good day," before rushing past. Shrews were excellent conversationalists (apart from the fact that they spoke far too quickly when excited and were sometimes difficult to understand), but Mr. Goodfellow had no time to spare this morning for idle chitchat.

Mr. Goodfellow was very annoyed at himself for having overslept, but the annual Sage Awards ceremony the night before had run seriously over schedule, especially (as usual) the musical numbers. Who'd ever had the brilliant idea of booking the jumping mice as chorus line extras should have his head examined! Their lengthy (and occasionally dangerous) antics had forced him to make his acceptance speech well into the wee hours of the morning. Had he not been receiving a Lifetime Achievement Award, Mr. Goodfellow might have ducked the entire affair and spent a quiet evening at home. His family, of course, wouldn't hear of it. They had proudly stood by while he donned his tuxedo suit: sleek black fur with white chest and cuffs and shiny pearl buttons. He had worn the very same formal attire to the captain's table on the maiden voyage of a grand ocean liner many years before. It had been quite some time since Mr. Goodfellow had seen an appropriate opportunity to wear it, due, in part, to the fact that it had only recently been reclaimed from a roving band of moles. Held in high regard by these creatures, the luxurious suit was one of the few articles of clothing that had failed to turn up after Mr. Goodfellow's missing trunk had been returned to him. When the item (along with the attending moles) was finally spotted by a troop of young Sage on a wilderness trek through the Rockies, it had taken Mr. Goodfellow a great deal of time and effort to get it back. Six months of negotiations and three pounds of cashews later, the moles had finally agreed to hand it over. Mr. Goodfellow had really just pursued it for nostalgic reasons, never dreaming that he would be standing in it so soon after its return, surrounded by family and friends, and about to receive one of the most prestigious honors known to The Sage.

And even though the tuxedo suit was considerably more snug than he remembered, everyone agreed that Mr. Goodfellow looked marvelous. There had been a moment of panic when two of the buttons at his expanding waist had suddenly popped off and flown across the room, but with a bit of quick thinking, a sharp needle and some industrial-strength thread, a catastrophe was averted. It was at that particular moment, though, that Mr. Goodfellow had an overwhelming desire to rush upstairs, trade in his pinching formal mouse shoes for a pair of comfortable old slippers and curl up on his bed with a good book and a mug of hot, milky tea.

"I really wish everyone wouldn't make such a fuss," he had lamented, fiddling with the bow-tie clip that was poking into his neck. "You don't suppose I still have time to forward a taped address to the ceremonies instead, do you?"

"What? And miss all the fun?" Mr. Goodfellow's older brother, Filbert, had joked, giving him a hearty slap on the back. "Why, it's your day in the sun, Jolly, old man. Enjoy it!"

"Will there be a lot of mice in the audience?" Mr. Goodfellow had asked nervously.

"But of course! Dozens, in fact," Filbert continued, trying very hard to stifle a laugh. "You don't think we could keep your most ardent admirers away, do you? You're a legend in your own time, Jolly. I understand there's a large contingent coming all the way from Chicago. They're still chattering about that Da Vinci flying mission that you and Edgar undertook—and all these mouse generations later, too! It's quite extraordinary!" Filbert paused just then and turned to his wife. "You *are* bringing an extra box of tissues, aren't you, Hazel? If I know mice, they're apt to get completely carried away with the emotions of the evening."

Mr. Goodfellow had groaned and seriously considered bolting from the room right then and there. But the look of profound pride on Edgar's face and the twinkle of love in Beatrice's eyes succeeded in putting any further thoughts of escape to rest.

"I'm so proud of you, Jolly," Beatrice had whispered into

his ear. Then she'd softly kissed his cheek. "And you look absolutely dashing, too!"

That was all the encouragement needed for a Sage nearing his 1,000th year. Mr. Goodfellow took a last look in the mirror, smoothed down his white chest fur one last time and beamed with satisfaction. Beatrice had a knack for saying just the right thing at just the right time. She gently took his arm and led him out the front door before he had the opportunity to protest any further. And after the ceremonies, when he returned home again—somewhat disheveled by all the mouse pawing, but full of happy memories and cheese puffs—he was secretly thankful that she hadn't let him miss a single second. Even though Mr. Goodfellow believed that the Sagely honor of providing centuries of unseen inspiration (all while disguised as a mouse!) to gifted humans was reward enough, he couldn't deny how satisfying it was to be considered worthy of such high regard by his peers.

As thoughts of the previous night slowly dissolved, Mr. Goodfellow thrust his nose high into the wind, licked the salt from his lips and peered out to sea. The intoxicating aroma of wild roses from the dunes mingled with the ocean breeze, flavored at this particular hour with the pungent seaweed smell of low tide. He lifted the binoculars that hung from a strap around his neck and scanned the waves.

"Whatever are you searching for at this hour of the morning?" asked an approaching voice.

The familiar scent of lavender floated into Mr. Goodfellow's nostrils. Beatrice, yawning as she rubbed the sleep from her eyes, stood beside him, a chestnut-brown mouse suit draped over one arm, mask and paws over the other.

"You really should be a bit more careful, dear," she continued sternly. "Rushing out like that without your things..."

"Yes, my love. I know! You're quite right, of course." Mr. Goodfellow grabbed the suit and gave her a quick peck on the cheek. "It's most irresponsible of me," he muttered, twisting himself around like a circus contortionist as he tried to zip himself into his suit and look through the binoculars at the same time. "But I promised Sam that I would keep a lookout, you see, and I'm afraid I may have missed him altogether. He was taking the new boat out at first light. I always like to encourage him in his hobbies. It's been quite an accomplishment for him, building that vessel all by himself."

"What's that?" asked Beatrice, shading her eyes from the sun. "Just coming around the rocks."

"What's what?" replied Mr. Goodfellow, tugging furiously at the unbearably tight legs of his suit. Good heavens! Just how many cheese puffs had he consumed last night? he wondered, unaware that he had accidentally slipped his feet through the suit's armholes. He abandoned the tugging just long enough to look through the binoculars again. A broad smile stretched across his face.

"That's him! Going at a fair lick, too! He warned me it would be fast. Just look at him go!" Mr. Goodfellow chuckled, then put his arm around Beatrice's furry waist and gave her a little squeeze. "That boy's full of surprises, isn't he?"

Beatrice looked him squarely in the face and raised her eyebrows.

"I can't help it," Mr. Goodfellow announced defensively. "No matter how hard I try, I can't help but look on him as a young lad—just as he was on the day we first met. I hope you don't find me too foolish, my love."

As Beatrice slipped her paw tenderly into his, she glanced down at Mr. Goodfellow's upside-down suit and the odd sight of his toes wiggling through the ends of the armholes.

"No, dear," she giggled. "Of course not."

Wishing again that he had not slept in so late, Mr. Goodfellow sighed and let the binoculars slip from his grasp. "It appears that Sam has already decided to head back in, my dear," he announced, as he reached for Beatrice's paw and suggested they return home for a spot of tea. "It couldn't have been a better morning for sea trials, though," he continued. "I do hope that the boat has performed to Sam's expecta—"

Without a word of warning, Mr. Goodfellow suddenly dove behind a cluster of rose hips, dragging a startled Beatrice with him. He lifted his paw to his lips and motioned for her to be quiet. Beatrice tilted her head in puzzlement. The beach-grass beside them rustled slightly, then parted down the middle, as the short-tailed shrew, accompanied this time by his family of eight, emerged and proceeded down the path. When they were far enough away to be out of hearing range, Mr. Goodfellow squeezed Beatrice's paw and breathed a sigh of relief.

"That was close!" he whispered into her ear. "Lucky for us their eyesight is so abominable."

"Really, Jolly! That's not at all neighborly of you," Beatrice scolded.

"I know, I know," he shrugged sheepishly. "But I'm absolutely parched for tea. I just couldn't face a lengthy shrew conversation at the moment. It would have taken that chap at least twenty minutes just to tell us what each of the little ones has been up to. And I can never remember all of their names, anyway."

Beatrice gave him a disapproving look. Feeling that it might be prudent to change the subject entirely, Mr. Goodfellow leaned closer to her. "Do we have any of those wonderful treacle tarts of yours left, my love?"

Beatrice turned and rolled her eyes at him before she started to climb the stone steps to their cottage. "I'll take a look," she replied dryly.

Mr. Goodfellow was inspired to stop just then and drink in his surroundings. He sighed with bliss. Blue Heron Cottage was as much a sanctuary to him now as it was a home. Years of wonderful memories of his life with Beatrice Elderberry lay within each of its small but tastefully decorated rooms and Mr. Goodfellow would not have traded it away for the grandest castle on earth. But as with every relationship—especially one that spanned a few hundred years—there had been one or two little bumps along the way.

Not long after they had exchanged their marriage vows in California, Mr. Goodfellow and Beatrice had returned to New England. They picked out a spot along the shore, sheltered by windswept dunes and tall grasses, with an unparalleled view of the ocean, and began construction in earnest. From this location, Mr. Goodfellow would have unlimited access to the nearby Jaffrey house, where his Sagely advice could still be secretly passed along to the aging Professor Hawthorne as he and Professor Jaffrey continued to promote their scientific findings about Mars. More importantly, Mr. Goodfellow's whispered inspirational words and nuggets of wisdom could also find their way into the ears of that budding young astronaut, Fletcher Jaffrey.

Everything else had fallen into place, too. Beatrice's beloved seaside cottage on the English coast did not sit empty for long, as Filbert and Hazel Goodfellow (Edgar's parents) happily took up residence and began to catch up on the 120 years they had been apart. Mr. Goodfellow's riverbank flat served as a welcome retreat for that famous Sage, Cornelius Mango, while he recovered from his terrifying flying squirrel accident.

While Mr. Goodfellow was busy with his duties, Beatrice decided to occupy her own time with something new and challenging, and it was in this spirit of adventure that the Blue Heron Bed and Breakfast was born. Mr. Goodfellow was a little skeptical about the whole arrangement, but he was still a new groom at the time, happy enough to indulge his bride in whatever caught her fancy.

Everything started off well enough. Small groups of Sage, hearing word of an idyllic new retreat by the sea, began to trickle in. For the most part, these were "between-assignment" Sage in search of a few days of rest and relaxation (some with young families in tow), a few pensioners and the occasional newlyweds. Engaging the assistance of the experienced Hawthorne house mice in the food acquisition and preparation department, Beatrice's new enterprise was off to a grand start. In no time at all, news of the Blue Heron and its five-star cuisine spread like wildfire. Just three months after its rather modest opening, it was already booking accommodations well into the following summer. It wasn't unusual for Mr. Goodfellow to have to fight his way past the deck chairs and umbrellas and buckets and spades that lined the porch just to get through his own front door. And more often than not, when he did, he was handed an apron by an officious mouse and whisked through to the kitchen to chop parsley or stir a pot of soup. Every now and then he would see Beatrice dart past in a blur of activity, followed by an entourage of chattering mice.

The fact that some of the Hawthorne mice were spending more time at *his* home than at Sam's was becoming a great source of irritation to Mr. Goodfellow. Though they assured him that everything was under control, he nevertheless felt compelled to remind them that their prime concern should be the security of the ancient scrolls that lay behind the walls in

Sam's house, and not the creation of the world's creamiest cheesecake. Thank goodness for Rollo, Mr. Goodfellow would often say. Heavens knows what they would do without the leadership and loyalty of the little black gypsy mouse! But even that thought was dashed one evening when Mr. Goodfellow returned home to find Rollo in the kitchen fussing over a soufflé. After that, half of the mice were sent packing, all the way back to the Hawthorne house. The Blue Heron Bed and Breakfast, Mr. Goodfellow announced sternly, would have to get by with a significantly reduced staff. For awhile, things did quiet down a bit. But it was really just the calm before the storm. Returning home unexpectedly and very late one evening, an exhausted Mr. Goodfellow tiptoed up the stairs. He slipped into his dark bedroom and under the blanket of his warm and inviting bed. He gave the sleeping figure beside him an affectionate pat. Just as he was drifting off himself, the bedroom door slowly creaked open and Beatrice popped her head inside.

"Is that you, Jolly?" she whispered softly. "I thought I heard you come in."

Mr. Goodfellow sat up in bed with a start and switched on the light. The figure beside him grunted and sat up, too. A little old Sage—well into his 1,300s and without a tooth in his head—politely asked him to turn off the light before he woke the two equally aged characters who were sleeping on the other side of him. Mr. Goodfellow looked forlornly at Beatrice. A foot, bearing one of his prized argyle socks, was dangling off the far edge of the bed. On the night table, a set of pearly white dentures, submerged in cleaning solution, grinned at him from the inside of his favorite cranberry glass tea mug.

"We're having to double up tonight, I'm afraid," Beatrice explained, as sweetly as she could. "We're overbooked again.

I'm with the group of ladies next door." Before Mr. Goodfellow was able to respond, Beatrice popped her head back into the hallway and gently closed the door behind her.

By the end of the following week, the last visitor had been politely ushered out and the Blue Heron Bed and Breakfast was closed indefinitely. The house mice made their way back to Sam's and life returned, for the most part, to normal. Fortunately, Beatrice wasn't unduly upset. What had started out as a part-time endeavor had gotten completely out of hand. It was like having a tiger by the tail, she'd admitted, and it was actually a relief to be finally free of it.

Mr. Goodfellow shook himself back to the present with a shudder. Thank goodness those days were behind them! The only person he wanted to share Blue Heron Cottage with now was, he hoped, busily setting out a little tray of treacle tarts and tea for two in the kitchen. Smacking his lips in anticipation, he trotted up the front steps and was just about to turn the doorknob when the sounds of laughter and voices drifted through to him from somewhere inside. His heart sank. How *could* he have forgotten? He turned around, slunk back down the steps and sighed. As he made his way along the path to the sea, all he could imagine were dozens of different-sized chins, each one wagging away with talk and laughter, and all of them covered in crumbs from those indescribably delicious tarts.

Whenever Jolly went missing, Beatrice needed to go no farther than the edge of the sand dunes to find him. He had installed a small wooden bench a number of years earlier and had enjoyed many peaceful moments of contemplation there, staring out to sea. Mr. Goodfellow was spending a great deal more time outdoors these days than usual, though. Since almost everyone in the immediate family had come to see him receive his prestigious award, Blue Heron Cottage was now, by Mr. Goodfellow's standards, painfully overcrowded. And with the birth of Edgar and Charlotte's baby just days away, everyone had decided to stay on to await the blessed event. His and Beatrice's little love nest had once more become a bustling bed and breakfast, and it was beginning to try his patience. Not that he could blame them, of course. It *had* been over a hundred years since a birth had been celebrated in the family, and everyone was understandably excited. Mr. Goodfellow just wished that they could be excited somewhere else.

In addition to Hazel and Filbert Goodfellow, the other set of grandparents, Ashcroft and Penelope Sparrow, had taken leave of their assignments in South America to offer their daughter and son-in-law their love and support. Charlotte's grandparents, Hartland and Edwina Sparrow, had traveled all the way from their Soaring Sparrow Ranch Spa and Vineyard in California. They had stopped in Colorado to pick up Charlotte's eleven-year-old (in human years!) brother, Porter, who had just completed an intensive two-week training course at the Cornelius Mango Mountain Climbing Academy under the tutelage of famed Sage adventurer Jasper Pike. As if that wasn't enough, Porter's parents—knowing all about their son's penchant for pets—had arrived with a large insect in tow.

"Wow! Neat!" Porter had exclaimed with delight. "I'm going to call him Jasper!"

Mr. Goodfellow grimaced. "Porter, I doubt the esteemed Mr. Pike would find that choice an entirely appropriate one—"

But his words fell on deaf ears. Porter had already left, sweeping the giant cicada up in his arms and rushing out of the room to search for something that might make a good collar for his new companion.

Perched on his bench by the dunes, Mr. Goodfellow looked out to sea and sighed again. It was going to be a long week. He had no doubt that even Porter's new pet was happily munching on a morsel of *his* treacle tart at this very moment. It wasn't as if Mr. Goodfellow didn't enjoy having family and friends visit, but lately, he'd felt the need for solitude and quiet reflection more than ever before. He couldn't quite put his finger on it, but there'd been something different in the air lately, and he was finding it a bit unsettling.

Mr. Goodfellow lifted his binoculars and scanned the three-acre island that lay at the mouth of the harbor. He rested his sights on the lighthouse at its easternmost tip and the sailboat that had just pulled into dock. He could see Sam as he eased himself off the boat and secured its lines. Two other figures made their way down from the keeper's house and joined him there, accompanied by a trio of bouncing dogs.

Feeling a tap on his shoulder, Mr. Goodfellow let out a gasp. When he spun his head around, the tip of his mouse mask collided with the fluted edge of a glistening treacle tart. Beatrice was standing over him. Mr. Goodfellow lifted his mask onto the top of his head and smiled as he reached for the tart.

"Thank you, my dear," he mumbled between mouthfuls of pastry and sticky syrup.

Beatrice sat down on the bench beside her husband and took his hand. She had always prided herself on being able to tell when something was troubling him. Suspecting that she might know what it was, Beatrice broached the subject as delicately as possible.

"You're not still fretting over the... um... incident, are you, Jolly? You mustn't keep blaming yourself, dear. No one else does, I can assure you. The awards ceremony last night should have been proof of that. That whole business was quite clearly out of your hands. You couldn't possibly have predicted what Winnie Redwood was about to do, and it has been five years now, after all."

Mr. Goodfellow took a deep breath. It wasn't an easy subject to talk about, even now, and he really wished that Beatrice hadn't brought it up. Not that he didn't think about it privately at some point every day, but he had learned to keep the more overwhelming worries about Fletcher and Redwood at bay. Now that Beatrice had brought it right to the surface though, it was suddenly impossible to block the words of Winchester Redwood's farewell note from his mind.

Dear Jolly,

By the time you read this thing, buddy, I'll be hurtling through space on my way to who knows where. Try not to get yourself all twisted up. I know what you must be thinking, but it's not what it looks like. Honest, chief. I'm not doing this for myself. I kept thinking of you going on this mission and leaving Beatrice all alone, maybe forever, and, well, it just didn't sit right with me. Besides, Fletcher and I have a lot in common, you know. I promise I'll look after him. Now don't go getting mad! You were right all those years ago. He needed someone like you and you were the best Sage for him. No doubt about it. But, hey, look at us now! Me and Fletcher—both footloose and fancy-free bachelors; no wives or kids or grandkids to blubber over us, right?

Remember when you told me about Fletcher's old friend at NASA letting him in on some highly classified information? You also told me what Fletcher was thinking of doing. Then you said you were worried about having to say

37

good-bye to Beatrice. You told me that she was trying to be brave, but that she was really crying herself to sleep at night? Well, I had to do something. So I called this guy I know at headquarters who owed me a really big favor and he kinda messed a few of the files around before anyone wised up and... Well, here I am—too late for The Council to do anything about it, right? I guess you must have figured out by now that the mousetrap emergency with your Uncle Duncan was just an excuse to get you out of the way. Sorry about that.

Anyway, I think that's all I gotta say. Except, don't be too angry, okay? You'd have done the same for me. Give Beatrice a great big kiss, tell her Winnie says good-bye, and say "so long" to everybody else, especially Edgar. He's a good kid. Oh, just one other thing, Jolly: I know we've had our differences in the last 700 years, and I'm sorry about all that stuff, but right now I'd really like to believe that you could think of us as true friends. It would mean a whole lot to me.

Your pal (I hope),
Winchester Redwood

Beside himself with anger, Mr. Goodfellow must have read the letter fifty times over during those first few days, not wanting to believe that even someone as outrageous as Winchester Redwood would attempt such an insane scheme. He must have been completely mad, Mr. Goodfellow complained bitterly to Beatrice. In truth though, it was simply too painful for him to admit that Redwood—a source of torment during all his years at school, that annoying and puffed-up practical joker—had plotted to commit the most incredibly noble act of love and friendship he had ever witnessed.

When the highly decorated (and long retired) astronaut Fletcher Jaffrey decided at the ripe old age of eighty-one to secretly slip aboard a NASA scout ship bound for an undisclosed location—quite possibly never to return—Winchester Redwood took it upon himself to take Mr. Goodfellow's place at Fletcher's side, so that Jolly might spend the rest of his years in the company of the woman they had both loved.

As they sat together on their bench by the sea, Mr. Goodfellow squeezed Beatrice's hand, looked into her eyes and smiled a little sadly. Beatrice had indeed struck a sensitive chord with her questions about Fletcher and Redwood. Was that what was really troubling him, though, or was it something else? Mr. Goodfellow had a strange suspicion that the incident that had unfolded five years earlier wasn't what was making him feel anxious now.

"You know, my dear, I'm not sure that it's about Redwood at all. At least not completely," Mr. Goodfellow tried to explain, fidgeting with his last morsel of tart. "It's a feeling I haven't had for ages, not since the scrolls were found again and given to Sam for safekeeping. Sam has been fulfilling his role most admirably, after all. The scrolls have remained safe for seventy-five years now, and thanks to the discoveries made on Mars, humankind has been given a chance to avoid similar devastation. It may be slow going for some years to come still, but there's been steady progress, hasn't there? And yet, I sense something stirring," he whispered. "It's a horrible feeling I remember from long ago and I can feel it deep inside my bones."

Mr. Goodfellow lifted his binoculars up one last time and trained them on the three figures by the island dock. Standing up from his bench, he scanned to the lighthouse beyond them. For years now, the ancient scrolls of Mars had lain side by side, safe and secret within the lighthouse walls, faithfully watched over by Sam, Edgar and the many loyal descendants of Rollo—the incomparable gypsy mouse. And there the twin scrolls were to remain, until the Earth and its inhabitants were ready to receive their message again. At least that was the plan.

Mr. Goodfellow shuddered as another strange and shivery feeling crept up his spine. Shaking it off as best he could, he took Beatrice's paw in his and headed back to Blue Heron Cottage.

3

Every Heart Has

Its Own Ache

"We were beginning to worry that you'd forgotten us!" said India.

She put her thin arms around Sam and gave him a hug. She had kept her hair long and silky, just as she'd had it as a young girl, but it was pure white now and woven neatly into a little braid at the nape of her neck.

"Well, it was really *me* who was getting a little worried," she continued. "Alice kept assuring me that you'd be here any moment. Grandad *never* forgets a promise, she kept saying. Right, Alice?"

Nodding in agreement, a girl of about thirteen stepped forward, raising herself on tiptoe to give Sam a kiss on the cheek. She was tall and slender, her long black hair pulled back into a ponytail with a red silk ribbon. She was, as Sam often noted, the spitting image of her Nana India when he'd first laid eyes on her.

Sam was also quick to point out that Alice was fortunate enough to have inherited a few attributes from his side of the family, too. Whenever Sam wanted his granddaughter's undivided attention, he would call her by both her first and middle names: Alice Hannah. This name had been passed down through time from Sam's great-great-grandmother and it was one that young Alice more than lived up to. The original Alice Hannah had been born in the northern English moor country. She'd been little more than a girl herself when she was left to run the farm after her father fell ill. According to family stories, Alice Hannah single-handedly fought off their unscrupulous landlord's numerous attempts to push her out. With a spirit that was remarkable for the time in which she lived, Alice Hannah gained a reputation in the surrounding area as a force to be reckoned with. Legend had it that she possessed a passion for riding bareback across the moors, her long, wild hair flying—like a heroine from one of the romantic novels that India still loved to read.

"How was the boat trip, then?" India asked, jolting Sam and his imagination back from the moors.

"Better than I'd hoped, actually," Sam smiled with satisfaction. "Goes just like the wind." He put his arm around his granddaughter. "Have you decided how you'd like to spend the day?" he asked. "Do you still want to see that new movie?"

"It's not a *movie*, Grandad," Alice sighed a little impatiently. "It's called a holospan. Remember?"

"Yes, of course. Sorry. Your old grandad's a bit out of step with these things, I'm afraid."

Alice slipped her arm through his and smiled. "You really liked the last one, though. I know you did."

"I suppose it was alright," Sam replied, "although I did find those odd seats a bit of a challenge. And what do they call that other thing...the 'smelly vision' part? Now back in my younger days, we would have thought that was really something—"

"You *have* to have the seats that spin around, or you'd never be able to see all the action!" Alice interrupted. "And its called 'smellovision.' I don't know how you could have ever watched shows without *that*. It just wouldn't feel real at all. And they were on those flat screens, too, weren't they? It must have been *so* primitive."

"You're absolutely right," Sam replied, chuckling. "It was downright backward, Alice. But somehow we managed to survive. Why, I remember some Saturday afternoons when your Great-Uncle Fletcher and I would spend hours at the movie theater. Nana India, of course, usually had her nose stuck in a book back then, but me and Fletch would buy a big bucket of popcorn each and—" Sam stopped talking just then and looked up at his wife. There was an expression of sadness on her face and he knew in the pit of his stomach what she was about to say. "They've announced something, haven't they?" he asked before she had a chance to speak. "Finally called it off?"

India nodded her head, then dabbed at her eyes with a tissue. Sam put both of his arms around her.

"Well, it's not totally unexpected, I suppose," said Sam, whispering into her ear. "They lost contact almost a year ago, after all. But I had hoped they might keep searching anyway... just a little bit longer, at least."

As he comforted India, Sam could feel the old, brown envelope rustling against the inside pocket of his jacket. He hadn't been able to bring himself to tell her about the letter's arrival. At least she had had one more week than he to cling to the hope that Fletcher and the rest of the ship's crew would be found safe.

"We don't have to go to the show today, Grandad," offered Alice quietly. "We could go another time if you want."

"No, Alice. A promise is a promise." Sam looked into India's sad eyes. "Maybe you should come with us?"

"No. I'll be fine," she replied. "I'm not a big fan of those holospans, anyway. They don't leave enough to the imagination, if you ask me. But you two run along. I know how much you enjoy your days together."

India loved to see her husband and granddaughter sharing similar interests. Sam and Alice were, after all (as India frequently observed), "like two peas in a pod."

"Sounds as if we're set then!" Sam announced.

The three boxer dogs that had been milling about suddenly decided to vie for Sam's exclusive attention, leaping into the air and pawing at his front and back. There was a muffled yelp from inside Sam's shirt pocket as one of the flailing paws made contact with his chest. Sam remembered Edgar, and then the key, with a start.

"There's a little side trip I'd like to make when we get to town, Alice, if you don't mind. I'll just get my things." He hurried up the pathway toward the house, the three dogs bounding at his side. "Wait for me by the boathouse!" he turned and called back.

With the dogs lunging in ahead of him, Sam entered the front door of the old wooden keeper's house, then made his way through the covered walkway that connected it to the light tower. At twenty-five feet tall, the brick structure was as solid now as it had been when it was built in the 1880s. All these years later, it was still directing mariners past the shoals of dangerous rocks that lurked offshore and guiding them into safe harbor. Even though the lighthouse beacon had been automated for close to a century, it was still essential that a trusted caretaker watch over the site. Apart from its historic significance, the island and its outbuildings had recently been

44

incorporated into a rapidly expanding area of reserve lands. These environmentally protected regions stretched for hundreds of miles along the coast now, and were administered by a local trust that was dedicated to the preservation and restoration of coastal habitats and resources, especially the delicate ecosystems of the dunes and salt marsh estuaries.

A woodworker by trade, Sam had jumped at the chance to man the island when the town council had offered him the job. It was the perfect place to pursue his vocation and fulfill his dream of handcrafting his own wooden sailboats. India had not needed much convincing, either. The scientific research possibilities were unlimited. Her early work in aquahibernation had proven invaluable on the first Mars expeditions, and when later interests led her into the study of marine ecosystems, the opportunity to live on a coastal island seemed ideal.

For the last fifty years, Sam and India had lived in the shadow of the lighthouse, enjoying the turn of the tides and the cycle of seasons. It was here that they had raised their daughter, Nellie (Alice's mother), and instilled in her a love of family, a respect for nature, and everything else they could teach her about integrity and compassion. Their island world was quiet, peaceful and remote; the perfect place for anyone seeking solitude—or with something very precious to hide.

As he continued through the walkway, Sam reached into his shirt pocket and pulled out a rumpled Edgar. Rubbing at a knee that had been pummeled on more than one occasion by overactive dog paws, Edgar made a passing comment about enrolling the boxers in another obedience course. Apart from his own injury, Edgar explained, he had recently been receiving a litany of complaints from the mice. Sam looked at him with a tired expression.

"We've been over this before, Edgar. It's not an easy thing using the words 'boxer' and 'obedient' in the same sentence," he chuckled. "Our little Tosca here has potential," he said, bending down and giving the youngest dog a tickle behind her ears, "but Fletcher's two are really hopeless. Maybe we should try giving them a bit more exercise?"

Sam looked behind him to where Fletcher's dogs, Carmen and Buttercup, were leaping wildly as they tried to capture the little beams of sunlight that were streaming through the small windows. It was hard to believe they were both nearing seven. He wondered if they still missed Fletcher as much as they had at first. But they were so much younger then, after all. They had actually lived most of their lives without him. It was rather silly, Sam supposed, to still be calling them Fletcher's dogs. He felt a pang of pain and longing in his heart.

When Sam finally reached the lighthouse tower, he quickly shooed the dogs away, closed the walkway door behind him and gently set Edgar on the floor.

"Do you have the key, Sam?" asked Edgar.

"The what?"

"The key! We *are* going to the Jaffrey house to search for the box, aren't we?"

"Yes, of course," Sam mumbled. "I'm sorry, Edgar. I was a million miles away."

"A *million* miles?" Edgar looked up at his old friend. "You miss him a lot, don't you?"

Sam nodded his head slowly, then pulled the wrinkled envelope that held the key out of his jacket pocket. "I wonder if we'll ever know what really happened."

Their conversation was interrupted by a soft voice calling from the opposite side of the room.

"Edgar, are you back? Thank goodness!"

It was Charlotte, and as she waddled toward them out of the shadows, it became clear that she was probably no more than a day or two away from motherhood. A handful of scurrying mice, each carrying a tiny satin pillow, attended her. Whenever and wherever she stopped, they would quickly plump up their pillows and arrange them in a pile at her feet. Charlotte looked at her husband with an expression of desperation.

"Are the mice looking after you, my love? Edgar inquired. "I did tell them to be particularly attentive while I was gone."

"Yes, I can tell," Charlotte replied with a sigh. "But perhaps they're just a bit *too* attentive. When I mentioned this morning that I fancied a piece of cheese for breakfast, they produced a basket of assorted dairy products that could have fed an army. Edgar," Charlotte whispered, trying not to unduly alarm him, "they're very sweet but do you think they would be terribly offended if we asked them for a few moments alone? I'm feeling rather tired."

At that announcement, Edgar rushed forward and threw his arms as far as he could around her waist. Charlotte looked up at Sam and rolled her eyes.

"I'm quite alright, Edgar. I just need to rest a bit, that's all." She glanced over at her group of chattering attendants. "Without all those pillows."

Edgar politely herded the mice away, then returned to hover over his young wife again.

"I think it might be better if you stayed with Charlotte today," Sam suggested.

Edgar glanced up at him with a look of relief. "Are you sure?"

"I'll be able to find Sanjid's box by myself," Sam assured him. "One thing I remember well about Fletcher is that he was never one to tidy things up. A typical bachelor, I guess. The old Jaffrey place looks the same as it did seventy-five years ago."

"What box?" Charlotte asked quizzically. "What's going on?"

Edgar flinched. "Well...they've finally called off the search for Fletcher and the ship, I'm afraid. Sam's been left a key that apparently opens a box at the Jaffrey place and—"

Charlotte wiggled her way out of Edgar's affectionate grip. "You should have told me right away, Edgar! I want to go back to the keeper's house immediately," she announced. "India will be needing me. This whole thing has been very trying for her, you know. This new development will be quite a letdown. A few words of encouragement will do her a world of good."

"But Charlotte," replied Edgar, wringing his hands, "your condition!"

"Really, Edgar," Charlotte said, looking at him sternly. "I'm perfectly fine!"

Charlotte spoke in a determined tone that Edgar (after 142 years) knew well. He tried once again to dissuade her, but it was hopeless. Charlotte Sparrow shared many similarities with the Elderberry branch of her family: an appreciation of good books, a love of lavender and a near-obsessive taste for gingerbread. But above all, Charlotte had that streak of Elderberry stubbornness that for centuries had distinguished them in Sage lore and made them formidable operatives.

"I'll leave you two alone to figure it out, then," Sam blurted as he bolted for the door. "Alice is waiting for me!"

Sam, who was more than a little relieved to have some-where else to go, would much rather have faced the trio of leaping, drooling dogs waiting for him in the walkway than one determined Sparrow on a mission.

4

WISDOM RIDES ON THE
RUINS OF FOLLY

With India bidding them farewell from the dock, Sam and Alice began the short voyage across the channel that separated the lighthouse from the mainland. It would have taken no more than a minute or two by electromagnet-propelled hover boat, but Sam still preferred the longer way; rowing across in a small wooden vessel he had built thirty years earlier. Apart from providing exercise, it was a virtually silent method of transport that afforded a much better opportunity to observe the passing marine animals and seabirds. This was a pastime that Sam and his granddaughter shared with great enthusiasm. They had spent many hours together, spotting whales and seals and porpoises and dozens of different birds, like the piping plover and the least tern, two rare inhabitants that had started a repopulation explosion in the area, after decades of near extinction. Alice would mark down each species and their estimated numbers in her small notebook, whenever Sam called them out to her. The uncommonly large flotilla of black ducks that constantly plied the waters of the channel had always fascinated and puzzled Alice, but not Sam. For all the years that he (and the scrolls) had inhabited the lighthouse, this loyal family of waterfowl had been providing a feathered ferry service to and from the mainland for both mouse and Sage.

After they had tied their boat to the town's public docks, Sam and Alice made their way across the adjacent rock pier to a short stretch of white-sand beach. This was a particularly favorite spot, a quiet little world littered with tidal pools. There was always an interesting assortment of creatures here, living in the deep crevices and water basins left by the receding tide: purple starfish, sea anemones and urchins, and the occasional hermit crab. At the water's edge, small groups of sandpipers scurried through foamy layers of swash left behind by the breaking waves. Jumping over the rows of small streamlets that trickled down to the sea, Alice searched the wet sand until she found the ultimate prize—an unbroken sand dollar, flat and round and gleaming white, deposited intact by the gently rolling surf. She held it up for Sam to see, then popped it safely into her pocket.

Alice moved along to another of her interests then—spotting small creatures that had crept too far up the beach for the ebbing tide to return them to the sea. She diligently scanned the clumps of drying seaweed below the long line of dunes, rescuing small crabs and starfish and carrying them back to the safety of the water in the hollow of a broken clamshell.

It was at times like this that Sam could see, in Alice, a clear reflection of himself as a boy. Stubborn and independent, Alice was an imaginative girl with an insatiable appetite for all things miniature, an abhorrence for cruelty of any kind and an unshakeable belief that all life, no matter how small, should be championed and defended. While Sam had done much to instill and nurture these characteristics in his granddaughter, there had been times when even he was surprised by the depth of her commitment. When she had been barely out of her toddler years, Alice began a personal mission to rescue and rehouse every stray cat in town. And at the age of six, after discovering a young seagull with a broken wing, Alice had insisted on feeding and caring for the bird until it was well enough to release—a task that would have challenged even the most devoted animal lover.

Alice was definitely in her element by the sea, and though she had lived here all of her life, her fascination with it had never waned. She had traveled with her parents to many interesting places in the world, but this small town by the ocean was the only one to which she felt truly connected. Were she to have known Mr. Goodfellow, Sam supposed, Alice would have wholeheartedly agreed with his observations. The sea, especially here, did have a way of soaking right into you and soothing your soul.

Leaving the beach, Sam and Alice climbed the steep row of steps that led up to the concrete seawall and the narrow road beyond. They began walking toward the center of town, past the restaurants and cafés, the antique bookstores and boutiques, on winding streets lined with tall oak and maple trees. It was a tiny, almost perfect little oasis here, a town deliberately preserved as a record of a time long past, in a world still struggling to harmonize the needs of humankind and nature. Outwardly, at least, it appeared that very little had changed here in the last half century or more. Beneath the surface, however, a steadily growing movement had begun to take hold and, more importantly, to spread beyond the confines of one sleepy seaside town.

It had all started with the creation of the Hawthorne-Jaffrey Society, a worldwide organization that had been founded fifty years earlier and still maintained its headquarters in some of the old university buildings at the edge of town. Sitting on its current board of directors were Alice's parents, George and Nellie Durham. Their roles as Society ambassadors had taken them around the world many times, and on those trips that fell during the school term, Alice stayed at the lighthouse with Sam and India.

Passionately dedicated to the protection of Earth's resources, and the promotion of renewable, nonpolluting energy sources, supporters of this new movement owed much to the dedicated work of its famous founders. It hadn't been easy in the early years, though. After the release of their paper "Mars: The Cradle of Civilization," local university professors Cedric Hawthorne and Sanjid Jaffrey suddenly found themselves exposed to the torment of public ridicule. Much of the controversy surrounding their findings was inspired by one Professor Avery Mandrake, head of the archeology department at the same university. To the handful of people—including Sam, Fletcher and India—who knew the *real* story, Mandrake was a dangerously unscrupulous man and a mastermind of deception. Even more menacing (as only Sam and The Sage were aware) was the fact that Mandrake had fallen under the influence of The Fen. These inspirers of evil on Earth, sworn enemies of The Sage, intended to possess the ancient Martian scrolls one day and use the power locked within them for their own gains.

Since Hawthorne and Jaffrey had no solid evidence to back their claims that Earth's civilization owed its very existence to a group of ancient survivors from the ruined planet of Mars, Professor Mandrake was able to attract considerable attention in his movement against them. He had no trouble collecting an enthusiastic group of academic naysayers who took great delight in humiliating Hawthorne and Jaffrey and discounting their "outlandish" theories.

A little more than twenty years after the paper had first been published, though, the whole world was turned on end. The first manned expedition to Mars, led by Fletcher Jaffrey, unearthed the first small clues that Hawthorne and Fletcher's father might have been right all along. There they found evidence that Mars had once been home to a highly advanced civilization—long since destroyed. That society's unfortunate fate had been sealed by its refusal to alter a path of waste and greed, eerily similar to the one that Earth and its inhabitants had chosen to travel. Though it had taken almost a quarter of a century, Fletcher's dream of vindicating his father's scientific reputation finally became a reality when he planted his feet firmly on the Martian surface in the year 2028. Subsequent expeditions confirmed Hawthorne and Jaffrey's earth-shattering claims, leaving Professor Mandrake with a great deal of egg on his face. In fact, he was never quite the same. He withdrew from society, refusing to see anyone but his own son, Basil. He even abandoned his obsessive passion for scuba diving: an obsession that had always puzzled everyone in town, except for Sam. Sam alone knew that the ancient and powerful scrolls that Mandrake was searching for had not been washed out to sea at all, but recovered by a courageous band of Scandinavian Sea Mice and returned to him and The Sage for safekeeping. In order to fully protect the scrolls and thwart the evil intentions of Mandrake and The Fen, this was something that Sam could reveal to no other soul, not even his closest friends or his family.

Frustrated over his failure to find the scrolls and humiliated by the success of his academic rivals, Avery Mandrake left town altogether one day. Word had it that he finally passed away at a remote spot somewhere in the inland mountains, a broken and bitter old man, unable to regain the respect of the academic community that had once eaten out of his hand. Basil Mandrake stayed on in town as the years passed, dabbling in real estate, and wheeling and dealing in a variety of unsavory business ventures, while he kept a constant watch on Sam. Ever since the scrolls had slipped from his father's grasp and been swept out to sea, Basil had a lurking suspicion that Sam knew more about their fate than he ever let on. It was as if Basil was waiting for Sam to slip up, even if that took the rest of their lives.

The work of the Hawthorne-Jaffrey Society had fanned outward in the years that followed. Ardent supporters of the new movement lobbied governments and businesses, imploring that Earth be given a chance to heal itself. Even so, it had been an unsteady start. For a number of years, the world passed through periods of global upheaval—energy crises, wars, famines and one environmental disaster after another. Decades of reckless technological advancement had depleted Earth's resources, melted the polar ice caps and choked whatever clean air was left with pollutants. In those dark years, crop circles appeared with increasing regularity in virtually every corner of the world, providing support for Professor Hawthorne's declaration that they were part of an ancient message system linked to the survivors of a fallen world and their plea for Earth's salvation.

Even as Fletcher and his crew made their first historic Mars landing, the world continued to teeter on the brink of disaster. It was only after analyzing the remains of the ruined Martian civilization that many finally began to see the parallel between the fate that had befallen Mars and the fragile balance that existed back on Earth. The grave consequences of living without regard for each other or the natural world were far too great to ignore any longer. It was time for Earth to change direction. Row upon row of tall, spinning wind turbines began to spring up around the globe, along with endless fields of corn for ethanol fuel production, and numerous green-roofs—a vast system of oxygen-replenishing rooftop gardens.

It was an encouraging beginning. But so much damage had already been done that Sam and The Sage could only hope it was not too late—that the tides of change would not suddenly turn back again. As they knew all too well, there were those still driven by greed, power and their own selfish desires. An underground movement, opposed to the newer, more responsible world, was already gaining ground. It started with a handful of displaced individuals who refused to abandon the wealth and status they had enjoyed in a wasteful and unstable world.

Among this group, there was none more enthusiastic than Dr. Ramona Mandrake, granddaughter of Avery and daughter of Basil. An accomplished scientist, Ramona dreamed of turning the clock back to the time when her experiments with genetic mutation would have been heralded as a brilliant achievement and not a moral outrage. Ramona was a prime target for The Fen, who lurked in the shadows, forever on the lookout for a receptive ear.

As for The Fen themselves, they had not slunk away in defeat when Sam and The Sage had spirited the scrolls to safety. Patient and unyielding, they were simply lying in wait for that rare chance, that golden opportunity, to infiltrate and corrupt. After all, the passage of time for creatures that lived for many hundreds of years was of little significance. They had busied themselves throughout the decades, worming their way into the cold hearts of people whom they could manipulate for their own evil purposes. Cunning and malevolent, they watched and they waited, biding their time while the fate of the world hung in the balance.

On the surface, it appeared that Ramona Mandrake was a kind and devoted daughter. She had recently announced that she would be taking some time off work to nurse her frail and aging father. The part of the story where Ramona's research funds had been suspended and her entire department placed under investigation for unethical practices had been conveniently omitted. She had also been experiencing an overwhelming desire to see the Mandrake family reputation restored in the scientific community. The stories of her grandfather Avery's humiliation at the hands of Professors Jaffrey and Hawthorne had been gnawing at her for years. If Ramona had her way, no one would ever again speak the name Mandrake without the respect it deserved. After moving back in with her father, Ramona set about establishing a makeshift laboratory where she could work on her pet projects, unencumbered by annoying visits from the scientific-ethics board.

Despite his advancing years, Basil was anything but feeble or needy. He had established a formidable reputation among the town's children as a nasty old curmudgeon. Even the neighborhood cats and dogs had taken to walking on the opposite side of the street whenever they passed his house. An obsessive sidewalk sweeper, Basil had a habit of lifting his broom and walloping any unsuspecting animal that ventured too close to his property. He really hadn't changed at all in seventy-five years. The cruel and spiteful boy who had challenged Sam in his youth had become a mean old man. For Basil, the worldwide fame of Fletcher Jaffrey and the resulting decline of his own father were almost too much to bear. His intense dislike for Fletcher and Sam grew steadily stronger, until it attained an almost folkloric quality. People in town would never have dreamt of inviting a Jaffrey or a Middleton anywhere that a Mandrake might turn up, even though Mandrakes were rarely on anyone's guest lists. Basil had already alienated the town council by attempting to open up a number of questionable enterprises in a dilapidated three-story building that he had purchased years earlier. One of his ventures had involved an attempt to profit from the illegal whalebone carving trade. This operation had been quickly detected and shut down and Basil had been forced to pay a hefty fine, but, as usual, he had managed to bounce back into some other business soon after. Fortunately, few of his seedy ventures survived for long, except for an old taxidermy shop on the main floor that was still in operation. For the past few years, Basil had been aided in this enterprise by his younger offspring, Lyle, a robotics-school dropout, who turned up every time the proceeds in his bank account began to run dry. Lyle (and the animal-stuffing store) were eyesores in an otherwise picturesque location, and rather an embarrassment, too, in a place that prided itself on its advances in wildlife conservation.

Sam thought on all these things as he made his way through town, glancing from time to time at Alice, who was strolling happily by his side. He wondered if the day he and The Sage were hoping for would come to pass in her lifetime. Sam was optimistic enough, most of the time, to imagine that it could, but today he had a strange feeling of foreboding instead.

Poor Alice always shuddered when she passed by the taxidermy shop's big front window, with its dust-covered and cobweb-infested display. But this was an unavoidable experience on most trips through the shopping district, as the store stood right smack in the middle of the town square. Alice had

tried averting her gaze whenever it came into view, but she was somehow strangely drawn to it.

Though they were long deceased, it was hard for Alice not to feel pity for the stuffed creatures, with their cold, glassy eyes. Despite their prominently visible price tags (some with numerous markdowns), none ever seemed to sell. With the recent restrictions on the taking of animal pelts, the profitable side of Basil Mandrake's stuffing business was in catering to the sportfishing enthusiasts. Despite growing public disapproval, and ongoing attempts to police their activities, they continued to flock to the area, eager to return home with a large trophy fish to mount on their den walls. In the front window, however, it was the same old mothballed bunch, year in and year out: a snowshoe hare, a striped skunk, a red fox, a great horned owl, a raccoon, a beaver, a young white-tailed deer and a tiny Eastern chipmunk. These had been arranged to encircle the largest (and most expensive) offering; a snarling, rearing, six-foot black bear—complete with flesh-tearing claws, jagged, pearl-white incisors and a gob of shiny, plastic drool running down its chin. This "window of death" as Alice called it was a shameful and ugly spectacle, but it was Basil Mandrake to a tee, Sam thought. Like father, like son.

Sam took Alice's hand and gave it a squeeze. "We should have taken the long way 'round today, shouldn't we have? Come on, let's get out of here."

With a few more years of experience under his belt than Alice, Sam had trained himself not to linger in front of the window. But something was different today. Something was new. It caught Sam's eye and drew it down to the bottom left side of the display, right beside the furry white foot of the snowshoe hare. It was nothing unusual, really, just the tiny stuffed body of a meadow mouse, crouched on his hind legs, his glass eyes staring into a kernel of yellow corn that he had been bent into position to nibble. But the sight of this particular little creature caused Sam to stiffen. Flustered, he reached his hand past his shirt collar and pulled out his magnifying glass.

"Poor little thing," Alice offered quietly. Then she continued with a tone of indignation. "Why is he making up new ones when he can't even sell the old ones he has? Mean old man!" She crouched down and stared at the mouse, then ran her finger gently over the glass. "I wonder where he came from."

Sam, peering intently through the magnifying glass, suddenly gasped. His mind raced. It couldn't be! It wasn't possible! But there it was, as plain as day. Knowing mice, as Sam surely did, it wasn't hard to remember that each one had a distinguishing mark. And this was a mark like no other; an unmistakable diamond-shaped patch of creamy fur at the throat that Sam had seen many times before. This little fellow was a lighthouse mouse. But how had he ended his days in Basil Mandrake's clutches? For every creature in the area, especially the mice who were dedicated to the guardianship of the ancient Martian scrolls, The House of Mandrake Taxidermy Emporium was to be avoided at all costs. Sam stared at the lifeless mouse again and shuddered. Only the day before yesterday, he'd seen the little fellow with a large chunk of Gorgonzola cheese wedged under his arm, chattering excitedly to his companions at home. He had just found (according to Edgar's mousespeak translation) a large, safe supply of gourmet cheese at an establishment somewhere in town. He had been so excited about his discovery, Sam recalled, that it was doubly heartbreaking to see what had become of him. And apart from the terrible tragedy of it all, this was a security breach that needed to be investigated immediately.

"Are you alright, Grandad?" Alice asked with concern. "You look kind of white."

"Um...yes, I think so," Sam replied, still trying to gather his thoughts. "Just a bit tired, that's all. Maybe a sit-down somewhere would help."

A sudden gust of wind blew through a pile of crimson maple leaves lying along the curb and hurled them against the dirty glass panes of Mandrake's front window. Sam shuddered again, then looked down the street, where his eyes fell upon a friendly and comforting sight: the old ice cream shop that had been serving its delectable wares for almost a hundred years. It wasn't exactly the same kind of treat that he had enjoyed as a boy—especially considering the newer, more popular flavors, like seaweed and dandelion—but they *still* had vanilla and for Sam, that was heaven. Alice, with as incurable a sweet tooth as her grandfather, needed no more persuading than a nod from Sam in the shop's direction. She ran ahead and secured one of the outside wrought-iron tables that faced away from the taxidermy shop.

Scattered autumn leaves crunched under Sam's feet as he made his way along the sidewalk. Still unnerved by what he had seen, he paused for a moment and turned back to look at Mandrake's shop one more time. For a split second, Sam was sure he could see movement in a small window on the third floor; a ripple of the curtain and a darting shadow. Wondering if they had been playing tricks on him, Sam rubbed his tired eyes. Either that, he thought, or someone had been watching them. He turned up the collar of his jacket and hurried over to Alice.

5

THE SMALLEST OF GIFTS SOMETIMES HIDES THE GREATEST OF TREASURES

Ever since she'd been very small, Sam had been bringing Alice to the ice cream shop regularly, for a treat and a story—usually one that involved her Great-Uncle Fletcher's exploits on Mars or an episode from the family's many encounters with the Mandrakes. From their spot on the shop's patio, Alice could just make out the big stone chimney of the Hawthorne house, Sam's boyhood home and the setting for all the exciting stories about the Hawthorne dynasty and the mysterious scrolls. The old house had been inherited by Sam almost twenty years before. He had decided to honor the memory of his parents by gifting the estate to the University Foundation on the condition that it be used to house Peggy and Trevor Middleton's extensive collection of Early American folk art so that future generations might study and enjoy it. History can teach us many things, as Mr. Goodfellow often remarked, and Sam was happy now to see that the art classes and history seminars held at the old house were an appropriate testament to the work that his parents had started there years earlier.

Abigail Spender, former administrative head of the university's art program, would have been overjoyed to know that her old department now included such a prestigious venue. The course of Ms. Spender's life (and that of Cedric Hawthorne's) had taken an unforeseen, but joyous, detour. Soon after she had finally ended her long and heart-breaking infatuation with Professor Mandrake, Ms. Spender and Professor Hawthorne (well into his nineties at the time) fell madly in love. They eloped and spent their remaining years breeding a line of prizewinning miniature poodles. All of the dogs could trace their bloodlines back to Ms. Spender's courageous companion François, a small but determined creature who'd distinguished himself one Labor Day weekend by defending his mistress's honor and biting off the tip of Professor Mandrake's long and pointy nose. This was one of Alice's favorite tales. She especially liked the part when her heroic grandfather had rushed to François' aid. With barely a thought for his own safety, Sam had risked his life in a brave attempt to save the little poodle who'd been cruelly tossed into the sea by Mandrake and left to drown. Sam loved to tell the story as much as Alice liked to hear it, although he always regretted that the best parts were the ones he couldn't share. The wise and steadfast Sage, the wicked, shadowy Fen and the brave band of Scandinavian Sea Mice that had plucked him and François from certain death—these were details for Sam alone to know and remember. Alice Hannah Durham, though, was a particularly perceptive girl. Sam couldn't help but notice that even as his stories came to the same ending time after time, Alice had an odd habit of holding her breath, as if she somehow suspected that there was a lot more to tell.

Sam tried to stop by the Hawthorne house as often as he could. He liked to make sure that everything was running smoothly, but he especially loved standing in his old room again, converted now to one of the gallery offices. It was there, on an autumn night seventy-five years before, that Sam had met a small Sage by the name of Mr. Goodfellow. It was a meeting that had changed his life forever. Sam had always felt a profound sense of peace in that room and whenever he stood there and closed his eyes, he could almost believe that he was twelve again. He could hear his parents laughing in the kitchen downstairs, and the excited barks of Figgy, his faithful boxer, as he tore across the landing. He remembered the sound that scurrying mouse feet made behind his bedroom wall, and Fletcher's voice, calling to him through an open window. On some days, the memories would be vivid enough to bring a smile to Sam's face, or (especially in these last few years) a tear to his eye.

After they had finished their ice creams and Sam had delivered yet another rendition of the François and Mandrake story, Sam and Alice continued their walk through town until they reached a street that had once been as familiar to Sam as his own. It was here, in a big, white, wood-framed house, that Fletcher and India had lived with their parents—Sanjid, the chemistry professor, and Leonora, the opera singer—and an ever-present pack of boxers. For the last thirty years or so, Fletcher had lived there alone—except for when he was touring about, giving lectures on his years in the Space Program or recounting the excitement of landing on another planet. The first words spoken at that monumental moment were etched forever in the history records. In a nod to the theories of Professor Hawthorne and his own father, Fletcher had composed a little poem: *From a distant world, through the blackness of space/ We, the sons and daughters of an ancient race/ Bring back the legacy of all things that remain/ Mankind will nevermore say 'you can't go home again.'* It was vintage Fletcher. It may have sounded a bit corny, but it was heartfelt and sincere, and there was definitely some Jolly Goodfellow input in the last line.

With Alice by his side, Sam stood on the front porch of the old Jaffrey house and pressed the code into the entry pad. With a faint beep, the door lock unlatched and Sam pushed his weight against it. It had been a few weeks since Sam's last visit. Now, with the onset of fall, the house was just beginning to feel a little cool inside. Sam shivered, more from the atmosphere than the temperature, as he stood inside the front hallway and fiddled with the climate-control panel. The house was darker and gloomier than he remembered, as if it sensed that its master might not return.

Sam made his way through the long corridor toward the study. Many years before, this room had been the scholarly domain of Professor Sanjid Jaffrey. After his retirement, Fletcher's father had transformed the room into a shrine to the Space Program and, of course, his famous son. The walls were lined with framed holographic pictures of each of the Mars expedition crews, with particular emphasis on the first seven, all of which had been captained by Fletcher. One entire bookshelf had been devoted to the literature and laser records that Sanjid had collected about the Red Planet and the discoveries made there. On the next bookshelf over were several old scrapbooks, including the one that Sam had started, when Fletcher revealed his secret dream to be the first astronaut on Mars.

Alice had visited the house many times before and had grown keenly aware of Sam's mood changes whenever he passed through the front door. He became much more reflective and melancholy, and it made Alice sad to see just how much her grandfather missed his best friend. Alice still remembered her Great-Uncle Fletcher, but less vividly as the years passed. She had been barely eight the last time she had seen him and now that she was older, Alice wished that she had not taken so much of her family's history for granted. There were many things she wanted to ask Fletcher, but it was too late now. As she stood in the study, surrounded by all these things from the past, Alice couldn't help but stare at the framed holographs and news articles with greater interest and a hint of regret.

There were fascinating scenes of astronauts posing with archeological finds, famous the world over now. In one of them, Fletcher grinned behind the visor of his space helmet as he straddled the nose of the giant Martian face—the one that had been the source of so much speculation and heated debate when it was first photographed by the Viking orbiter in the 1970s. Far below him, their elbows resting on hydraulic metal diggers, several other crewmen were looking up and smiling, too, taking a break from unearthing what lay beneath the red soil at their feet. Here were dozens of intricately carved stone heads, stacked one on top of another like a gigantic totem pole. It was a structure that X-ray imagery had revealed to be almost 100 stories high. In another scene, astronauts crowded around the base of something strangely similar in size and shape to the great Egyptian pyramid of Cheops, but this one was a transparent structure that on closer inspection appeared to have formed part of a magnificent rooftop atrium. All of this and much more lay beneath the tons of red silt that the receding Martian floodwaters had deposited thousands and thousands of years before. Sprawling cities of metal and glass, bridges that spanned mile-deep canyons, exquisite art-work and sculptured crystal waterfalls—all in ruins and all just as Professor Hawthorne and Sam had seen in the holographic message balls deep in the core of the crop circle. And all as described in the Hawthorne/Jaffrey papers.

On the big cherry-wood desk in the center of the room, one of the scrapbooks lay open to display the news releases that Sam had continued to paste in over the years. There was the intriguing story of aging astronaut and international hero, Colonel Fletcher Jaffrey, and his mysterious disappearance five years before: "MARS PIONEER VANISHES FROM FACE OF THE EARTH." This news had led to a considerable amount of speculation and even more headlines, especially in those sensational weekly tabloids dedicated to printing the supremely unbelievable. Sam had even included a couple of these, purely for fun. "WISCONSIN FARMER CLAIMS SPACEMAN NOT MISSING AT ALL—REPORTS STRANGE GOINGS-ON AND EXTRA COW IN HERD." And Sam's personal favorite; the picture of a woman holding a blanketed infant with the face of a 1960s space chimpanzee. The accompanying headline read: "I HAD FLETCHER JAFFREY'S SPACE BABY." This ongoing besmirching of one of the space community's most honored heroes was becoming a monumental embarrassment to NASA. And so, a few weeks later, another headline appeared in one of the more respectable publications: "PERSISTENT RUMORS FORCE NASA TO REVEAL EXISTENCE OF SECRET SPACE MISSION. PURPOSE AND DESTINATION AS YET UNKNOWN— MISSING SENIOR ASTRONAUT BELIEVED TO BE ABOARD."

Sam and India were greatly relieved that Fletcher had been found alive, but despite repeated requests for further information, NASA wasn't willing to reveal much more. Every so often, the space agency executives would release a brief statement that included friendly messages from the astronauts, but that was all. Then, four years into the mission, word came that communications had been temporarily lost. Despite assurances that the problem was a simple technical glitch, attempts to re-establish contact with the ship proved fruitless. "NASA EXPERTS UNABLE TO SOLVE COMMUNICATION SNAFU. FATE OF MYSTERY SHIP AND CREW IN QUESTION." These ominous headlines, months old now, were the last ones in the scrapbook for Alice to read. Sam would have to add the final clipping sometime later; that fateful announcement, only hours old, that ship and crew had been declared officially lost and their covert mission terminated.

While Alice was engrossed in her reading, Sam scanned the bookshelves. He fingered the key in his pocket, hoping that it might help him remember which book Professor Jaffrey had used to hide the wooden box; the same small box he had concealed the scroll sliver in so many years before. Had Fletcher decided to move it? Sam wondered. All of Sanjid's old chemistry texts were still there, along with just about every book of note that had ever been written about planets and space travel and the origin of the universe. Works by Clarke and Sagan and Hawking swam before Sam, swirling together into one hazy blur until one of his eyes finally came to rest on a brightly bound book, set a little apart from the others. Sam turned his head sideways to read the title—*One Thousand REALLY Funny Jokes*—and started to chuckle. This *had* to be the one, he thought, remembering a summer long, long ago when Fletcher's brief but annoying flirtation with practical joking had almost driven him mad. Fletcher would have wanted the last laugh, especially at a somber moment like this. He reached for the book and pulled it all the way forward to the edge of the shelf, then stood up on his tiptoes and peered behind. It was impossible to make anything out in the small, darkened space, so Sam stretched his arm as far as he could, groping in the shadows until the ends of his fingers collided with an object that was hard and sharp. Stretching just a bit farther, Sam grasped one corner of the thing and pulled it toward him. The light from the window glinted off the strip of gold-colored metal piping that adorned Sanjid's old wooden box.

Holding the box in one hand, Sam fumbled around inside his jacket with the other. When he had extracted the gold key, he slowly slipped it into the lock and turned it clockwise until he heard a soft click. Sam paused then and held his breath. A dozen questions filled his mind: What on earth could be inside? What had Fletcher felt compelled to squirrel away for so many years? And why could he have it only now, when Fletcher was gone?

Sam pulled the key from the lock and gently lifted the box lid. Folded neatly into a square and fitting snugly inside the box was a piece of yellowed writing paper. Sam pried it loose with his fingernail and pulled it out, revealing a small mound of crinkled tissue paper. Underneath *that* lay a tiny book, not much bigger than a packet of matches, its thick cover decorated with an arrangement of ornate geometric patterns. In several places, tiny, multicolored gems had been embedded deep into the cover's surface. They shone and sparkled in the light that was filtering through the study window. Sam ran his finger across the cover, then picked up the small book and carefully opened it. With the aid of his magnifying glass, he attempted to read the markings on the shining silver pages; line upon line of black strokes and squiggles, faded in some places, almost rubbed away with time and wear in others—all in a script that he had never seen before.

Sam looked up and turned his head. Alice, with her back to him, was still poring over the contents of the scrapbooks. After returning the wooden box to its place on the bookshelf,

Sam quickly slipped the odd little book into his jacket pocket, unfolded the yellowed paper and began to read.

Sam,

    Well, here we are. Or, I guess I should say, here you are. After all, if you're reading this letter now, then I'm already gone, right? I hope it was a respectable departure (something to do with space, at least). When you've been in the limelight as much as I have, you always worry that you'll end your days slipping on a banana peel or ingesting a tainted oyster or something. Wouldn't be a real classy way to go out for a guy who's been to Mars twice, would it?

Sam stopped reading. Fletcher had been to Mars *seven* times in his illustrious career, not two. He must have written the letter before his most famous mission of all.

Whatever it was, I hope that it didn't end up being something dumb or embarrassing for the rest of you. Anyway, I guess I should get to the point. You must be wondering by now why I left this little thing for you. Actually, I've been hanging on to it for awhile—since the last mission to Mars—trying to figure out what to do with it. As you know, that trip wasn't the great success we were all hoping for—a bit of a disappointment (archeologically speaking, that is). Just the same sort of stuff we found the first time—a few scattered artifacts, like this one here. But now that NASA's finished analyzing all the aerial and underground surveillance data, they think they may have found something really significant. That's why we're going on another mission right away. I have a feeling that this is going to be the big one. I can't wait to go back into space,

Sam! It may sound funny, but I feel that I kind of belong there. I can't help it! I guess it must be in my blood or something. I don't know why, but somehow I think you'll understand what I'm trying to say. By the way, my dad is really excited by what we might find this time. His only regret is that old Professor Hawthorne didn't live long enough to see all of this. (But hey—reaching 110 was a pretty amazing accomplishment in itself, wasn't it?)

Now, about this little book. I shouldn't have kept it, I guess. I should have handed it over once we returned to Earth, but I just couldn't. It didn't seem right for the book to end up in a science lab to be picked apart and then put on display in a stuffy old museum somewhere. When I first found it, I couldn't help but feel that it really belonged to someone else. I figured it must have been a Martian kid's toy, or something. But as soon as I picked it up, I had these really strange feelings. All I could think about was you, Sam—maybe it was because of all those miniature things you loved so much when we were kids. Whatever it was, I had to give it to you someday, no matter what.

I'm not the kind of guy who gets all mushy about stuff too often, Sam, but hear me out. I figure that I've been living on the edge for a pretty long time now. You never can tell what's going to happen up there. Space is an unpredictable world to hang around in, even though it feels like home to me. Anyway, I'm putting this little thing in Dad's old box and leaving a letter and key with the folks at NASA, just in case I don't come home one day. I was going to give it to you a million times myself, but something kept holding me back. I wanted the book to mean something real special—a kind of final gift to you when the time came, so that whenever you looked at it, you'd remember me.

Well, that's it I guess. I'm starting to get all choked up here, anyway. Hey, maybe I'll live to be 110, too! Wouldn't that be something? And if you go first, then I've just written this whole letter for nothing!

You've been like a real brother to me, Sam. Thanks for everything: for standing there and cheering for me, and keeping an eye on everybody else while I was floating around in space—especially India. By the way, are you guys ever going to get together? Faint heart never won fair lady, you know!

Fletch

Sam folded the old letter back up, popped it into his pocket alongside the book and scratched his head. That was exactly the same proverb that he and Edgar had recited to Mr. Goodfellow about Beatrice, seventy-five years ago. And years later—not long after Fletcher had written his letter and as he was speeding back to Mars on his third and most important mission—Sam had finally proposed to India Jaffrey and Fletcher had become his brother-in-law, after all.

When the time came to leave the Jaffrey house and its memories behind, Sam made a quick survey of all the rooms, and Alice returned the scrapbooks to their place on the bookshelf. They finished up their Saturday afternoon trip to town by catching the latest holospan epic. It was a remake of *Lawrence of Arabia*, made even more spectacular than the original with the simulated desert atmosphere, date-flavored popcorn topping and the pungent aroma of camel that hung over the audience. Sam nearly jumped out of his revolving seat when one of the holographic mammals suddenly ambled up to him and snorted something very unpleasant into his face.

Sam had some reservations about this type of entertainment, particularly as it didn't really fit in with the town's usually stringent dedication to historic preservation, but Alice enjoyed the show immensely. She talked nonstop about it all the way back through town, dancing about and gesturing excitedly as she relived her favorite scenes, distracting both herself and Sam from the fact that they were wandering straight toward the taxidermy shop's front window.

"Slow down, Alice Hannah," Sam warned. "You're going to collide with something!"

But it was too late. Grimacing as she suddenly came face-to-face with Mandrake's snarling bear, Alice stopped her girlish twirling and began to stumble. As Sam grabbed her by the arm and heroically swept her across the street, he turned his head to take one last look at the sad sight of the stuffed lighthouse mouse. To his amazement, the space at the foot of the snowshoe hare was no longer occupied. His eyes searched the length and breadth of the filthy window, but the mouse had vanished. Sam shook his head. Had he imagined the whole thing? No, of course not, he reasoned. Alice had seen it too, hadn't she? He thought about asking her, then quickly changed his mind. From the strained expression on her face, Sam could see that Alice had had enough of the window of death for one day. And he had no intention of telling her about the shadowy movements behind the third-floor window, either—at least not right now. He would wait for a more fitting opportunity to bring it up. Anyway, it was time to go home. India would be expecting them. Sam suddenly felt very tired. It was probably just his aging eyes playing tricks on him, he supposed. Or maybe he *had* imagined both the stuffed mouse and Alice seeing it, too. Sam sighed. It wasn't easy growing old.

6

A Babe in the House Is a
Wellspring of Joy

S am shared a quick supper with Alice and India, then
made his way through the lighthouse walkway to
show the mysterious little book to Edgar. He was
eager to know what his friend might make of Fletcher's
strange gift and was both disappointed and concerned to find
Edgar and Charlotte missing. From the agitated condition of
the mice, Sam knew something was up. There had been many
times over the years that he wished he could converse in
mousespeak, but never so much as now. He tried a form of
primitive sign language, extending his arms in front of him
and moving them over his belly to represent Charlotte's condition. At first, the mice seemed utterly confused. Then one
of them, a bright little black-and-white creature known to
Sam as Lydia—Rollo's great-great-great-granddaughter (many
times removed)—suddenly scurried into the wall cavity and
returned with a small piece of paper clutched in her paw.
Employing his magnifying glass, Sam discovered that it was a
brief and hastily written note from Edgar that the rest of the
mice had forgotten about in all the excitement. *Charlotte feeling a little strange*, Edgar had frantically scrawled. *Me, too! I*

think this is it! Gone to Blue Heron Cottage. Will send word by mouse later.

Thinking that it was probably best to let nature take its course, and knowing that India would find his sudden urge to take a stroll along the beach in the pitch dark a bit puzzling, Sam resisted the temptation to dash over to the Goodfellows' that night. He might as well have, though. A trip across the channel would have been a welcome relief from all the tossing and turning he found himself enduring in the final hours before dawn. It had come as quite a shock when he'd returned home to see the formerly stuffed mouse from Mandrake's, complete with the distinctive diamond-shaped patch of cream-colored fur at his throat, alive and well and in the company of the other lighthouse mice. As bizarre and unpleasant a realization as it was, Sam concluded that he really *must* have imagined the whole thing. What other explanation could there be? He decided not to bring up the window incident with Alice again, after all. He wasn't about to have her worrying about him.

When Sam did make his way to the Goodfellows' very early the next morning, he discovered that everything at Blue Heron Cottage had been turned upside down. His concerns about his own mental state soon melted away. Charlotte had indeed given birth the night before, not to one, but two, tiny Sage; twin boys, in fact. Edgar was a little overcome, and totally unprepared for his role as the father of two, but he had performed admirably as a steadfast and able coach for Charlotte, repressing the urge to faint until much later.

Over the next few days, as news of Winston and Little Jolly's arrival spread throughout the Sage world, dozens of congratulatory cards and baby presents began to arrive by mouse courier. When a fair number had collected in the front sitting room, and Charlotte and Edgar began to feel overwhelmed by the mountain of unanswered greetings, it was decided that everyone should lend a hand. On the fifth morning after the birth—a crisp but sunny autumn day—Mr. Goodfellow insisted that he was quite capable of entertaining the twins while the rest of the family was occupied with their correspondence.

"I know that you all think a childless old Sage can't handle a couple of youngsters, but we'll be fine," he assured them. "I'll take them outside for a breath of fresh sea air. Just leave them with their Uncle Jolly. It's time we boys spent a few moments getting to know each other better, anyway."

A miniature wicker basket that had once held a chocolate-coated peanut butter Easter egg (courtesy of Sam) was the perfect size for two newborn Sage, each no bigger than the tip of Sam's thumb. While Sam waited outside the front door, Mr. Goodfellow carried the basket onto the covered porch and gently set it down. Sam stared at the babies. Each had a very short cap of red hair at the top of its head, the same color as Edgar's, standing up like a fuzzy halo just above two bright button eyes, deep and brown like Charlotte's. They were handsome little boys, pink and plump, looking a bit like baby mice, but endowed with considerably stronger vocal chords than any rodent Sam had ever encountered. It was truly remarkable, he thought, that two things so small could make that much noise.

"Goodfellow lungs!" shouted Mr. Goodfellow over the noise. "Edgar had them, too, as I recall!" He tried rocking the basket back and forth with the tip of his mouse claw, wincing slightly and covering his ears as the babies' cries grew even louder. "Of course, the stereo effect is something new, I must admit." He nervously peered back through the window for reinforcements, but the rest of The Sage, oblivious to the hideous screaming outside, were up to their elbows in shiny bows and colored paper.

"I say, everyone! I say—" But Mr. Goodfellow's words were drowned out by a loud chorus of excited "oooo's" as Charlotte and Edgar held up a matching pair of teeny beige-colored mouse suits, a gift from Great-Uncle Cyrus.

Mr. Goodfellow turned back to the babies with a look of creeping desperation on his face. "There, there now, Winston, my boy," he whispered lovingly, lifting one baby out of the basket and giving it several frantic pats on the back.

Squinting his eyes, Sam leaned farther over. "That's Little Jolly," he casually remarked.

"Really?" Mr. Goodfellow replied with surprise, holding the baby out in front of him to examine it. "Are you sure?" His eyes darted to the baby in the basket and then back again. "How on earth can you tell? They're identical!"

"Not really. Take a closer look," Sam suggested. "Winston's much more jowly around the chin. See?"

Mr. Goodfellow returned the little bundle to the basket and stared down at both babies with an expression of embarrassment. He really had no idea which screaming child was which. But that was the least of his worries right now.

"Sam," he suddenly cried out in panic, "are the little tykes supposed to turn purple?"

Mr. Goodfellow was even too distracted to call Porter to task. As the boy dashed out of the front door with a beach ball under one arm and Jasper under the other, it appeared he had managed to craft (without permission) a very attractive pet collar and leash from a pair of Mr. Goodfellow's best suspenders.

It seemed to Sam that his dear old friend was clearly into this baby business way over his head. When Jasper (possibly inspired by all the crying) decided to do what cicadas do best and join in with his high-pitched, chain-saw-like acoustics, it looked as if Mr. Goodfellow might lose his composure altogether. Feeling very sorry for him, Sam tried offering the twins a distraction. He quickly pulled the chain out from around his neck and jangled his tiny Scandinavian Sea Mouse knife over their basket. When that proved ineffective, he took hold of his magnifying glass. He was a parent and grandparent himself, after all. Maybe the poor little things were feverish or had something sharp poking into them. No sooner had he leaned over the basket and lifted the glass up to his eye to get a better look than one of the babies stopped crying and started chortling, followed almost immediately by a flood of gurgles from the other.

"I say! What's happening in there?" Mr. Goodfellow whispered excitedly, as he bent over the basket.

"I'm not sure," Sam replied. "Maybe it's the magnifying glass." He tried to move it out of their line of sight, but the babies giggled even louder.

"I'm more inclined to think that it's you, Sam," Mr. Goodfellow concluded. "You're a hit! Always did have a way with the younger crowd, didn't you? Just like Edgar."

Sam shrugged. "I don't know what it could be, really. I wasn't even trying that hard."

"The point, exactly! Children can't be fooled by contrivances. They appreciate the unexpected. The sight of your distorted features behind that glass must have struck them as hugely comical. You seem to have won them over, at any rate. And not a moment too soon, I might add," he whispered, peering through the window into the front sitting room. "It looks like the party's breaking up in there!"

Mr. Goodfellow was immensely satisfied at the moment, particularly since it would appear to all of his relatives that they had not misplaced their trust in him. By the time Edgar emerged from the house to take the twins back to Charlotte for their ten o'clock feeding, Winston and Little Jolly were back to their normal pinkish color, and as happy as clams.

"Lovely boys! And no trouble at all," Mr. Goodfellow reported, when Edgar returned to join his uncle on the porch. Settling himself into an old wooden rocking chair, Mr. Goodfellow gave Sam a wink. "Why, I was just telling Sam here how much the little fellows remind me of you when you were a youngster. It seems like yesterday to me, Edgar. It's hard to believe that you're a father yourself now."

Mr. Goodfellow stopped rocking his chair as a look of melancholy swept across his face. He took a folded white handkerchief from the inside of his suit and gave his nose an impressive blow.

"All our sweetest hours fly the fastest," he said, his voice quivering. "Remember when I told you that proverb years ago, Edgar? Those little lads of yours will be grown before you know it. Don't let the time in between slip away too soon, my boy." He quickly blew his nose again and returned the hankie to his suit.

Edgar nodded his head. The three of them sat quietly for the next few moments, lost in their own thoughts of friends and family.

Sam looked up first, sensing that now might be an appropriate time to show them the artifact that Fletcher had tucked away five decades earlier. When Sam pulled the miniature book out of his pocket, Edgar and Mr. Goodfellow made their way down from the porch and onto the soft sand. It was obvious from the expression on Mr. Goodfellow's face that this was not the first time he had seen the book. He looked it up and down, then slowly ran his paw across the bright jewels and strange markings that adorned its cover.

"I always regretted that I didn't have a chance to take a closer look at this all those years ago," Mr. Goodfellow remarked. "It wasn't as if I didn't try, mind you. There was something immensely intriguing about it, but Fletcher had a one-track mind about the thing. For some reason, he wanted it just for you, Sam, and no whispered suggestion otherwise could dissuade him. He brought it back to Earth inside his space suit and immediately concealed it in that box. Later on, he wrote the note to you and hid everything in the bookshelf, forwarding the key to NASA with strict instructions concerning its delivery."

"You knew about it all along, then?" Sam asked.

"Well, of course I did! I was there when he found it! It was on the second Mars expedition, if my memory serves me; the one to the Elysium region, not long after the first expedition had uncovered a small but promising nest of artifacts buried deep within a system of caves in the Valles Marineris. The scientific discoveries on that second trip were somewhat disappointing, relatively speaking. Just a few bits and pieces were found: simple, everyday remnants of Martian life. It wasn't until the next mission two years later—to the Tharsis region at the foot of the great mountain, Olympus Mons, that the most spectacular archeological relics began to be unearthed. By then, the Elysium expedition and its small finds were all but forgotten, save for a few samples that Fletcher and the other astronauts gathered up to bring home."

"But you *knew* that Fletcher had left this for me fifty years ago! Why couldn't you tell me about it?" asked Sam.

"Because it was a confidence that I could not betray," Mr. Goodfellow replied. "This was to be something between you and Fletcher; something with which I, even as his Sage, could not interfere. I hope that you understand, Sam. Its existence had to be revealed to you in a manner and at a time chosen by Fletcher himself—"

"The time of his *death*?" exclaimed Sam.

"It was as *he* wished, Sam."

"But why?"

"All I know is that it was something Fletcher felt very strongly about. He cared for you a great deal, you know. You were there with him every step of the way as his career with the Space Program progressed. You bolstered his spirits as he set off on each new mission, and took pride in his successes with never an ounce of regret or envy. Fletcher understood that. It was almost as if he knew, too, deep in his heart, that the destiny of his best friend, a lighthouse keeper, might be far greater than his own. Perhaps Fletcher wanted to leave you this gift as a final affirmation of brotherly love—something he was certain you would appreciate, a thing so rare and special that you could not possibly forget him when he was gone."

"But that's crazy! I don't need anything to help me remember Fletcher!" Sam sighed in frustration.

"Nevertheless, Sam, it was important to *him*," Mr. Goodfellow replied.

"But what did he mean when he said he had a strange feeling that it belonged somewhere else, and that he thought I might know what to do with it?"

Mr. Goodfellow scratched his head. "I'm afraid I'm not entirely sure about that."

Edgar, who had been quietly studying the small book while Mr. Goodfellow and Sam were speaking, suddenly looked up.

"There's something really odd about this thing, Uncle Jolly. I think you'd better take a closer look."

Mr. Goodfellow shuffled over to where Edgar was balancing the opened book on his knees, and peered over his shoulder.

Edgar pointed a mouse claw to a symbol at the top of a page and whispered softly, "That looks just like part of the—"

"High Crest of the Governing Council!" Mr. Goodfellow interrupted. "My goodness, so it does, Edgar! How extraordinary!"

"But how could that be, Uncle Jolly?" Edgar asked, looking puzzled. "Here, in a book that Fletcher Jaffrey found on Mars—"

Just then, Mr. Goodfellow dropped onto the sand beside Edgar and took the book from his grasp. He flipped through the pages from front to back and then back again. His face grew flushed and his paws began to tremble.

"Uncle Jolly..." Edgar began again, his voice straining, "you don't think that it's..."

"The Book of The Sage, Edgar?" Mr. Goodfellow finished in a dry whisper. "It couldn't be."

Edgar gulped. Mr. Goodfellow looked up and stared at him with eyes that were wild with wonder.

"It's just a story, Edgar. Everyone knows that."

Intrigued, Sam leaned forward. "What's this Book of The Sage thing, anyway?"

"It's a mythical relic that was supposedly lost long, long ago," Mr. Goodfellow replied. "It is so old and ancient, so steeped in fancy, that I don't think anyone truly believes that it really exists. It's a tall tale that every young Sage hears around the family hearth at least once."

"But what does it say?" asked Sam. "If it really is this old book, what's it all about?"

"It's about us," said Edgar quietly.

"Or so the myth goes," Mr. Goodfellow interjected. "It's supposed to contain the knowledge of the ancients of our race, our origins and, in fact, the very reason for our existence." He hesitated a little before he continued. "The book is also reputed by some to contain a darker element in the history of The Sage. What this might be has always been a source of great speculation. All I can tell you is that this part of the legend usually makes the younger Sage move a little closer to the comfort of their fireplaces on cold, dark nights."

Even now, enveloped in the warmth of his mouse suit, Edgar couldn't help but shiver. Mr. Goodfellow continued to examine the book's strange black script.

"If we could understand the written language of the old ones, perhaps these mysteries would finally be revealed. But those who might have understood any of this are long buried, I'm afraid. The Book of The Sage—if indeed this is what we are holding—would, according to legend, be tens of thousands of years old. It comes from a time when we Sage may have been altogether different from what we are now."

"But what was the book—or The Sage who wrote it—doing on Mars?" asked Sam.

"That, my dear friend, is the million-dollar question," said Mr. Goodfellow, "with an answer, I fear, that may be locked forever in this book." He shook his head in frustration at the meaningless lines of script that lay before his eyes. "Unless..."

As he often did when he was deep in thought, Mr. Goodfellow furrowed his brow and absently began to tap his claws together. A slow smile spread across his face.

"What, Uncle Jolly?" asked Edgar. "What is it?"

"More correctly, Edgar, *who*. There is only one soul on Earth I can think of who might be able to make some sense of this. The most senior member of our community comes to mind, older by far than even Great-Uncle Cyrus."

"Delphinia Shipton?" asked Edgar, barely able to whisper the name.

"Precisely, my boy!"

"But no one has seen her for years!" Edgar exclaimed. "She's *really* ancient, Uncle Jolly! Nobody's sure where she lives, either, and besides that, she might not be alive anymore."

"Oh, she's alive, Edgar," Mr. Goodfellow replied with conviction. "You can be sure of that. We would know if such a great Sage mystic were no longer among us. I have no doubt that the passing of someone with her vast stores of knowledge about Sage history and tradition would send a sizable energy ripple throughout our world. She occasionally comes out of hiding, I'm told, with the right amount of persuasion. In my humble opinion, Edgar, the esteemed elders of The Governing Council would do well to find Delphinia Shipton as soon as possible."

At that, Mr. Goodfellow tucked the thick book under his nephew's arm and ushered him toward the cottage, then pulled a notepad and pen from the inside of his suit. Edgar immediately transferred the book into the palms of both paws, carrying it as far out in front of him as he could safely manage, with a newfound sense of reverence and a little terror.

"If we've stumbled upon what we suspect, Edgar, then the others must see the book at once," Mr. Goodfellow called after him with a tone of urgency in his voice. "Then send for a courier, if you will, my boy. I'll compose a message for Great-Uncle Cyrus. He's Delphinia's oldest friend, you know. If anyone can find the elusive Mrs. Shipton, it would have to be Cyrus Goodfellow."

Despite all the technological advances over the decades, it was still common practice among The Sage to employ the services of the elite mouse courier service, as it provided the safest and most discreet means of communication. While

Edgar showed The Book of The Sage to the rest of the family, Mr. Goodfellow remained outside with Sam. Using shorthand, he quickly wrote down everything he needed to say to Great-Uncle Cyrus while the thoughts were still fresh in his mind. Then he pulled a crisp, white sheet of paper from his notebook and proceeded to execute a letter in his best hand-writing. Painfully conscious of what a stickler old Cyrus was about penmanship skills, Mr. Goodfellow felt as nervous as a schoolboy as he rounded his vowels, dotted his "i's" and crossed his "t's" with extra care and precision. Whenever his hand slipped, or his pen discharged an unsightly ink blob, he would sigh with frustration, crunch the paper into a tight lit-tle ball, throw it onto the sand and start all over again. When he began to utter a few milder curse words as well, Sam decided it might be best to head home and leave him to it.

Alone with his work, Mr. Goodfellow paused every now and then, whenever he needed to rest his cramped hand, stop-ping altogether when he detected a faint rustling in the wild-rose bushes beside him. He cocked his head to one side and listened intently.

"Drat!" he whispered to himself. "Shrews again! They'll be wanting to prattle on for hours about the weather conditions or something." Mr. Goodfellow quietly collected his papers and started tiptoeing toward the cottage. "I have no time for such folly right now," he mumbled.

Careful not to make a sound, Mr. Goodfellow slowly crept across the sand, glancing back several times to make sure he had successfully eluded his would-be companions. He had almost made it to the bottom of the cottage steps when he suddenly collided with someone who was doing a little creeping of his own. White papers flew everywhere. When Mr. Goodfellow bent down to retrieve them, two paws reached forward to assist him. These were mouse paws, though, not shrew's. Mr. Goodfellow breathed a sigh of relief as he looked up into the muzzle of a lighthouse mouse.

"Lucky for me it turned out to be you, old chap!" he exclaimed. "I thought you were a shrew or two, you know, and I wasn't looking forward to explaining my behavior to them. They're so easily offended, aren't they?"

The mouse, twitching his whiskers, looked right into Mr. Goodfellow's eyes, then grinned in a peculiar way. Before Mr. Goodfellow could inquire as to the reason for his visit to Blue Heron Cottage or if he required any assistance, the mouse turned to leave. As the midday sun glinted off the patch of diamond-shaped, creamy fur at his throat, he quickly shoved a pawful of papers into Mr. Goodfellow's arms and scurried off in the direction of the town, as if he was in a great hurry to be somewhere else.

Mr. Goodfellow struggled to straighten his papers as he climbed up the cottage steps. He made a mental note to ask Edgar what the mouse had been doing there. Perhaps he had delivered a message of some sort. But as his mind wandered back to more pressing thoughts—The Book of The Sage, his letter to Great-Uncle Cyrus, and, of course, whether they would be able to find Delphinia Shipton—Mr. Goodfellow soon forgot all about the lighthouse mouse and whatever business he might have been on.

7

A Little Knowledge Is a Dangerous Thing

After all the excitement generated by the discovery of The Book of The Sage, the next few weeks seemed interminably slow as Mr. Goodfellow and the others waited for a reply from Great-Uncle Cyrus.

Unable to delay their return to South America any longer, Ashcroft and Penelope Sparrow finally bid a tearful farewell to their new grandsons, promising Charlotte that they would come for another visit as soon as they were able. Hartland and Edwina Sparrow decided to return home, too, to their Californian ranch/spa and vineyard. Harvesttime had arrived and since experienced help was hard to come by, Hartland had been forced to leave his precious grape crop in the care of an itinerant chipmunk family. Mr. Goodfellow was secretly delighted that Blue Heron Cottage was finally clearing out, although he did his best to appear quite disconsolate over the various departures. Beatrice had not been fooled by his behavior for one second, and had sent him some very disapproving looks. When she invited Filbert and Hazel to stay on for a while longer, he hadn't dared protest. Porter, on an extended school break, also remained, urged by his parents to spend some quality time with his big sister and his new nephews. Jasper, too, was still about, although Mr. Goodfellow never stopped hoping that the call of the wild would lure him home one day.

Even at that, Blue Heron Cottage had managed to regain much of its former tranquillity. This was especially noticeable on the days when Charlotte—with the twins, Edgar, his parents, and Porter and Jasper in tow—insisted on returning to the lightkeeper's house to see how India was faring. Mr. Goodfellow relished those days, especially when Sam came by to visit and they could wander out to the old bench by the sea dunes and contemplate the world together.

It was on one of these occasions—when the fall winds had begun to carry a distinctly winter-like chill—that the peaceful atmosphere of Mr. Goodfellow's dune sanctuary was abruptly invaded by the arrival of an express mouse courier with an urgent delivery.

With great anticipation, Mr. Goodfellow tore the letter open to discover that it was indeed what they had all been waiting for. Great-Uncle Cyrus began by apologizing for the length of time it had taken to reply, then proceeded to relate the story of how he had managed to track down the elusive Delphinia Shipton. Knowing that Delphinia would not reveal herself to just anyone, and in spite of his greatly advanced years, Cyrus had decided to take on the assignment himself. The whole operation read like a complex detective novel, but one that unraveled at a much slower pace than most, as Cyrus shuffled valiantly from one clue to another with the aid of his walker. Armed with tips from a host of traveling Sage and assorted forest creatures, Cyrus finally located Delphinia in a place that seemed an appropriate home for a 1,800-year-old mystic: a cave high atop a cliff on the windswept Cornish

coast—a stone's throw from Tintagel, legendary birthplace of King Arthur. It was also the home of Delphinia's girlhood, where, as Sage lore had it, she had counseled the great wizard Merlin. This rumored relationship did much to fan the flames of mystery that flickered around Delphinia Shipton and her strange powers. And Delphinia, choosing to live the life of a hermit and never to speak of those years, had done nothing to explain or dispel the stories.

Cyrus had been relieved to find Delphinia in such remarkable shape for her age. She had been delighted to see her old friend, and had welcomed him graciously. The dark, damp and drafty cave he had expected to find was actually warm and inviting. Several wall-mounted torches provided adequate heat and also illuminated the vast collection of beautiful artifacts that Delphinia had collected throughout the centuries: polished wood furnishings, marble sculpture works and some absolutely stunning hand-woven carpets. And as much as this was not the typical home of a hermit, neither was Delphinia Shipton a typical hermit. There was not a trace of a rag or a tatter anywhere. Smartly attired and coiffed, Delphinia quite successfully belied the fact that she had been around since the fourth century. She was, however, rather reluctant to speak of times past. She had retired, she declared adamantly, and that was that—at least until Cyrus revealed the reason for his visit. When he began to describe the mysterious book, she soon became very excited and animated. With her gray eyes sparkling and her long white locks (that up until then had been artfully contained in a hand-crocheted snood) flying in all directions, she began firing dozens of questions at him. Questions that poor Cyrus, going on the limited information that Mr. Goodfellow had included in his letter, could not answer.

"It became apparent to me then," Great-Uncle Cyrus had relayed (in the most exquisite handwriting that Mr. Goodfellow had ever seen), "that Delphinia Shipton will not rest until she is able to lay her own eyes on this book of yours. It is imperative that you arrange for it to be delivered to her as soon as possible—with, of course, the utmost discretion and care. Delphinia has asked me to stay on with her here for the time being. Trusting to hear from you soon, Great Uncle Cyrus."

The next days brought long hours of discussion at Blue Heron Cottage as Mr. Goodfellow and the rest of The Sage considered how best to safely transport the book into Cyrus and Delphinia's hands.

Edgar, having always been keenly interested in the mystical world, could not take his eyes off The Book of The Sage. And when he wasn't staring at *that*, he was reading Great-Uncle Cyrus's letter over and over again, trying to imagine what a 1,800-year-old Sage was really like. But it was while he was leaning over the twins' basket one night, preparing to gently kiss each one on the forehead, that his responsibility as both a father and a Sage suddenly hit him. When it was finally decided that the book should be personally delivered, Edgar stepped forward to volunteer.

Edgar had not journeyed overseas in a great many years. He was delighted to discover from his well-traveled parents that the four-and-a-half-hour express hover-ship journey would be a lot less nauseating than a turbulent aircraft flight or a four-day crossing by sea-swelled ocean liner. In fact, the last traces of Edgar Goodfellow's disdain for traveling seemed to float away like the early morning mist that blanketed the coast on the day he prepared to set off for England.

While Edgar made last-minute preparations, Mr. Goodfellow

carefully secured the book in layers of wrapping, then constructed a convenient carrying handle with a length of braided string. Charlotte helped by packing a small duffel bag with just a few essential items.

It was harder than Edgar had imagined to leave Charlotte and the twins, even for just a short time, but the sense of pride and duty he felt when one of his boys gurgled and smiled at him was enough to dispel any feelings of doubt.

Edgar bid good-bye to everyone, and then Sam—who had come by to offer Edgar transportation to the harbor pier where he could catch a shuttle-boat into Boston—picked him up and deposited him in his pocket. It was just like old times.

The two friends talked of many things as they made their way into town; the odd circumstances surrounding the discovery of the book, Fletcher's rather cryptic note and the strange journey Edgar found himself on now.

"It's important for me to do this alone, Sam," said Edgar, feeling as if he should explain.

Sam smiled and nodded his head. He knew Edgar well enough to imagine why. Safely delivering the ancient book to The Sage's oldest and wisest mystic was, of course, Edgar's prime objective. But there was also a little part of Edgar that wanted to prove to Great-Uncle Cyrus—the patriarch of the Goodfellow family—that he was no longer the shy, clumsy little boy who had been such a worry to his relatives all those years ago. Even though his Uncle Jolly had helped him find the courage to confront one of the most evil and notorious Fen, Edgar was never quite sure that he had gained Cyrus's respect.

A devoted father himself, Sam understood how hard it was for Edgar to leave his new family behind. Before he left him at the pier, Sam promised Edgar that he would guard the boys with his life.

Apart from a brief note to advise them that he had arrived safely at Delphinia's cave, there was no further word from either Edgar or Great-Uncle Cyrus for what seemed like an eternity. The winter holidays came and went. Then Groundhog Day, too. Mr. Goodfellow took to sitting by himself at the dunes more frequently, in spite of the harsh, biting winds and occasional snow squalls. Sam joined him whenever he had the chance and whenever the weather allowed. This time of the year was a rather bleak one for Sam, especially when March break rolled around at school. It was one of the times that Alice's parents returned from their travels abroad. It was wonderful for Sam and India to spend some time with their daughter and son-in-law, but it was never for long enough. No sooner had they arrived, it seemed, than they were dashing off on another exotic adventure, this time with Alice in tow. Sam missed having a young person around and was always relieved when Alice returned home.

Others at the lighthouse tried different ways to occupy themselves. Filbert took up highland dancing, but soon grew tired of his daily practice routines on the front porch, especially when the drifting snowbanks became too high to leap over. He moved inside and began to whittle instead, producing an assortment of intricately carved wooden puzzles and toys. Despite their grandfather's enthusiasm, Winston and Little Jolly were still far too tiny to play with any of them. For her part, Charlotte began fretting over little things. How could she have known that Edgar would be gone for so long, she complained one day. And then, after lamenting that she should have packed more than two pairs of underwear, Charlotte ended up in a flood of tears. It was just the strain of waiting. Beatrice and Hazel tried to help as best they could, especially with the care and feeding of the twins. Porter, on the other hand, was simply bored. There were no other kids his age to play with and Jasper, in partial hibernation mode, was no fun at all.

It was a chilly day in the first week of April when Sam decided to pay the Goodfellows a surprise visit. His arrival at Blue Heron Cottage coincided almost precisely with that of an exhausted mouse courier. Struggling up the front steps, his fur caked with huge chunks of ice from a vicious spring storm he had just passed through, the poor creature collapsed at the door before he could ring the bell. Alerted to the emergency by Sam, Mr. Goodfellow and Filbert carried the mouse inside and warmed him by the fire for a least an hour before they were able to prize his frozen paw from the letter he was carrying. While Hazel gently rubbed some feeling back into the rodent's extremities and Beatrice administered a hot cider toddy, Mr. Goodfellow opened the window wide so that Sam could hear, then quickly tore open the note. It was scribbled in Edgar's handwriting and contained a considerable amount of flawed grammar and sloppy penmanship. It was nevertheless readable, and when Mr. Goodfellow began to recite what Edgar had written, it became apparent to everyone why his mind might have been racing and his hand a little unsteady.

Greetings and love to all—from Great-Uncle C. too. Trust everyone is O.K. Sorry about the wait—I never imagined I'd still be here, but it's all taking longer than expected and Cyrus seems to need me. Really don't know where to begin! Cyrus can't take time to write—he's too busy helping Delphinia. And Delphinia—well, she's in some kind of trance, I think—glued to the book—she hasn't slept in days.

Anyway, it really is The Book of The Sage!— Delphinia's positive! And it's turning out to be everything

the legend cracked it up to be—maybe even more. There's
too much in it to tell you everything—the record of thou-
sands and thousands of years—I'll try and give you the
main points—at least, for now. There are parts that
Delphinia hasn't figured out yet—she needs you to help her
with something—but I'll get to that later. Here's what she's
come up with, so far. In fact, I'm going to copy down the
exact translation that Delphinia wrote on some scraps of
paper here, just to be sure I get it right. By the way, if
Porter is still there with you, it might be a good idea to
send him out of the room. Some of this stuff might scare
the little fellow. If he is there, well...I hope you didn't just
read that part out loud...oops...

"Oops, indeed." Mr. Goodfellow stopped his recitation of Edgar's letter and looked straight at Porter. Porter, jumping up and down, was about to open his mouth to speak, but Mr. Goodfellow waved off his protest.

"Calm down, Porter," he sighed. "It's entirely my fault. I should have read the letter over first. Anyway, it's too late now. I sincerely hope, however, that what you are about to hear won't scar you for life."

Porter beamed from ear to ear as Mr. Goodfellow found his place and continued reading. It seemed that, conscious of the importance of what he was now writing, Edgar had been able to settle both his thoughts and his shaking hand. The rest of the letter was much more legible.

The Sage are considerably older than any of us have
ever imagined. The book itself, which was written by The
Sage to record all that should be remembered, dates back
many thousands of years. The accounts and stories

95

contained in it, however, go back even further—beyond the histories of either Earth or Mars. The book makes reference to a time and place so long ago, and so far removed from the known physical world, that it is almost impossible to comprehend. In this other realm, the creatures we know as Sage and Fen were not distinct from one another as they are now. Instead, they existed as a single group; glorious, immortal beings, winged and pure in spirit. Here they lived side by side with many types of similarly blessed creatures, until a huge catastrophe befell them all. A great evil had managed to infiltrate their lofty world, dividing it in two and shattering their peaceful existence. A colossal struggle ensued, and those who had chosen to follow the path of evil were cast far away to live in a realm of darkness. The smallest beings—a group that, like the others, had now split into two—became lost in the enormous confusion that followed. Both sides tumbled helplessly from their own divided world to a place that was neither here nor there; the physical world of the planets and stars. These creatures had been the lowest order among all their brethren, and the smallest in size, too—so small, in fact, that no one seemed to notice that they had vanished at all. Wingless now, and no longer immortal, they found themselves marooned in the physical world, forgotten by all the other beings they had once known, doomed to dwell forever among humankind. And though it may have appeared to be a par-adise that they had first fallen into, it was a paradise that could never last—for while those who came to be known as The Sage remained dedicated to inspiring good in all around them, those called The Fen devoted themselves to the causes of evil.

Mr. Goodfellow stopped reading and cleared his throat. There was absolute silence in the room and not much movement either, except for Porter. Fidgeting in a corner, the boy had twisted his arm behind him and was now busily poking at one of the bony knobs that jutted out of the top of his back.

"As for the names Sage and Fen," Mr. Goodfellow continued, "these may have been garbled somewhat over the millennia. There are parts in The Book of The Sage that have not stood the test of time or the great Martian flood as well as others, and—"

"Angels," murmured Sam under his breath.

"Pardon?" asked Mr. Goodfellow. He looked up from the letter and out the window to where Sam had made himself a comfortable seat on an old piece of driftwood.

"Something I'd forgotten about, I guess," Sam replied, staring up into the sky. "When I was a boy, I made up a game. It was a silly word thing, with anagrams and missing letters. Just kid stuff. In fact, India ended up helping me with it. From SAGE to AGES to ANGELS. Yes, that was how it went. I remember now."

"And The Fen?" Filbert asked.

"That's easy," piped up Porter, who was standing with his back to the hallway mirror and his sweater pulled up over his head, staring with a newfound appreciation at his shoulder knobs. "You just take an A and two L's and stick them in after the F. It's easy—FALLEN. And if The Fen were the same as us once, I guess that would make them angels, too, only fallen ones."

"Indeed," said Mr. Goodfellow, feeling the blood rush to his face. "Out of the mouths of children . . ."

It wasn't as if The Sage assembled at Blue Heron Cottage had never considered that the strange knobs on their backs and those of The Fen were connected. Speculation about their relationship to each other had abounded in Sage lore for centuries. But this was altogether different. Here it was now, spelled out for them in black and white in an ancient book that up until a short time before had been no more than a myth; a part of legend. And as each soul gathered at Blue Heron Cottage that day would have to agree, none of them would ever feel quite the same again.

The balance of Edgar's letter contained, as he had mentioned it would, a special request from Delphinia Shipton. The Book of The Sage, she had determined, was incomplete. A square indentation set within the hard back cover had once contained a carved, flat piece of crystal—possibly a map—which was referred to within the body of the book. Somewhere along the way, the book and map had been separated. While this could have happened at any time during the book's voyage across the heavens with The Sage, Delphinia strongly suspected that it had probably occurred during the cataclysmic flood on Mars. After all, the book seemed to have ended its journey there. For some reason, The Sage who escaped to Earth with the fleeing Martians were unable to save it in the rapidly rising waters.

If this missing map had been left behind on Mars, as well, Delphinia suggested, then perhaps it might still be retrievable—if, of course, it hadn't already been discovered. The map was an important and integral piece of the book. According to Delphinia, information about all the wanderings of The Sage might be locked inside, perhaps including a reference to the site of their very first encounter with human life. Whatever had become of it, she stressed, an investigation should be undertaken immediately.

"That's a bit of a tall order, wouldn't you say?" Beatrice

commented, after Mr. Goodfellow had finished reading.

"Like finding a needle in a haystack, my dear," Mr. Goodfellow replied, with a sigh and a roll of his eyes.

Sam, however, was already deep in thought. The map had not been found by Fletcher—that much he knew—but he did remember something that Mr. Goodfellow had said about that second expedition to Mars. Disappointed at the limited success of their journey to the Elysium region, the astronauts had gathered up the few odd artifacts they could find before returning home. Fletcher had been strangely compelled (against orders) to keep the small book he had found for Sam, but the other crewmen most likely turned over their discoveries to the scientists at NASA. Might the missing map be among their finds? At the very least, it was a place to start.

When Sam suggested this possibility to The Sage, Mr. Goodfellow looked up from his brooding with a startled expression, as if he had just been hit by a bolt of lightning.

"Great heavens, of course!"

"What is it, Jolly?" exclaimed Beatrice. She had seen this sort of look on his face before, whenever he found himself on the verge of a great revelation.

"The lost mission, my dear! The one that Fletcher and Redwood were on," he announced excitedly. "It was to an undisclosed place, known only to NASA!"

"Discovered through the study of an artifact they had found fifty years ago—determined later to be a crystal star map—that must have taken their top scientists decades to decipher?" asked Filbert.

"Precisely!" replied Mr. Goodfellow.

"But that doesn't seem possible," suggested Charlotte, as she cuddled Little Jolly. "We'd know about something like that, wouldn't we? It would be recorded in the files at headquarters. A scientific discovery of that magnitude would have required an expert Sage."

"Or a similarly experienced Fen," said Hazel, absently bouncing Winston on her knee.

Everyone turned and looked at her. Edgar's mother was a quiet, thoughtful woman, but when she did offer an opinion it was often with uncanny insight.

"True enough, I'm afraid," Mr. Goodfellow responded with a whisper. "We can only hope otherwise."

The room fell silent again. Charlotte shuddered and held Little Jolly a little closer.

"The first thing we should do is contact headquarters and see what type of activity has been occurring at NASA in recent years," Mr. Goodfellow suggested, as he gently placed Edgar's letter back into its envelope. "Perhaps there's a way we can get to the bottom of this. After all the work she has done so far, I'd hate to let Delphinia Shipton down now."

"Leave it with me, Jolly," said Filbert with a nod. Then he spoke in a slow, southern drawl. "I'm on it like a hound."

"I beg your pardon, Filbert?"

"It's an expression, Jolly," he grinned, "Texan in origin, I believe."

"Let me see, now," Mr. Goodfellow replied drolly. "It *must* be one of Winchester Redwood's."

"Why, yes it is!" replied Filbert. "How did you know?"

"Just a lucky guess. His mother hailed from Amarillo, if I'm not mistaken. And by the way, Filbert, your accent is dreadful."

Filbert made an unpleasant face. Mr. Goodfellow sighed as he walked out of the room. Was he to be eternally haunted by the memory of Winchester Redwood and the selfless sacrifice he had made by taking his place on that lost ship? Or might there be a chance for some sort of closure, after all? If what really happened out there in space could ever be determined, perhaps poor Winchester's soul may be laid to rest once and for all. Mr. Goodfellow could only hope.

As Sam returned home, carefully navigating his way across the ice bridge that would join the lighthouse island to the mainland for only a few more weeks, his mind churned with everything he had heard. More great mysteries had been revealed to him, and once again there was not a single human soul he could tell. It was almost too much to bear. He opened the door to the keeper's house and found India in a very characteristic pose, curled up in a big armchair by the fire with her nose in a book. Carmen, Buttercup and Tosca, happy to be inside on such an unseasonably cold spring day, were stretched out at her feet. Frozen to the bone, Sam held his hands in front of the fire, then bent over and kissed the crown of India's snow-white head. She gazed up at him and smiled. Seventy-five years had passed, but Sam's knees still felt funny whenever she looked at him that way. He had an overwhelming desire to blurt everything out—to ask her if she could recall a silly word game they had played when they were kids. Would she have remembered? Probably. India had always had a remarkable memory. Would she believe him if he told her the truth about everything? Maybe she would, he thought. India was remarkable in many ways. But Sam bit his tongue. He was relieved when Alice picked just that moment to bounce into the room.

"I spent the whole morning looking for you, Grandad!" she exclaimed. "It's Saturday, you know!"

"I've been out for a breath of fresh air," Sam replied defensively, suddenly remembering that he had promised to spend some bird-watching time with her. "And to do a little groundwork for you," he quickly added. "It's still bitterly cold out there, but I'm happy to report that the ospreys have finally returned to their nesting site. Get your things and we'll go have a look!"

Alice ran to the front closet for her coat, then lifted a pair of binoculars down from a hook. When she opened the front door, Sam pulled the collar of his coat tighter around his neck as a blast of cold air hit him. He would not have disappointed his granddaughter for anything in the world, even if it meant braving the frigid conditions of an early April in Maine for the rest of the afternoon.

8

DO NOT ASK WHICH IS THE RIGHT WAY FROM A MAN WHO CANNOT SEE

Over the next few weeks, Filbert launched an in-depth inquiry into all the appropriate files at headquarters. When he had finally exhausted his search, he called everyone together to share his findings.

"According to the information I've been able to track down," Filbert began, "the only name that keeps popping up is Sir Percival Davenport. Sir Percival was the world's foremost expert in astronomical mathematics before he passed away from a heart attack a few years ago. For the last fifteen years of his life, he worked as a guest lecturer at a number of universities as well as occasionally providing consultation to NASA. His Sage, I'm told, was none other than Cornelius Mango. The rest is a bit sketchy. The files, I'm afraid, are not entirely in order."

"The great Cornelius Mango?" Mr. Goodfellow exclaimed. "I wasn't aware that he'd returned to active service again! Are you absolutely sure?"

Filbert paused and scratched his head as he stared at his file. "Well, that's what it says here. Mango was a bit of a hero of yours once, wasn't he, Jolly? Unless of course, there's another Cornelius Mango out there somewhere."

"There's only one Cornelius Mango!" Mr. Goodfellow stated with conviction. "I can assure you of that! But I was under the impression that he was still suffering from the after-effects of that dreadful flying squirrel collision, seventy-five years ago, and that he'd remained in retirement. The last I heard, he was allowing his prestigious name to be used by an assortment of popular franchises—young Porter's climbing school comes to mind." Mr. Goodfellow scratched his chin. "He suffered a significant blow to the head in that accident, Filbert. How on earth did he convince The Governing Council to allow him free rein again? Among other things, as I'm sure you will recall, the poor soul had taken to wearing his under-garments on the outside of his suits! I can't help but feel troubled by this news," he continued, as he began to pace. "It may, however, explain the incomplete state of the files." Mr. Goodfellow scratched his chin again. "I think it may be prudent to pay Mr. Mango a visit. Where exactly is Cornelius residing at present?"

Filbert quickly scanned his eyes over his notes.

"Um...southern Florida, apparently," Filbert replied with a smile. "Ahhh...orange groves, sunshine and warm seas. I'll get the beach umbrellas, Jolly!"

"That may be wishful thinking, I'm afraid. Better pack the rain gear, too. I believe that hurricane season is about to begin."

His smile slowly vanishing, Filbert wandered off to find his rubber-lined mouse feet and foul-weather ears.

It didn't take long for Mr. Goodfellow to pull a few belongings together for the trip south. Assuming that it would be only a very short visit, he elected to leave his traveling trunk behind. He still shuddered whenever he recalled how it had been lost in a farmer's field during his and Edgar's frantic crop circle search for Professor Hawthorne. It had finally been recovered, of course, but not before its precious contents had suffered the indignity of being picked over by a pack of moles. He was not about to risk that again, at least not on this trip. He prepared a small overnight bag instead, which he slung over one shoulder, balancing himself off on the other side with his best umbrella, the one with the brass horse's-head handle.

When he was ready, he tickled the twins and gave Beatrice, Hazel and Charlotte a kiss each on the cheek, assuring them that he and Filbert would be back home in a day or two. Calling for his brother, Mr. Goodfellow hurried out the front door and down the stairs, barely avoiding a collision with Porter who was crouched on the middle of the bottom step, his face pressed into a book.

"Good heavens, Porter!" Mr. Goodfellow exclaimed, as he quickly hopped to one side. "Please find a more suitable reading perch if you will, my boy. You could cause a most regrettable accident sitting there like that!"

Porter looked up at Mr. Goodfellow and shuffled over to the very edge of the step.

"Sorry," he mumbled apologetically.

Just then, Filbert stuck his head out of the small half-moon–shaped window in the cottage attic and announced that he would need a few more minutes to prepare. Mr. Goodfellow sighed and sat down at Porter's side.

"What do you have there, lad?" he inquired, turning his head sideways and straining to read the title.

"Just school stuff," Porter answered. "I have to read it before the start of next term. It's kind of boring, though."

"Indeed," replied Mr. Goodfellow. "By the looks of it, I believe it's the very same textbook that we used. When you think about the hundreds of years that have passed since then, it's quite shocking, isn't it? I do hope that some of the teaching reforms that Edgar has been working on so diligently all these years will finally be adopted at the next Governing Council Educational Forum. It's high time for a change. What's that chapter you're reading, now?"

"It's Chapter Three," Porter replied unenthusiastically. "'How to Whisper Effectively.'"

"Absolute nonsense!" Mr. Goodfellow exclaimed. "Why, you can't teach a thing like that in a textbook! You have to get out there, into the middle of it, and roll up your sleeves."

Porter shrugged and closed the book. "Well, I'm all signed up to apprentice with my dad in South America next year."

"Next year! How old are you now, my boy?" Mr. Goodfellow inquired.

"I'll be 166 on my next birthday."

"Really? High time you were out in the field, if you ask me!" Mr. Goodfellow exclaimed. "Edgar was barely 105 when we went on our big summer trip, you know."

Mr. Goodfellow paused, recalling how his great-uncles and cousins had skillfully maneuvered him into taking on the highly accident-prone Edgar, far earlier than usually recommended.

"Of course, that was a unique situation, I suppose," he quickly mumbled. "But, nevertheless..."

Mr. Goodfellow paused again, but this time with a glint in his eye.

"I have a compelling idea, Porter, but first you must understand that Filbert and I will be on important Sage business. Not the traditional kind, either, but something a little more investigative in nature. You might find it of interest, but you must agree to be on your best behavior."

Porter nodded slowly.

"Alright then. What would you say to a little trip to Florida?"

Porter quickly jumped up from the step. He was grinning from ear to ear.

"I can see that the idea intrigues you. Let's go find Charlotte and Beatrice and Hazel and tell them the good news. Then you can pack a few things while I hunt Filbert down and tell him to get a move on. I'm afraid, though, that Jasper will have to remain here."

After Porter had been assured by the ladies that they were quite capable of the care and feeding of a cicada, he and Filbert and Mr. Goodfellow were on their way. Mr. Goodfellow had been anxiously waiting for an excuse to try out the new magnet-powered super-train that was plying the East Coast and this seemed to present the perfect opportunity.

Cornelius Mango, it turned out, wasn't the easiest person to find. He had listed his current address in the central filing system as Palm Tree 24, accompanied by a badly drawn map. But Mango lived on a particularly long stretch of sand, and he'd failed to update Sage headquarters about the extensive beachfront erosion that had altered the lay of the land in the years he'd been there. Arriving at the crack of dawn the following morning, in a blinding rainstorm, Filbert, Jolly and Porter eventually discovered that Palm Tree 24 was now Palm Tree 9—but not before rousing a number of Cornelius Mango's irritated neighbors from their warm beds. When they finally arrived at the right front door, dug into the trunk of an old coconut palm, Mr. Goodfellow was in as foul a mood as the weather.

When repeated pressing of the chime button elicited no response, Mr. Goodfellow rapped loudly on the door with his umbrella handle. The sound of slowly shuffling feet could be heard on the other side. The door unlatched with a click and a beak-like nose emerged through a narrow crack.

"I've told you before, no thank you!" a voice chirped abruptly from inside. "Whatever it is you're selling, I'm not interested."

As the crack in the door began to close, Mr. Goodfellow managed to push in the end of his umbrella.

"Mango, I presume?" Mr. Goodfellow bellowed a little impatiently. The nose, still visible beyond the crack, began to quiver with apprehension.

"Cornelius?" offered Filbert, in a more friendly tone.

The door slowly creaked open until Cornelius Mango's whole head popped out.

"Do I know you?" he asked. He frowned as he looked Filbert, Mr. Goodfellow and Porter up and down suspiciously. "Or are you just trying to sell me something?"

"Good heavens, man! Let us in!" Mr. Goodfellow shouted, as streams of rainwater dripped off the end of his nose mask. "It's not a fit day for Sage nor beast!"

The door began to close again.

"Cornelius! Wait!" Filbert implored. "We're the Goodfellow brothers: Filbert and Jolly. We're Archer Goodfellow's sons. Surely you remember him? Or our Great-Uncle Cyrus? And our young associate here is Porter Sparrow. You may have heard the family name. They're well known in the West Coast spa business."

"Ah-hah! I should have known!" Mango exclaimed. "This is all about a health club membership, isn't it?"

"No, Cornelius! I assure you!" Filbert responded.

There was a long pause as the door remained still for a moment.

"Well...I *do* remember the Goodfellow family," Mango slowly began. "Archer's sons, you say? Let me see now. Filbert was the older one, I remember. Nice chap. Used to go around with that foreign exchange student, Hazel Almondo. But Jolly? I'm not sure....Wait! Ahhh, yes! How could I forget? He was always the butt of that American chap's practical jokes, wasn't he? I think his name was Redwood or something. Yes! That's it! Winchester Redwood. What a card!" Mango began to chuckle uncontrollably. "I remember hearing about an incident at their school graduation ceremonies. Apparently, Redwood had smuggled in this whoopie cushion and—"

"That does it, boys!" Mr. Goodfellow cried. "I'm going in!" He shoved his large mouse foot through the front door, leaving Mango no choice but to open it all the way and let them inside. "We have something important to discuss with you, Mango!" Mr. Goodfellow continued, as he pushed his way into the front hallway. "We don't really have the time to reminisce about silly schoolboy pranks, do we, Filbert?"

"No, I suppose we don't," Filbert replied, trying very hard to stifle a chuckle of his own.

As Mr. Goodfellow, Filbert and Porter paraded over his threshold, Mango blinked helplessly at them through the glasses at the end of his beakish nose. They had a green tint to them, like old bottle glass, and were just as thick, giving him a strange, bug-like appearance. At the very top of his head were two little strands of gray hair that had been combed across his crown and back again several times to give the illusion of more hair. His mouth was very small and he had an odd habit of pursing it repeatedly, as if he had just sucked on a big slice of lemon. Mr. Goodfellow cringed behind his mouse mask. Surely this was not the debonair, sophisticated operative that he had admired and patterned himself on?

Mr. Goodfellow, Filbert and Porter removed their suits and masks, shook the excess water onto the hall mat and stared with awe at the scene before them. There wasn't one square inch of Mango's front hallway, apart from the very small area in which they now stood, that was not covered with objects and memorabilia. A ceiling-high brass hat rack containing every conceivable type of headgear loomed in one corner. In another, stacks of house slippers and ungroomed mouse shoes reached halfway up the wall. There were umbrellas and beach balls, carry bags and surfboards, a scuba tank with mask attached, and an old, dust-covered telescope. Hanging from the ceiling were dozens of raggedy, faded banners from countless birthdays and New Year's Eves past. They dangled down to the floor, intertwining along the way with long threads of sticky spiderweb. It looked more like the abode of a pack rat than a respected Sage.

"Neat!" announced Porter, admiring a scene that would have impressed most eleven-year-olds. Mr. Goodfellow's reaction was somewhat different.

"What's become of him, Filbert? He was once so great," Mr. Goodfellow whispered into his brother's ear. He was clearly crestfallen to see the conditions in which his erstwhile hero was now living.

"Well, at least he's not wearing his undies on the outside anymore," Filbert whispered encouragingly. Porter muffled a giggle behind his hand.

Shaking himself back to the matter before them, Mr. Goodfellow began to speak again. "We've come here concerning one of your past assignments, Mango and—" The

sound of labored breathing and some strange sucking noises distracted him. "Porter!" he cried. "Please take that thing off immediately!"

Porter removed a deep-sea-diving helmet and quickly returned it to the hat rack. Mr. Goodfellow turned and looked quizzically at Filbert. Oblivious to his brother's glance, Filbert was staring down the long hallway and into the dozens of rows of gleaming eyes that shone out from the shadows.

"It's alright, everyone," Mango called out in a soft, soothing voice. He turned to Mr. Goodfellow and gave him a cold glare. "You've frightened them with all your shouting, you know."

"Oh...I'm terribly sorry, of course," said Mr. Goodfellow. He raised his eyebrows at Filbert and shrugged his shoulders. "It's just that the weather's absolutely horrible and we've been out in it for quite some time and—just a minute, Mango— frightened *whom*, exactly?"

"My houseguests, if you must know," Mango snapped. When he turned to address the rows of eyes behind him, his voice softened again. "You might as well come out. I don't *think* these gentlemen are from the bylaw committee." He turned his head back around and snapped again. "Are you?"

"No...of course not," Filbert replied as dozens of small creatures began to creep down the hallway toward them. There were slow-moving sow bugs, swaying centipedes, hairy gray spiders, a daddy longlegs with at least two of his appendages missing, and what appeared to be a troupe of hobbling circus fleas.

"What are you running here, Mango? A hotel of some sort?" Mr. Goodfellow inquired.

"More of a retirement villa, by the looks of it," declared Filbert, as he observed the elderly state of the residents.

"Wow!" Porter cried out, unable to believe the incredible good fortune of landing in such a wonderful place.

"Sshh!" Mango implored, rushing forward to close the small crack he had left in the front door. "I'm in enough trouble already. There are some very tight rules in our little palm tree community, you know. Strictly single-family residences." He looked sympathetically at the group of aged insects. "They had nowhere else to go, I'm afraid. It all started when my last assignment passed away a few years ago. Sir Percival Davenport's home was a veritable haven for insect life. He was an absolutely brilliant man, but a dreadful housekeeper."

"I wonder where he got that from," Mr. Goodfellow whispered into Filbert's ear.

Mango shot him an unpleasant look.

"Sir Percival had a heart of gold, I'll have you know! Wouldn't hurt a fly!" Mango paused and took a deep breath. "Made pets of them, instead; especially the old and injured ones. And that is how I inherited this unique collection of associates. Sir Percival had no family of his own. He left all his worldly possessions to charity. His house was cleared out in a matter of days, and all of the furnishings sold at auction. I barely had time to gather my own belongings and return home to Palm Tree 24 here."

"You mean Palm Tree 9," corrected Filbert.

"Really?" Mango seemed genuinely surprised. "How extraordinary! *That* explains why I've been receiving Evangeline Puffadder's mail these past months." He glanced over at a mountain of frilly, heavily scented letters in another jumbled corner of the front hall. "Anyway," Mango continued, "these poor souls here followed me home. When creatures in need are taken in from the wild and nurtured and befriended like they had been by Sir Percival, they cannot be left to fend for themselves any longer." He gestured toward the troupe of now wheezing fleas. "I ask you—how could they hope to find employment in that condition? I could do no other than bear the responsibility for the kind work that Sir Percival began. I was honored to spend so many fruitful years with him. He was a remarkable human."

"Indeed, Mango," observed Mr. Goodfellow. "Highly commendable behavior. However, it's the rather large gaps in your fruitful working relationship with Sir Percival that have brought my brother and I here today. We're most interested in his intriguing consultations for NASA. We are investigating the destination of a space mission that has just recently been declared missing. We have a note here from one of the Governing Council members giving us permission to search—"

"Gaps? Whatever do you mean?" asked Mango with a puzzled expression. "I can assure you that it's well documented, gentlemen. I'm sorry you had to come all this way for nothing. A quick call to the filing department at headquarters would have answered your questions—"

"We've checked into that already, Cornelius," Filbert interrupted. "The files were never handed in. That's why we're here."

"Never handed in! That's preposterous!" Mango exclaimed. "Come with me!"

He waddled through the hallway with Mr. Goodfellow, Filbert and Porter at his heels, entering a small room that was even more disheveled than the hall. He quickly moved aside two drooping palm fronds that were propped up in one corner (and the three elderly aphids that were nibbling at them), to reveal an old filing cabinet. He tugged at the handle of the rust-encrusted middle drawer, but it would not budge.

"I can't understand this at all," Mango puffed, as he continued to struggle with the drawer. "I was in here just the other day, doing a bit of tidying up."

Mr. Goodfellow opened his mouth to comment, but Filbert gave him a firm nudge in his side. Mango finally resorted to giving the drawer a swift kick with his foot, and it flew open. There was a loud and piercing sound of metal squealing against metal, and dozens of papers flew into the air, accompanied by a flapping Monarch butterfly that had been trapped inside the drawer.

"Oliver!" Mango exclaimed. "There you are, you rascal!" He turned to Mr. Goodfellow and Filbert. "It's a good job you fellows came by today, I suppose. Heaven knows when I would have had an occasion to look in here again!"

"Indeed," Mr. Goodfellow observed drolly. He picked the butterfly up from the ground and gently dusted him off. Oliver fluttered awkwardly out of the room and headed for the kitchen.

"Last year, the poor boy had the misfortune of colliding with a flock of Canada geese heading the other way," Mango explained, as he fingered through his files. "His migrating days are over now, I'm afraid. It's shocking how a simple aerial mishap can cause so many long-term problems."

"Really?" Mr. Goodfellow replied. He turned to Filbert and raised his eyebrows yet again. "Apparently there's a lot of that sort of thing going around," he whispered.

Mango pulled a thick wad of pink papers out of the drawer "Ah...here's what we're looking for, I believe," he announced with satisfaction. "I have kept all the appropriate copies, as you will see."

As Mango turned to hand the papers over, a look of absolute horror suddenly swept across his face.

9

BEAUTY IS OFTEN FOUND
IN THE MOST UNLIKELY
OF PLACES

Mr. Goodfellow and Filbert looked down at the papers in Mango's hand. Peeping out from underneath the pink duplicate copies was a thin pile of white ones.

"It appears that you have indeed kept all the appropriate copies, Mango. And a few other items to boot," announced Mr. Goodfellow.

Mango's face turned ashen. "The originals!" he cried. "It can't be! How did this happen?" He tried to pull the white papers free from the rest of the pile, but they were stuck together with something hard and tacky.

"What the devil *is* this?" he lamented, growing more frustrated with every tug. He broke a tiny piece of the sticky material off and touched it to the end of his tongue. As the papers finally pulled free, he staggered backward into the filing cabinet and slowly slid to the floor. "Dried sugar icing," he mumbled, staring off into space. "They all love it when I bake, you know. I must have been doing some filing one evening while I was preparing dinner..."

Filbert, who had been down on all fours examining the interior of the filing cabinet drawer, suddenly stood up, holding an empty tube of liquid icing sugar in his hand.

"Been missing something, Cornelius?"

Mango looked up, then dropped his head into his hands and started to tremble. "Oh...this is simply dreadful!" he wailed in anguish.

"Now, now, Mango!" Mr. Goodfellow said sternly. "Get a grip, man!"

But Mango couldn't take his eyes off the white and pink papers, all covered in a thin, crusty film. The writing on them had run together into swirling black rivulets of dried sugar mixture. Whatever information had once been there was now totally unreadable.

Filbert sighed. It looked as if the trip had led to a dead end. Mr. Goodfellow, however, wasn't about to give up that easily.

"You must remember something about those files, Mango," he suggested. "What exactly was Sir Percival working on for NASA?"

Mango looked up. His eyes were blank and staring. "Um..."

"Come on, Cornelius, old man! Think!" Mr. Goodfellow implored.

Mango straightened up. The fact that Mr. Goodfellow had called him Cornelius had a strangely encouraging effect.

"Well...let me see," he slowly began. "It was top secret stuff, I do remember *that*. Sir Percival was summoned to join an international team of scientists that had been assembled by NASA. He was given a square, flat, crystal-like object to examine. It was very, very small, as I recall. Something of Martian origin, they said, that had been uncovered on one of the early missions to the Elysium region. Sir Percival was to study it and attempt to ascertain its meaning." Mango's eyes began to sparkle as he spoke faster and more confidently. "Yes!" he exclaimed. "I remember it now! Other scholars had long suspected that it was a highly significant artifact, but after years and years of toiling, they were unable to translate its full message. Even Dr. Eustace Slocumb, the world-renowned astronomer and head scientist on the team, had failed to crack it. It was rough going at first and Sir Percival needed my constant encouragement. He soon determined— as others before him had—that the strange markings on the artifact coincided with established star maps. But there was another element to the thing; more puzzling than anything Sir Percival had encountered before. Almost by accident, when he was about to give up completely, he fell upon a series of complex mathematical sequences that seemed to suggest that there was a directional aspect to the map and with it, the means to finding a very special destination. Trying to deter- mine where on the map this place might be caused him no end of frustration."

"But Sir Percival finally did solve that puzzle, didn't he, Cornelius?" asked Mr. Goodfellow, banging his fist excitedly on the filing cabinet. "He pinpointed an actual place and a specific way to get there!"

"Indeed, he did," Mango replied with satisfaction. "Sir Percival was the hero of the day among the other scien- tists, you know. Although, I think there may have been some ill feeling toward him from Dr. Slocumb."

Mr. Goodfellow raised an eyebrow in interest.

"A case of professional jealousy?" Filbert interjected.

"Quite possibly," replied Mr. Goodfellow, furrowing his brow with concern. "Or perhaps Eustace Slocumb represented something considerably more ominous." He stared straight ahead then, reciting the name over and over to himself. "Eustace Slocumb, Eustace Slocumb, Eustace Slocumb." Mr. Goodfellow closed his eyes. "I know I've heard that name before, Filbert," he announced with conviction. "But where?"

Mango stared off into space again for a few seconds as if *he* was trying very hard to remember something, too. Then he shook his head vigorously a couple of times and turned back to face his visitors. He was beaming now from ear to ear. He had surprised even himself with the way he had managed to gather his thoughts together under such stress.

"But *where* did Sir Percival's discoveries finally lead him, Cornelius?" asked Filbert, still waiting for Mango to finish his story. "*What* information did he uncover? You must remember. You *were* his Sage, after all."

Mr. Goodfellow sighed impatiently, as Mango began to fidget.

"Well, you see," he said slowly, tugging at his collar with the tip of his finger, "that's where it becomes a little more complicated, I'm afraid."

Mr. Goodfellow and Filbert looked at each other with exasperation. Mango's satisfied look began to dissolve.

"The rest is a bit foggy," Mango explained defensively. "My memory's not what it used to be." He hung his head and began to twiddle his thumbs.

"Your memory's not been the same since you took that blasted flying squirrel joyride seventy-five years ago, Mango! I can't believe you were allowed to meddle in matters of such importance. It's inexcusable!" Mr. Goodfellow let loose, unable to control any longer the supreme disappointment of discovering just how far his old hero had fallen.

Filbert glared at his younger brother.

"Steady on, Jolly," he interjected, glancing sympathetically at Mango and the crowd of aging insects that were slowly gathering at his side. Porter, who had been happily playing in the corner with the aphids, looked over to see what the hubbub was about.

Mango sighed.

"No...he's absolutely right, of course. There's no excuse. I never should have lobbied so fiercely for the assignment." Mango grabbed the damaged file papers and clutched them to his chest. "I can just imagine what you're thinking. It's quite obvious that Sir Percival, and the rest of the world, would have been better served by someone else, isn't it?" A single tear slid down his cheek. "I'm a disgrace to the profession," he sniffled.

Feeling a little guilty over his outburst, Mr. Goodfellow rummaged around inside his suit, extracted a clean white handkerchief and tossed it into Mango's lap.

As Mango's shoulders began to shake, a scarab beetle sidled closer and nudged him with one of its protruding horns. Without looking up, Mango gave its head a reassuring pat. The creature persisted in its overtures, though, prodding even more vigorously each time.

"Thank you, Cromwell," Mango mumbled, dabbing at his eyes with the hankie. "I appreciate your concern, but I don't think there's anything you can do to help." He patted the beetle's head again. "That's enough now. Off you go."

Cromwell, however, would not be deterred. Mango began to grow a little annoyed, especially after the beetle hooked one of its horns into the sleeve of his cashmere cardigan and began to tug.

"What on earth is it, Cromwell?" Mango exclaimed. When he stood up, trying desperately to shake the beetle off, Cromwell held on even tighter.

"I think he wants you to go somewhere with him, Cornelius," Filbert remarked.

Mango looked at him blankly. "Really? How curious."

With a frustrated sigh, Mr. Goodfellow took Mango firmly by the shoulders and turned him toward the doorway, in the direction the beetle was tugging. "Out there, man!"

When he was sure he had everyone's attention, Cromwell let go and tottered down the rest of the darkened passageway and into another small room. The beetle emerged a short time later, struggling behind the weight of a very large and very fragrant ball. By the slow and loving way that Cromwell was maneuvering the thing down the hallway—taking great care not to scrape it against the walls—apparently it was something of immense value. It was, in fact, his most prized possession; a project he'd been working on for many years.

When he had rolled the giant ball directly in front of them, Cromwell stopped and shuffled to the side. A little taken aback by the onslaught to their senses, especially noticeable in the cramped quarters of Mango's palm trunk abode, Mr. Goodfellow, Filbert and Porter quickly covered their noses, but Mango seemed unmoved.

"The dung ball *again*, Cromwell?" he sighed. "I know how much it means to you, but I really don't think it's something these gentlemen need to see." He turned to Mr. Goodfellow and Filbert and whispered. "I'm dreadfully sorry about this. I tried every trick in the book to get rid of that thing when they all moved in, but the beetle wouldn't have it. He's hopelessly attached to it, you know. Started building the thing years ago, in Sir Percival's lab—"

"Really?" interrupted Mr. Goodfellow. He tapped his fingertips together, in that certain way he did whenever an interesting thought was crossing his mind. "Back at Sir Percival's, you say?"

Mango looked at him with his now familiar blank stare. Filbert, significantly more clued in, however, glanced at his brother with an expression of growing interest.

Mr. Goodfellow trotted back into the front hall for a moment, returning with an umbrella from Mango's vast collection. He was not about to use his own beloved brolly, no matter how intriguing the theory that was formulating in his mind. Standing as far back as he could from the beetle's dung ball, Mr. Goodfellow made several exploratory taps. Then, throwing all caution to the wind (and after glancing towards Cromwell for permission to proceed), Mr. Goodfellow leapt forward with the grace of a skilled swordsman, launching the sharp, pointed tip of the umbrella directly into the center of the hard, round ball. He instantly withdrew it with a great flourish, then stood back and waited. Everyone else, Sage and insect alike, gathered around in silent anticipation. But nothing happened. Mr. Goodfellow furrowed his brow. With umbrella extended, he stepped forward to try again. At that moment, a little speck of dirt slowly trickled down the side of the ball, followed by another and another, until the entire structure began to crumble before his eyes. With a shrill little cry, Mango dove out of the way. Struggling for a moment to open the hall closet door, he disappeared behind it, returning to the calamitous scene a few seconds later, holding onto a flimsy dustpan and brush. Eyes wide with wonder, Mango dropped the useless tools to the floor with a clatter as the disintegrating dung ball, looking a lot like Mount Vesuvius during one of its more spectacular eruptions, continued to spill forth.

The ensuing evacuation of the hallway proceeded at a remarkable speed, considering the age and infirmity of

Mango's assembled houseguests. Within seconds, the area had completely cleared. Mr. Goodfellow, however, remained steadfast, convinced (as he continued shouting to everyone above the din of a thousand stampeding legs) that the silver lining of Cromwell's handiwork might soon be revealed. He was not to be disappointed. Mr. Goodfellow's calculated gamble had paid off. Sparkling through the last vestiges of grime was a small, square piece of crystal; the missing map from the legendary Book of The Sage. It was the final piece of the puzzle of the ages, hidden away by Sir Percival Davenport in the last place most people (except Mr. Goodfellow, of course) would ever think to look—the dung ball of a scarab beetle.

Beaming with obvious satisfaction, Mr. Goodfellow removed a white handkerchief from his pocket and stepped forward. He brushed most of the remaining dirt from the crystal block, picked it up with both hands and gave it a vigorous shake. Filbert, Porter, Mango and the insects cautiously crept back into the hallway.

"There you go, Filbert," Mr. Goodfellow exclaimed, giving the map a victorious hug before he deposited it into his older brother's hands. "Once again the merits of searching for that proverbial silver lining have not steered us wrong, have they?"

"Brilliant detective work, Jolly," Filbert admitted, holding the still soiled map at arm's length. "But how did you know where to find it?"

"Elementary, my dear Watson," Mr. Goodfellow replied with a grin.

Filbert rolled his eyes. He knew what was coming next. Mango, hopelessly confused, glanced around at everyone in the room. "Watson?" he inquired.

"It's just an expression, Cornelius, old man," Mr. Goodfellow explained. He smiled with satisfaction then and took a deep breath. "My years of guiding Sir Arthur Conan Doyle and an understanding of the deductive reasoning capabilities of his literary creation—the great detective Sherlock Holmes—have evidently proven most useful to me in this instance. I believe I may have come up with a theory that makes perfect sense. It's quite simple, really. After studying the crystal map, Sir Percival clearly understood that he was in possession of an object of monumental importance. When Eustace Slocumb revealed himself to be an intensely jealous man and quite possibly one of questionable ethics, too, Sir Percival decided to place the map where it would not be exposed to further exploitation. A man of remarkable intelligence and integrity, Sir Percival believed that what he had uncovered should be imparted to all humankind at once—but in a way that would not endanger or compromise the information it contained. Sir Percival was determined to see the map belong to all of Earth's inhabitants and not just a handful of self-serving scientists like Eustace Slocumb." Mr. Goodfellow nodded his head toward Cromwell just then. "Sir Percival had no family or close friends to confide in, so it seems only natural that he would think to hide it with one of his most trusted associates, biding his time until the right course of action presented itself. Regrettably, Sir Percival did not live to see the dawn of that day. I have reason to believe, now, that his untimely death may not have been natural at all, but the result of foul play. There are many drugs that could be secretly administered to mimic the effects of heart failure; drugs that would be readily available to a man of science."

"Like Eustace Slocumb?" Filbert suggested, raising an eyebrow.

Mango sank to his knees, put his head in his hands and began to shake. "How could I have been so blind!" he exclaimed. "I should have been more attuned to what was happening! I had been entrusted as Sir Percival's Sage, after all! Surely I should have been able to help him! I've ruined everything..."

"Don't be too hard on yourself, Cornelius," Mr. Goodfellow replied, in a tone that had become noticeably more sympathetic. "When the darkest of forces are at play, as I now believe they were, it may have been beyond the control of any *one* of us."

Mango looked up. There was a little spark of hope in his eyes.

"Just think of it," Mr. Goodfellow continued. "None of us could have been fully prepared for all that has happened lately and the many strange mysteries that have been revealed to us. No one could have foreseen or prevented any of it."

"And what of Eustace Slocumb?" Filbert asked.

Mr. Goodfellow slowly rubbed his chin. "A very interesting question, Filbert. As soon as Cornelius first mentioned that name, it rang a very loud bell with me. As I have since recalled, I came across it in a small news item that popped up a few years ago. The article concerned the abrupt resignation and subsequent seclusion of a top NASA scientist. That scientist was none other than Eustace Slocumb. It was a story that was completely overshadowed at the time by a much bigger one—the disappearance of one of our most beloved national heroes, Colonel Fletcher Jaffrey. Dr. Slocumb is a brilliant individual, Filbert, but one, I suspect, who is primarily motivated by greed and jealousy. We have seen his type before, I'm afraid. And I would not be surprised to discover that he has, like many other humans driven by sinister desires, frequently benefited from the counsel of The Fen. Since he had been put in charge of the scientific team entrusted with the map, it must have been infuriating to Slocumb that he had been able to only partially decipher it. Sir Percival, however, *was* able to complete his analysis of the information—something that I believe he may have ultimately paid for with his life. When he began to suspect Slocumb's unsavory intentions, Sir Percival managed to protect the map itself inside Cromwell's dung ball. But I fear that Slocumb may have succeeded in extracting the secrets locked within it from his dying colleague, anyway. We know that Sir Percival did not pass his findings to anyone else before his death, so we must assume that Slocumb was the one who presented this critical information to NASA, most probably as his *own* work. The secret mission went ahead, after all."

"If this theory of yours is correct, Jolly," Filbert remarked, "then Eustace Slocumb got away with murder."

"Indeed. And more than that." Mr. Goodfellow raised his eyebrows. "I believe he may have *gotten away* entirely."

"What?" asked Filbert, sounding confused.

"If you investigate a little further," Mr. Goodfellow explained, "I expect you will find that Eustace Slocumb is not really in seclusion after all. As hideous as the possibility may be, we have to consider that there was more than one stowaway on that mysterious trip."

"Eustace Slocumb?" Filbert exclaimed, as Mango, still crouched on the floor, gave a sizable shudder.

"I'm afraid so," Mr. Goodfellow replied. "A man capable of coldly murdering another human being surely would not have been content to merely hand over such sensitive information without discovering firsthand what kind of knowledge and riches lay at the end of the journey. I'm even inclined to think that Slocumb probably presented NASA with a considerable amount of misleading information, too, keeping the true coordinates that Sir Percival had discovered to himself, until he had gained complete control of the ship."

"But if that's true," Mango suddenly piped up, his voice quivering, "it would mean that Slocumb and—"

"It would mean, I'm afraid," interrupted Mr. Goodfellow, "that Fletcher Jaffrey and Winchester Redwood and everyone else on that voyage were in grave danger from the very start. We can only hope that they realized before it was too late what kind of threat lurked among them."

Filbert was staring ahead, deep in thought. "Perhaps if we knew exactly where they were going and what they might encounter there..."

Cornelius Mango, humming softly to himself, slumped forward on the floor and began to mumble through the side of his mouth. "I wish I could remember. I wish! I wish! I wish!" With each new lament, his forehead bumped against the hard floor of the hallway.

Mr. Goodfellow took him gently by the shoulders and helped him onto his knees. "It will do no good to go on like this, Cornelius," he said softly. "It's time to show what mettle we're made of. Right, old chap?"

Mr. Goodfellow turned to Filbert. "Now that we've located the map, we'll return it to its place within the book as soon as possible. Delphinia Shipton can continue her expert analysis from there."

"Book?" Cornelius Mango mumbled as his eyes flew open. "Analysis?" You haven't been talking about *the* Delphinia Shipton, have you? The great mystic?"

Mr. Goodfellow looked back nervously. Mango turned to glance at the crystal map that had been stored in his house for so long, concealed in Cromwell's dung ball. He began to tremble. "What *is* th-th-that—thing?" he cried in fear.

"We're not entirely sure just yet, Cornelius," Filbert

replied, patting him on the shoulder. "Don't worry yourself about it. We're going to take it back where it belongs."

"It's from The Book of The Sage," Porter piped up innocently, wondering why neither Mr. Goodfellow nor Filbert had thought to offer Mango this fascinating piece of information. "You know, that knowledge of the ages book that everybody whispers about." Filbert gave the boy a stern glance, but Porter, still revving up, was oblivious to it. "Mrs. Shipton thinks the map part is all about the wanderings of The Sage," he continued, "ever since she figured out from the book that the reason we have shoulder-knobs is because we all used to have wings and were related to The Fen once and everything—"

Cornelius Mango uttered a faint little cry and toppled forward again. His eyes were blank and staring.

"Well, Porter," said Mr. Goodfellow nervously, as he began to usher the boy from the hallway. "I can see that we're going to have to review that chapter on not revealing information that might be deemed too sensitive or distressing to certain people. Chapter Four in our textbook, if I'm not mistaken."

"Okay, Mr. Goodfellow. Whatever you say," said Porter, looking puzzled.

"Well, I suppose we really should be leaving now, anyway, Cornelius," Mr. Goodfellow offered in a loud and cheery voice as he hurried down the hall. "Don't bother getting up, now. We can see ourselves out."

Cornelius hadn't budged. In fact, he seemed incapable of moving. He hadn't uttered a word, either, except for a few incoherent gurgles.

"Do you really think we should be leaving him like

this, Jolly?" asked Filbert with concern. "He seems a tad disoriented."

"I suspect that he'll recover shortly," Mr. Goodfellow assured his brother. "Cornelius's attention span is not long these days. I doubt that he'll remember us, or any of this visit for that matter, by tomorrow morning. He's quite safe here and he's in the company of friends."

Mr. Goodfellow gently swung the front door open and pushed Porter and Filbert (still holding the crystal map in front of him) back outside and into the rain. As he was exiting himself, Mr. Goodfellow cordially waved his umbrella at Cromwell. The beetle returned a slightly awkward but equally cordial wave of one horn, as he gathered the remains of his beloved dung ball together to begin his next project.

10

The Wickedness of a Few
Is the Calamity of All

Nothing could have prepared Jolly or Filbert or Porter for what greeted them upon their return home. It was a scene of utter pandemonium. Their triumph at having found and secured the missing map from The Book of The Sage was dashed in seconds when they arrived at Blue Heron Cottage to discover Beatrice trying desperately to comfort a sobbing Charlotte and Hazel. In their woven egg basket in the corner, Winston and Little Jolly, upset by all the loud and unfamiliar noises, were screaming their heads off. As soon as she saw Filbert walk through the door, Hazel rushed over and threw herself into his arms.

Beatrice, her eyes red with tears, could do no more than point to a recently delivered mouse-e-gram that lay on the kitchen floor. Mr. Goodfellow ran to pick it up. It was addressed simply to Goodfellow—Blue Heron Cottage. The words were short and painful.

ACCIDENT AT SEA CLIFFS STOP CYRUS DEAD
STOP EDGAR MORTALLY WOUNDED STOP

HAVE INFORMED GOVERNING COUNCIL
STOP COME AT ONCE STOP   DELPHINIA

Mr. Goodfellow felt heartsick. He passed the note to Filbert and heard his brother gasp. He stood trembling for a moment, not knowing what to do. His mind was awash with grief. How could such a horrible thing have happened? The great Cyrus Goodfellow was dead and Edgar lay dying. It was almost too much to comprehend.

Porter looked up at him, frightened and confused. "What's going on, Mr. Goodfellow? What is it?"

"Something terrible has happened, lad," he replied in a dry croak. The painful lump that had formed in his throat was making it difficult to get the words out. He put his arm around the boy's shoulder. "There's been a tragic accident at Mrs. Shipton's cave, Porter. Our Great-Uncle Cyrus has died, I'm afraid, and Edgar is... well, Edgar is very, very sick."

Awkwardly shuffling his mouse feet, Porter looked down. Tears welled in his eyes and he tried to wipe them away with the back of his furry sleeve. "What are we going to do now?" Porter sniffled.

"That's a very good question, Porter," Mr. Goodfellow replied, trying hard to pull himself together. Lost in their grief, no one else in the room seemed capable of taking charge. It was all up to him. He walked over to the twins' basket and swept a baby into each arm. He bounced them up and down and cooed to them until they stopped crying. Then he called out to Beatrice.

"The mouse courier, my dear. Where is he now?"

Beatrice looked around the room. "I don't know," she replied, her voice shaking. "He was here a moment ago. With all the confusion, he must have decided to leave."

"That's odd," Mr. Goodfellow replied. "Not waiting around, or even offering to help? Why, we may have wanted to send an immediate reply. It's most unprofessional."

"Perhaps he had somewhere else to go," offered Beatrice, still trying to comfort the sobbing Charlotte. "Or another message to deliver?"

Mr. Goodfellow shook his head in frustration. "Inexcusable!" he muttered. The babies started squealing again. Mr. Goodfellow resumed his bouncing and cooing. "Porter," he called out, "I need you to do something for me."

Porter shuffled forward.

"Now listen carefully, lad. I want you to go to Sam's. To the lighthouse."

Porter nodded his head earnestly.

"When you get there, tell Sam what has happened and bring him back with you, alright?"

Porter nodded again. He pulled his hood and ears tightly around his head and repositioned his mouse mask over his nose. Mr. Goodfellow, still carrying the fussing twins, walked him to the front door.

"I don't have to remind you to be extremely cautious when you're passing through town, do I, Porter? When you reach the pier, find the black ducks and tell them where you want to go. They'll ferry you across. Now, take care, lad, and hurry!"

Mr. Goodfellow watched from the front porch as Porter ran down the steps and onto the sand, disappearing into the tall grasses as he made his way down to the beach and on into town.

Mr. Goodfellow hoped that Porter's errand was not too dangerous. But he remembered then that Edgar, at the same age, had already been on the run for many years, dodging the vengeful Shrike Fen and living by his wits.

It was difficult for Mr. Goodfellow to think of Edgar without wondering if he might already be gone. It was hard, too, to imagine that Great-Uncle Cyrus was truly dead. He had been such a powerful presence in the Goodfellow family and, of course, a respected member of the Governing Council for centuries. Thank goodness that Delphinia, at what must have been a profoundly shocking moment, had had the presence of mind to inform the Council of the tragedy. They would have taken matters in hand already, contacted the rest of the family and started the appropriate funeral arrangements. A Sage of Cyrus's high standing would no doubt be receiving full honors, Mr. Goodfellow surmised, perhaps even a special memorial service under Westminster Abbey.

He turned and walked back into the cottage to face the very difficult task of determining the next course of action. But it appeared by the look on everyone else's face that they had already decided.

Charlotte, in the midst of packing a small bag, was adamant that she was going to Edgar's side, and as soon as possible. Filbert and Hazel, anxious to be with their only son at this terrible time, were also determined to go. Mr. Goodfellow's more conservative plan—that he should go first and assess the situation—was shouted down unanimously. He stood, powerless, balancing Winston and Little Jolly on his hips, as everyone else lobbied to be heard.

"Just a moment!" he exclaimed. "Hasn't anyone thought to consider these little tykes?"

"Well, of *course* we have, Jolly!" answered Beatrice a little indignantly. "What a silly question! I'm going to watch the twins while the rest of you go. Porter can help me."

Mr. Goodfellow opened his mouth to speak, but Beatrice glared at him.

"It's all been decided," she said sternly. Then she sidled up to him and whispered, "It has to be this way. Charlotte and Filbert and Hazel would never forgive themselves if they didn't take this last chance to see Edgar again, even if it may just be for a brief time. And you must go too, dear Jolly. I know how much he means to you." She brushed away a tear that was trickling down her cheek. "I should be the one to stay here with the little ones."

Mr. Goodfellow sighed, then nodded his head in agreement. "You're right, my dear. But please allow me one indulgence. I have sent Porter for Sam, and I would feel much better if you and the children moved over to the lighthouse while we're away. He and the mice can watch over you much better there."

"Yes, of course, Jolly," Beatrice replied. "If it will give you some comfort."

Mr. Goodfellow's endless bouncing and cooing had finally paid off. The twins were fast asleep in his arms. He gently placed them back in their basket and tucked the blue blanket around them. He couldn't help but pause and stare. In sleep, their tiny faces seemed so calm and peaceful, as if they were visiting a kinder and gentler world. Every now and then, one of them would smile or sigh or blow a bubble. Mr. Goodfellow was thankful that they were still young enough to be oblivious to the great sadness around them and the even greater sadness that might yet come. But when he balanced that against the thought that they might never know their father, the brave and loyal Edgar Goodfellow, his heart filled with despair and his eyes with tears.

He went outside on the porch again, hoping that some fresh air might clear his head and ease his trembling. Still lost in sad thoughts, he did not notice the sly parting of the sea grass next to him or the brown courier mouse that was peering out, grinning in a strange and unnatural way, before it suddenly turned on its heels and darted away.

By the time Porter returned with Sam, everyone else was packed and ready to leave. Sam, of course, had taken the news of the fatal accident with shock and disbelief. Even after arriving at Blue Heron Cottage and hearing the words directly from Mr. Goodfellow's mouth, Sam still could not believe that such a senseless tragedy had befallen his friends. Naturally, he also wanted to see Edgar one more time, but The Sage asked him to stay behind. Edgar's children might need him, they explained, and Sam knew in his heart that his dear friend would have expected no less of him.

The next moments were difficult for everyone. Filbert and Hazel, looking tired and old beyond their years, said goodbye; first to Beatrice, Porter and the babies, and then to Sam. Even in their own overwhelming grief, they told him that they understood how painful it must be for him, given the special bond that he and Edgar shared. Charlotte, her eyes still brimming with tears, touched him tenderly on the hand.

Beatrice and Mr. Goodfellow embraced for a long time and whispered some words into each other's ears. Then Filbert announced that they should leave. The luggage of the four transatlantic travelers (including a special pouch to house the crystal map) was outweighed by the baby equipment and supplies that were going no farther than Sam's, approximately three miles away. It was fortunate that Sam would be rowing everything across the channel in his boat. Transporting all of the packages across the island by duck ferry would have required an entire flock of birds.

Placing The Sage and their luggage into the pockets of his shirt and jacket, Sam set off down the beach and up through town, dropping his first load at the shuttle dock. Mr. Goodfellow, Charlotte, Filbert and Hazel would have to wait about twenty-five minutes until the next vessel was scheduled to depart for the city. An enterprising family of water rats who lived under the docks, however, had provided a comfortable waiting area for passengers and an impressive display of food items for barter. The arrival of four Sage immediately caused a stir amongst the rat population, until it became apparent that none of these travelers had the stomach to eat.

It was hard for Sam to sort out his emotions as he gripped the ends of the wooden oars and began to row his boat toward the lighthouse. He had been devastated by the news of the horrible accident. It had never occurred to him in all his long life with The Sage that Edgar might be taken first. It didn't seem right or natural. Whatever years he had left on Earth now, Sam thought, they would seem desolate and lonely without Edgar Goodfellow. He hadn't even had the opportunity to properly grieve for his friend, now that the overwhelming responsibility of caring for Edgar's two boys had fallen partly to him. The precious cargo that he was carrying back home was beginning to make him feel anxious and edgy.

But had Sam known what was transpiring at that very minute, just a short distance away in the dark, dank, moldy basement of The House of Mandrake Taxidermy Emporium, his anxiety would have turned to sheer panic....

"Idiot!" snarled a voice from the shadows. "Look at all the sand you've dragged in!"

The figure who had just spoken raised a long, bony arm, then struck out with a vicious blow. The brown courier mouse staggered backward and fell, sliding awkwardly across the floor before it landed against the wall in a crumpled heap.

"Get outside and clean up your tracks before someone sees them! NOW!"

But the mouse did not respond. Its beady eyes stared straight, its face frozen in an eerie grin.

"BOGG!" the voice snarled. "Get over here! This stupid thing is acting up again!"

"Right away, Uncle Shrike!"

A figure emerged from the shadows and scurried over to the limp body of the courier mouse. He gave it a kick with one sharp-nailed foot, then reached down and grabbed hold of an ear. There was a tearing sound as he pulled upward, lifting a layer of fur and skin from the mouse's face to reveal a grizzly skeleton of silver tubing and multicolored wires. He removed one of the staring eyeballs and probed the empty socket with the tip of his long, jagged fingernail.

"Central circuits seem to be burnt out, Uncle Shrike," he announced nervously, before replacing the eyeball with a plop.

"AGAIN?" the other voice shrieked.

Shrike slid out from the shadows and moved across the floor. The wicked old Fen had changed little in the seventy-five years since Sam and the Goodfellows had thwarted his plans. Still obsessed with destroying the creatures who stood between him and his own dreams of glory, Shrike would have liked nothing better than to rid Earth of every last Sage, especially the one known as Edgar Goodfellow. And now that he found himself closer to attaining his goals than ever before—with the spoils of victory just outside his grasp—he had grown even more vicious with impatience.

"These changelings are nothing but useless pieces of junk!" he roared. He swept his black cloak to one side, then pressed a button that was implanted in his bony hip, just above a shiny metal leg. With a whirring sound, the leg lurched forward then fell across the mechanical mouse's body with a loud thump, scattering tubes in every direction. Tangled pieces of wiring writhed and twisted on the floor, sending little sparks of sizzling light into the air. The acrid smell of burning fur filled the room.

"That'll teach you to ignore the great Shrike Fen!" he gurgled with satisfaction, just before the bottom section of his robotic leg began to rotate. Shrike shrieked, then staggered sideways, struggling to remain upright. Bogg rushed to his side. The leg, oscillating out of control now, suddenly broke free. It flew up into the air like a spinning can, then arced down, coming to rest with a great clang on the other side of the room.

"This damnable appendage!" Shrike screamed, as he crawled forward to retrieve it. "It's no better than those hideous rodent contraptions!"

"But Uncle Shrike," whined Bogg, leaning over the mouse as he tried to untangle a jumbled ball of crushed wires. "Maybe if you weren't quite so rough with them—"

"Don't give me your pathetic excuses anymore, Bogg! Lyle Mandrake's a worthless parasite, just like his father! It's no surprise that his attempts to profit on those useless robotics experiments of his have failed so miserably. You've wasted too many years on both of those fools! They're hapless oafs." He turned then and stared straight at his nephew. "Or maybe it's just *you*, Bogg," he hissed. "Funny how the Mandrakes whom I've been responsible for have always had a little more cunning about them, isn't it? Why, that Ramona is quite a devilish genius, if I do say so myself. Her dear grandfather would have been very proud."

Bogg grimaced. He'd been listening to this sort of thing

since he was a boy. He glanced up at Shrike who was crouched over with his back to him, attempting to reattach his leg. Bogg clenched his white, bony fists. What he wouldn't give to get his hands around that scrawny old neck and give it a good throttle.

"Well, *I'm* done," Shrike announced, standing up and giving his robotic leg a good shake. "Have you fixed *your* thing yet?"

Bogg looked up from the hopelessly crushed remains of the courier mouse. Parts of it were still smoking.

"No, Bogg? What a surprise!" Shrike snarled, before his nephew had a chance to respond. "The least we can do now is spare ourselves from its insipid grin. Why is it that you can't eliminate those irritating expressions, anyway?"

Shrike raised his leg one more time, then ground it down into what was left of the mouse's face, completely obliterating the whiskered muzzle.

Bogg could no longer contain himself. "Now look what you've done!" he screamed in frustration. "I might have been able to fix him! Now he'll never be able to tell us if he completed his mission!"

"We'll find out soon enough," Shrike chuckled. "I've sent the other one—the creature with the diamond patch—to check up on those stupid Sage." Shrike stared at the crumpled courier mouse for a moment and then at Bogg. "Which reminds me, nephew," he sneered. "I trust that you adequately disposed of the original body this time; the one that this hopeless machine here replaced?"

"Yes, Uncle Shrike," replied Bogg hesitantly. "I-I buried it deep in the woods... just like you said."

"Well, let's hope that you did!" Shrike continued with a snarl. "I'd hate to think that you made the mistake of leaving it lying around like the first one! When that doddering old fool, Basil Mandrake, found it, he had it gutted and stuffed and shoved out in his front window before I knew what was happening. It almost ruined all our clever little plans, you know, especially when that meddling Sam Middleton stumbled onto it. That oversight could have spoiled everything, Bogg! I sincerely hope, for your sake, that it never happens again!"

"Yes, Uncle Shrike," replied Bogg, clenching his jaw and grinding down on his chisel-sharp teeth.

"Good! I'm so glad we understand each other," Shrike slowly hissed. "And I don't have to ask you about the fate of the real message that original courier was carrying, do I?"

"Um..."

"BOGG?"

"I took it back to the woods and burned it, of course! Right after we read it!" Bogg cried out, staring at the floor and fidgeting with his jagged nails.

"Excellent," Shrike gurgled.

Bogg continued to look down, terrified of catching his uncle's gaze and being caught out in a lie. With the sleeve of his black cloak, he quickly wiped away the little beads of glistening sweat that had broken out on his forehead. He was thankful that his uncle hadn't seemed to notice his distress. Maybe he'd gotten away with it, he pondered, at least for now. He'd searched everywhere for that blasted note. It must have slipped from his cloak on the way back to the forest. He'd planned to return and search for it again, but Shrike always seemed to have another tiresome job for him to do.

"Of course, we'll be needing a replacement for this one now," announced Shrike, kicking at the smoldering robot mouse. "So you'd better get cracking! You'll have to acquire another subject to copy, won't you? And see if you can't do something about that blasted grin this time. Slipping those things into a crowd of real mice is all very well, Bogg, but one day someone's going to take a closer look and the jig will be up!"

Shrike paused just then as he made a final adjustment to his leg.

"And although I do so regret to admit it, Bogg," Shrike continued, slowly tapping his long fingernails on the tip of his white, pointed chin, "those furry little spies have been useful in some ways, I suppose. Odd, how one's view of things can change overnight, isn't it, nephew? All these long years we've been stalking those loathsome Sage and that human accomplice of theirs, hoping to uncover the fate of the Martian scrolls, and now that we know where they've been hiding them, it seems of little consequence. Who could have imagined that we would be fortunate enough to discover something else? Thanks to that letter, we now know something so deliciously toxic to those miserable creatures that we might be able wipe them *all* from the face of the earth. It's Fennish justice, I tell you!" He shot Bogg a chilling grin. "Now get moving!"

Bogg looked up from the hopeless repair job and opened his mouth to speak, but Shrike, still shouting instructions, had already turned his back on him.

"I must be off!" Shrike announced. "I have important work to do with Ramona. She's making significant progress with her new genetic mutation trials, you know. If all goes well, Bogg, those crude robotics experiments of her idiot brother's will soon be a thing of the past. I believe I might suggest that she's ready to apply her genius to a few rodent subjects. After all, if she's intending to eventually experiment on the human species, she'll have to start off with something a little smaller, won't she? If all goes according to *my* plan, Ramona will soon be turning heads in the underground scientific community. The great name of Mandrake will be notable again. Or perhaps *notorious* would be a more fitting expression!" Shrike hissed with delight. "We'll soon be able to replace those troublesome mouse machines with something much more formidable. Let's see how well The Sage can deal with a few dozen genetically altered mouse helpers! It's such a delightfully devious prospect! For the time being, Bogg, I trust that you won't be fouling up *your* assignment." Shrike suddenly stopped speaking and spun back around. "I will not tolerate any more foolish mistakes, Bogg! Or any trivial distractions, either! Have I made myself *perfectly* clear?"

Bogg, muttering something under his breath, trembled with rage.

"Have you something to say to me, Bogg?" Shrike croaked, flashing his cold, steely eyes. "Don't speak behind my back, boy! Speak your mind! I despise secrets, you know."

"Yes, Uncle Shrike. I mean no, Uncle Shrike," Bogg replied, flustered. "I mean—I have nothing to say."

"It seems as if you've got quite a lot of work to do though, doesn't it, nephew?" crowed Shrike, rustling his cloak as he turned to leave. "So see to it! And meet me back here before daylight. I trust you haven't forgotten about our special mission?"

Bogg shook his head earnestly.

"Just checking, boy. I never know *what* to expect from you," he sneered. "And one more thing, Bogg," he whispered with particular malice. "If you ever choose to challenge me, I'll have you gutted and stuffed before you know what's hit you! Understand?"

"Yes, Uncle Shrike," Bogg replied, swallowing hard. "Of course, Uncle Shrike."

Trembling now with fear instead of rage, Bogg released the mass of tangled wires he was still holding in his hands. It fell toward the floor, expelling one final spark of light before coming to rest in a smoldering heap.

After his uncle had left, Bogg crawled into the damp, moldy tunnel they had bored through the basement wall and up the almost vertical clay pipe that led out to a filthy alleyway.

Scrambling to get out, Bogg could still hear his uncle's voice drifting down from the third floor, echoing through the hollow walls of the building. "Ahhh, how delightful! It's finally just you and me, my dear. Alone at last." Shrike's words dripped into Ramona Mandrake's ear like thick syrup. "Let's see what delicious things we can dream up tonight, shall we?"

Popping out of the end of the clay pipe and into the alley, Bogg stumbled over some leftover mouse bait; a chunk of perfectly ripened Gorgonzola cheese. As he picked himself up and brushed down his dusty cloak, the words "I despise secrets... I despise secrets..." played over and over in his mind. Cringing at the memory of his uncle's cruel threat, Bogg knew full well that if Shrike ever discovered what other secrets he was hiding from him, he would be dispatched as quickly and as brutally as a pitiful mouse.

As Bogg was scuttling off into the fading light of day, something was stirring deep within the forest. The winds of fate, it seemed, had chosen just that moment to swirl softly through the trees, where they picked up the last decaying leaves and pine needles of the previous autumn and lifted them high into the air. Floating in the middle of this mass of nature's debris was a very, very small piece of wrinkled white paper holding a message that had traveled all the way across the sea in the paws of a brave and dedicated mouse courier. The paper had managed to escape the clutches of The Fen, but its journey was far from over. It was not destined to sit forever in the forest, but to continue traveling back toward the sea. Another gentle breeze captured it there and carried it farther still, where it hovered for a while above the town square. Here it began its descent, finally landing at the foot of a small lighthouse mouse known as Lydia, who had just arrived to check out a new stash of cheese that one of the other mice had been insisting she investigate. Lydia picked up the curious piece of paper and turned it over in her paws. Like other mice, she could not read, but she was a particularly intelligent little creature and there was one row of odd squiggles that immediately caught her eye. She had seen one of these squiggles many times before and was almost sure that it meant "Goodfellow." And although Lydia's sensitive nose had already locked onto the exquisite smell of cheese in the vicinity, she tucked the paper under her arm and quickly turned for the harbor docks instead.

11

THEY WHO WILL NOT
BE DECEIVED MUST HAVE
AS MANY EYES ON THEIR
HEADS AS HAIRS

Sam was thankful that both India and Alice were otherwise occupied when he returned home. It was final-examination week at school, and Alice was probably in her room, busy with her studies. The sound of water running in the kitchen gave away India's whereabouts.

The twins had slept peacefully on the trip across the channel but had started to fret a bit since docking. Beatrice was having difficulty calming them, and Porter, instructed to keep Jasper under control, seemed to be having considerable problems of his own. Humming loudly to drown out the baby cries and the sounds of a cicada tuning up, Sam shuffled past the kitchen door and offered India a hasty greeting. As he made his way toward the lighthouse tunnel, Carmen, Buttercup and Tosca trailed through from the sitting room where they had been having a late-afternoon nap. Sam gave each of them a quick pat on the head, squeezing himself and his passengers through the walkway door before the dogs had any opportunity to investigate the strange noises coming from his coat pocket.

It was a relief for Sam to finally unload his special cargo in the sanctuary of the old lighthouse. He lifted Beatrice out first. She emerged, cradling a twin in each arm, with her usually immaculately brushed hair knot in total disarray. Strands of silver-streaked hair that had slipped out from under her mouse hood were now being tugged at with unexpected force by four tiny pink fists.

"Everything alright?" Sam inquired.

Beatrice flinched, then gazed up at him with a limp smile.

"I think so, dear. Some dry nappies and a spot of supper and I'm sure they'll be as right as rain."

The brave Sage who had stood by Winston Churchill's side in the darkest hours of the Second World War and helped him to stare down the likes of Adolph Hitler was not about to admit defeat at the hands of two fussing infants, each no bigger than a peanut.

Sam felt around his pocket for the six bags of baby supplies and the woven egg basket, and deposited them at Beatrice's feet. He had a little more trouble extracting Porter, who was engaged in a battle of wills with Jasper. It was proving to be quite a struggle for him to return his pet to the knapsack while keeping a tight grip on the creature's wings.

This rather noisy arrival had already alerted the lighthouse mice, who quickly emerged from the complex tunnel system behind the brick walls. Their joy at seeing the Goodfellow twins soon turned to despair when Beatrice told them of the terrible accident that had befallen their father. By virtue of his enormously kind and patient nature, Edgar Goodfellow had gained a special place in the hearts of the lighthouse mice and they were shattered by the news. There wasn't a dry eye between them. It was heartbreaking for Sam to see twenty-three tiny creatures so overcome with grief. Once again, he wished he could communicate more directly with them, if only to offer some simple words of comfort. The mouse with the diamond-shaped patch of fur at his throat must have been especially touched by the news, Sam presumed, as he observed him clasping his paws over his mouth and shaking from head to foot.

Even through this debilitating flood of tears, the mice still managed to offer their usual hospitality, ushering Beatrice and the babies past a small hole in the wall and into their haven beyond. There they cleared a quiet spot to set up the egg basket with enough space left for Beatrice's and Porter's cots.

Beatrice emerged from the tunnels a short time later to provide Sam with an update. Winston and Little Jolly had finally settled down after a change and a feed, and Porter, exhausted by all the recent events, had collapsed on his cot and fallen fast asleep, too. Even Jasper, appearing to sense the heightened emotions of those around him, had offered little resistance when Beatrice had tethered him inside Porter's knapsack.

Sam looked down at his watch. Mr. Goodfellow, Charlotte, Filbert and Hazel would have arrived in Boston harbor by now. They may have already managed to secure their transportation overseas. It would be a sad and difficult journey for them all, he predicted. Whether they would arrive in Cornwall in time for...before Edgar...Sam swallowed hard. His eyes filled with tears, and he was too overwrought with sadness to finish his thoughts. He glanced at Beatrice. She looked strained and exhausted.

"I think we should all get some rest," he suggested. "It's been a long day."

Beatrice nodded her head.

When he returned to the keeper's house, Sam had enough energy left to take a light supper with India. Alice, engrossed in her books, came out of her room just long enough to collect a sizable plate of food, and then wander back. Complaining to India that he must be coming down with something, Sam took to his bed a little earlier than usual, even before the last rays of evening light had disappeared, and fell into an exhausted sleep.

Later that night, deep in the woods (not far from where he had disposed of the brown mouse courier), Bogg Fen scurried under a thick bed of moldy leaves, hoping that he might be lucky enough to stumble onto the lost letter. He shuddered, not even wanting to imagine what Shrike might do if he should ever discover that it hadn't been destroyed. Bogg tried to shake all thoughts of his uncle from his brain. After all, he had other things to worry about. He felt under his black cloak, making sure that his package had not suffered the same fate as the letter and slipped onto the forest floor beneath him. Relieved to discover that it was still there, Bogg hurried ahead until he reached a familiar patch of soft, mossy ground. The ground soon gave way to puddles of thick, smelly mud. It squished and burbled beneath his feet, oozing up between his Fen nails, cool and inviting. It felt good. Bogg smiled. He looked ahead to where a huge, rotting tree trunk lay across his path, then glanced behind to make sure he hadn't been followed. When he felt it was safe enough to proceed, Bogg darted into the trunk, making his way halfway down the hollow interior until he reached a piece of old bark that had been wedged between the trunk's inner walls like a door. He rapped his hand against it, uttered a strange little shriek, then stepped back and waited. The piece of bark slowly moved until a small crack appeared, followed by the sharp fingernails of a long, bony hand.

"What have you brought me this time?" a female voice rasped.

Bogg struggled to untie the package at his waist.

"More of the same, Rook. Just as you asked," Bogg replied. "But these ones are much fresher," he added. "I'm a good provider. You'll see."

"Give them to me, then," the voice demanded, as the hand stretched farther through the crack.

"Can I come in this time?" asked Bogg, straining to see through the thin opening. "I want to see her again. Oh, and you, too—of course."

"No! It's not convenient! Come back later!" the voice snapped.

"Please, Rook. I've come all this way. I won't stay long. I promise."

"Very well, then," the voice replied brusquely. "Are your feet all covered in that smelly mud, again?"

"Yes."

"Come on in then."

Bogg squeezed himself through the crack in the door before Rook had a chance to change her mind. He gave her a quick peck on her white forehead, right below a tuft of dirty, matted hair. She pushed him aside, but not before grabbing the package from his hands and tearing it open with the ends of her pointy nails.

"Mmm...fresh grubs," she hissed, as she peered greedily at the wriggling contents.

With Rook suitably occupied, Bogg nudged past her, out of the hallway and into a larger room, filled with crude furnishings of bark and stone. Navigating his way past several piles of refuse that littered the floor, Bogg raced to the back of the enclosure where damp leaves had been scooped together in a pile. In the middle of the sagging heap lay a squirming infant with facial features not unlike those of a very small vulture. Bogg leaned over it, and hissed happily.

"There you are, my little Grakul," he gurgled with delight, fawning as proudly as any father would over his new baby daughter.

Bogg picked her up and held her, admiring all of her tiny, but sharp, little nails, one by one. He looked over at Rook and smiled.

"Look at that! I think she has my nose," he announced, but Rook was too preoccupied with her bag of grubs to notice.

Grakul started to fuss. Bogg quickly bounced her up and down on his bony knee. Maybe if he could prove to Rook that he was not only an able provider but also a useful father, she would let him stay a little longer next time.

Unlike The Sage, the society of The Fen was not an equal opportunity institution. Not all Fen were created quite the same, and Rook and her family could be found farther down The Fen social scale than most. They were regarded, in fact, as little more than slaves to the more fortunate. Bogg, still young and impressionable, had not considered the implications of this when he had encountered the alluring Rook. She, in contrast, was sly and worldly—and well aware of Bogg's lofty social status. She had taken every opportunity to present herself as a captivating companion. Bogg had been taken in by Rook's charms at first, and even though those charms had long since evaporated, he was tied to her forever by the child they had brought into the world together.

Every moment that Bogg could steal with Grakul was

precious to him, but after the grubs were gone, Rook soon tired of his presence and made her move to throw him out. By the time Bogg emerged from the hollow trunk and looked up at the slowly dawning sky, he realized that he had probably stayed far too long. He started to shiver. There was no possible way he could hope to acquire a new mouse courier victim and make it back to the rendezvous point in time for the mission. Shrike would be livid. Bogg had no idea how he was going to explain himself. He thrashed through the forest back toward the town and then on to the harbor as quickly as his bony Fen legs could carry him, trying desperately to think of another good lie along the way.

Sam awoke with a start and sat up in bed. He was sure that someone had called his name, but after a few seconds, he determined that it must have been a dream. Except for the eerie red glow of his old alarm clock, the room was completely dark and still. It was 5:00 a.m. As his eyes adjusted to the light, Sam could make out the gray shape of India, breathing softly beside him. He *must* have been tired, he thought. He hadn't even stirred when she'd slipped into their bed. It took Sam a few moments to gather his thoughts, and when he remembered all that had transpired the day before, his heart began to ache. He sighed, holding his head in his hands until the sound of rustling drew his attention to the floor. Trying not to awaken India, Sam carefully rolled down the covers on one side of the bed, then swung his legs to the floor, where he began searching for his slippers with the tips of his toes. He found the first one easily and pushed a foot inside.

"Psst! Sam!"

Sam stopped moving and listened in the dark. The voice was familiar. He felt the other slipper being pushed against the side of his bare foot. He hooked it with his big toe and slipped the rest of his foot inside.

"Porter? Is that you?" Sam whispered.

"You have to come right away! Something's happened!" Porter whispered back. Sam couldn't decide whether he could detect fear or excitement in the boy's voice.

"Quickly! Please!" Porter pleaded, tugging at the end of Sam's pajama leg.

Sam picked Porter up, carefully feeling his way to the end of the bed, and then to the door where he plucked his robe from a hook and slung it across his shoulders. Before he squeezed out of the room, Sam turned back to stare at India who was slowly stirring. He held his breath while she turned over and absently mumbled his name before she drifted back to sleep.

When they reached the lighthouse, Sam could tell by the look on Beatrice's face that something very troubling had happened. Still in her bathrobe, Beatrice had obviously been disturbed from her sleep, too. Lydia and the rest of the mice were gathered around looking at the wrinkled piece of white paper that Beatrice held in her small hands. She looked up at Sam.

"Thank goodness you're here, dear."

"What is it? What's happened?" Sam asked, reaching for the paper with one hand and his magnifying glass with the other.

"It's a note, Sam. It appears to be from Edgar."

"What?" Sam replied, puzzled. "How could that be? When did it arrive?"

"That's just it. It didn't arrive at all. Lydia found it. In town."

"There's brown stuff all over it," Sam complained, as he moved the magnifying glass across its surface.

"They're dried bloodstains, Sam."

Sam looked up and grimaced. "Sage?"

"Mouse," Beatrice replied quietly. The mice at her side began to tremble.

"But I don't understand," said Sam. "What's going on? I can barely read this."

"It's addressed to Jolly. Apparently, it never reached its intended destination," Beatrice explained. "I suspect it may have been intercepted. Look at the date."

"Two days ago," said Sam, straining to read Edgar's handwriting at the top of the page.

"And the message about the accident at the cliffs?" asked Beatrice.

"That was dated Tuesday, too, right?" Sam replied, his eyes opening wide. "How could Edgar have written to us on the same...There must be some mistake!"

"Perhaps," Beatrice replied. "Or else our mouse-e-gram was a red herring. Anyone could have sent it, if you think about it. It wasn't handwritten like this message, after all. Whoever sent it would have to have had the cooperation of a courier mouse, or been able to trick one. That would not have been an easy thing to accomplish."

"But if all this is true, then Edgar and Great-Uncle Cyrus might still be alive!" exclaimed Sam.

"Well, they may be," answered Beatrice. "But I've been too afraid to get my hopes up. If the dates on the messages *are* correct, and the mouse-e-gram proves to be a ruse, then we may have more to worry about than we think. Someone wrote that horrible message about the accident to lure as many of us away from here as possible. I don't imagine they intended us to find the first message at all. The reasons aren't clear to me yet. I'm hoping that whatever Edgar has to say may enlighten us. I had only just started reading when you came in."

"Here. I'll do it," offered Sam. He positioned his magnifier over the paper and began to read.

Dear Uncle Jolly and everyone at Blue Heron,
*   Cyrus and Delphinia send their best. I miss you all very much. I can't believe that so much time has passed already. I bet that the boys won't even remember who I am when I get home!*

Sam stopped reading and looked down at Beatrice. She had already taken one of her trademark lavender handkerchiefs from her bathrobe pocket and was dabbing at her eyes. Sam took a deep breath and started into the letter again.

How is the search for the map going? Hope you are having some luck there. Delphinia has been engrossed in her translations of the remaining parts of The Book of The Sage for days now. I suppose it took you all some time to digest the unsettling aspects of my last correspondence. Well, I'm afraid I must warn you now that the rest of what Delphinia has uncovered in the book may prove to be considerably more disturbing. Here it all is in Delphinia's translated words. By the way, you may want to suggest to Porter right now that he go outside and play or something.

Sam stopped reading and rolled his eyes. Porter just looked up and shrugged his shoulders.

"Well, I guess you're about to become the most enlightened youngster in Sage history, Porter, whether you like it or not," observed Sam, as he turned his eyes back to the letter.

There is something about the connection between The Sage and The Fen that must never be revealed, save to the few who are entrusted to guard this ancient book and keep its secrets safe forever. It is something that must never, ever, become known to The Fen. Because The Sage and The Fen were one and the same at the beginning of time, the means of our destruction lies within their grasp. According to the words of the ancients, the way to our end would be through our smallest and most innocent—our beloved children. If one of them were somehow to be taken from us as an infant and raised as a member of Fen society, then at the time of their maturity and full acceptance into that Fen world, all that is Sage would end. Every one of us would cease to exist.

Sam stopped reading and looked down at the floor. Beatrice had turned white and Porter stood frozen, looking as if he wished he'd left the room when he'd had the chance. For the next few minutes no one could speak or move, until Beatrice suddenly broke the silence with a great cry of anguish.

"The twins!" she wailed. "The Fen want them! They've seen Edgar's note! They know everything!"

Before Sam had a chance to react, Beatrice leapt through the mouse hole like a speeding bullet. The mice, tripping over each other in the confusion that followed, were trying desperately to squeeze in behind her, while Porter, still frozen in fear, had not budged an inch.

Sam dropped to the floor and crawled over to the hole, where he attempted to untangle the squirming ball of mice that was wedged against the wall. He noticed that the mouse with the diamond-shaped patch was not with them. Sam felt a strange and queasy feeling in the pit of his stomach. He gave Porter a little shake, rousing the terrified boy to action. Gently pushing the remaining mice aside, Sam ushered Porter through the hole. When he had disappeared, Sam sat back on his haunches feeling frightened and helpless. If something had happened to Edgar's little boys he would never forgive himself. He waited for what seemed like forever, until he heard the sound of footsteps rushing back through the tunnel. He held his breath, praying that Beatrice would pop out in front of him, babes in arms. But Porter emerged instead, shaking from head to toe. Tears were streaming down his face. In his arms he held two chunks of Gorgonzola cheese, roughly molded into the shapes of babies, their features carved out with the distinctively jagged edge of a Fen nail.

"They-they put these awful things in the basket!" Porter cried.

Still clutching Edgar's bloodstained letter, Sam's thoughts dissolved into a confusing tangle of fear and disbelief. When the chilling reality of what had just transpired finally began to sink in, Sam felt the panic rise in his throat. He placed a trembling finger on one of Porter's shoulders. "Where's Beatrice?" he whispered.

"I think they've taken her, too!" Porter sobbed. The hideous cheese babies crumbled in the boy's arms, then fell to the floor in pieces.

12

SEEING IS BELIEVING

Slumped with his back to the lighthouse wall, Sam cradled his aching head in his hands. What was he to do now? After successfully guarding the priceless Martian scrolls for all this time, he had ended up losing something infinitely more precious and it had all happened in an instant. If Edgar *was* still alive, what on earth could Sam possibly say to him? How could he explain the unfortunate circumstances surrounding the disappearances of Winston and Little Jolly? He had let Edgar down miserably. If The Fen *had* read Edgar's note, and had in fact plotted to kidnap the twins in a bid to destroy The Sage, it might soon be too late to try to explain anything anyway. Sam tried to read the rest of Edgar's letter through his blurring vision, and as he did, every word pierced his heart like an arrow.

"I'm sorry to be passing on such frightening information," Edgar had written at the end. "Heaven help us if The Fen ever get wind of this. It would be devastating. Let me know as soon as you discover any information about the map. Delphinia is dying to get her hands on it. I will write again soon. Give Charlotte and the *boys a kiss for me and guard them dearly. It eases my mind to know that you are all there with them. Love, Edgar."*

There were no words to describe the terrible pain and guilt that Sam was feeling now, or to soothe his suffering. He felt utterly helpless. Not knowing what to do either, Porter was still sniffling quietly, clutching a piece of Sam's pajama leg in his fist.

A handful of the mice had managed to pull themselves together enough to execute a quick search of the wall tunnels, but soon returned to tell Porter that Beatrice and the babies had vanished without a trace. They also reported that a new unguarded opening had been detected in the lighthouse wall, presumably where the invaders had entered and exited again. There were some scattered footsteps visible on the dusty ground outside, but the mice had lost them at the edge of the sea. There were also the telltale signs of a struggle back inside the tunnels in the vicinity of the baby basket. Beatrice had probably surprised the kidnappers at the scene, Sam surmised, and tried her best to defend the children. Instead of finishing her off then and there, The Fen must have decided to take her, too, perhaps believing that she would be more useful to them alive than dead. Beatrice's bathrobe lay in a crumpled heap on the ground, her mouse suit was missing from its hook on the tunnel wall and some of the baby supplies had been taken. Porter's knapsack was missing, too. Whoever had picked up the last item may have been unaware that Jasper was still tethered inside. When the mice reported the disappearance of his knapsack (and Jasper, too), Porter began to sob even louder. The kidnapping of his baby nephews had been terrifying enough, but the vision of his beloved pet's beautiful wings being plucked off by a Fen was almost too much for the boy to bear. He sank to the floor, curling up into a little ball of grief. It was at that moment that Sam, feeling so old and exhausted and hopeless that he could no longer hold it in, began to feel the tears welling in his eyes, too. He closed them tight and dropped his head to his chest.

In her bedroom, Alice opened her eyes and stared straight up. The first rays of morning light had already begun to filter through her window shade and flicker playfully on the ceiling. She had been awoken, she thought, by a troubling dream about her impending algebra exam. But as she lay still in the half-light, she became aware of a curious noise. She slipped from her bed and out into the hall, where the sound was louder. It seemed to be coming from the lighthouse walkway.

Turning the knob of the walkway door, Alice stepped inside and made her way down the long tunnel. She rarely ventured there alone. The old lighthouse itself was relatively weatherproof, but the thin-walled walkway, built directly over the flat stone bed of the island, was cold and damp and drafty even on the warmest and driest days. And, apart from the telescope that Sam had installed in the tower many years earlier, the lighthouse itself held little attraction for Alice. Wishing that she had taken the time to put on her warm slippers, Alice considered turning back. But the strange, pitiful sounds continued to draw her down the length of the tunnel. It sounded like a small voice crying, she thought, but there was something very different about this particular noise; it was not animal, but not completely human, either, and every now and then it was accompanied by a strange chorus of chilling squeaks and wails. Alice shuddered. Committed wildlife rescuer that she was, she had never been able to ignore the cries of an animal in distress, however unnerving. Perhaps some poor injured creature had taken refuge in the shadow of the lighthouse. Or perhaps something had crawled inside, given birth to its young and then found itself and its babies hopelessly trapped.

When she reached the end of the tunnel, Alice very quietly turned the doorknob and crept inside, trying not to alarm whatever it was that was suffering so. But no amount of imagining could have prepared Alice for the scene that awaited her on the other side of the door. There, sitting cross-legged on the wooden floor, was her beloved grandfather, gently patting the head of what appeared to be an *extremely* small boy, who was sobbing uncontrollably. The two of them were surrounded by a dozen or so equally distraught mice who were wringing their paws and emitting a series of impassioned squeaks, stopping every few moments to wipe their noses with the backs of their furry arms. That is, until one of them suddenly spied Alice, and squealed out a warning to the others. Within seconds, the entire group had disappeared through a small hole in the wall, leaving Sam and his tiny companion alone on the floor.

Sam looked up and let out a gasp, then threw himself in front of Porter's small body. Alice gasped, too. Still sobbing, Porter fumbled hopelessly as he tried to tie his mouse hood in place. Alice stared at Sam and Sam stared back, each one waiting for the other to either move or speak. All of the color had drained away from Alice's usually bright and rosy cheeks. She started to sway back and forth. Sam jumped up to grab her just as her knees began to buckle.

With her grandfather's arms supporting her, Alice slowly slipped to the floor, coming nose to nose with Porter, who had finally managed, in light of what was *now* transpiring, to reduce his sobbing to a few loud sniffles. With his mouse mask sitting crookedly at the top of his head, Porter held his breath and eyed Sam furtively, not knowing whether he should stay or rush through the wall hole after the scurrying mice. Sam stared back at him and shook his head. It was too late now.

"It's alright, Porter," Sam whispered. "Stay where you are."

Her eyes wide with wonder, Alice opened her mouth to speak, but the words caught in her throat.

"Don't be frightened, Alice," said Sam quietly, trying his best to calm her.

For Sam, however, it wasn't all that easy to brush aside the fact that his granddaughter was now a witness to something that no human being in history (apart from himself) had ever seen before. He imagined that she was feeling much as he had seventy-five years earlier when—frightened, alone and confused—he'd first encountered Mr. Goodfellow in the darkness of his bedroom. To Sam's surprise, however, Alice seemed to be recovering much faster than he had. The initial shock of stumbling onto a Sage was apparently wearing off. Alice even managed to smile reassuringly at poor beleaguered Porter before she looked up and stared knowingly at Sam. It was that same look he had seen on her face many times over the years, whenever he had finished relating one of his stories to her, with all Sage references deleted, of course. Sam had always thought she could sense that there was more.

"I *knew* it," Alice whispered with a quiet conviction. "I *knew* it all along," she declared again, as if she had finally put her finger on something that had been mystifying her for ages.

"What do you mean you knew it?" asked Sam. "Knew what?"

"It's in your eyes, Grandad," Alice answered with satisfaction. "Always has been." She smiled. "Like you were holding in a secret so fantastic that it was almost bursting to get out."

"Really?"

"*Really.*"

"Well, I certainly hope that I haven't been *that* obvious to anyone else," Sam announced in an anxious tone. "I'm supposed to be the only one, you know, although I have wondered from time to time whether your Nana ever figured out..."

"No, I don't think so," Alice replied, sounding quite sure of herself as she gazed with utter fascination at Porter. "I'm pretty sure it's just you and me, Grandad. I can feel it." She very gingerly extended her finger toward Porter. "Hello. I'm Alice."

"Um...Porter," he replied shyly. "Porter Sparrow. Pleased to meet you." Porter gave Alice's finger a tap with his hand. He was starting to feel a lot more comfortable, especially when she smiled at him again.

"Well, we actually have met before," Porter began more confidently. "But then you wouldn't have known about it, I guess. You see, I know you quite well, but you don't really know me," he babbled. "Do you?"

Alice screwed up her face in confusion.

"What Porter here is trying to say, Alice, is that he has known *you* for many years. Since your birth, in fact," explained Sam. "And your mother before that. Right, Porter?"

Porter nodded his head vigorously.

"But that's impossible," Alice exclaimed. "You're just a kid! Younger than me, I'll bet!"

"I'm 165!" Porter protested.

Startled, Alice stared at Porter for a few more moments.

"Are you...like...an elf or something?" she asked with hesitation.

"Hardly," Porter replied with a smirk. "There's no such thing as elves."

"A sprite?"

"Don't exist."

"A leprechaun?"

"Do I *sound* like a leprechaun?"

"No...but...Okay, a fairy, then?"

"Never seen one."

"A troll?"

Sam took that opportunity to leap into the conversation. "I can almost guarantee that Porter is just about to say that there is no such thing as a troll—"

"Actually," Porter interjected, "contrary to popular belief, trolls do, in fact, exist."

"They *do*?" exclaimed Sam. "Really?"

"At the present time, only in the remotest parts of Norway," Porter continued. "And although they have been unfairly maligned throughout the centuries, as I'm sure you are aware, they are actually quite highly regarded in that part of the world. I, for one, wouldn't dream of saying an unkind word about a troll to a Scandinavian Sea Mouse, for example—"

"A Scandinavian *what*?" asked Alice.

Realizing that the conversation had just moved into highly uncharted territory, Sam rolled his eyes and jumped in again.

"Another time, Alice. For now just know that Porter and his relatives are called The Sage. They are *extremely* old creatures, aging only one year for every fifteen of ours. They have dedicated themselves to inspiring the human species to do great things for many centuries. They disguise themselves as mice in order to remain undetected, and—"

"Ohhh..." interrupted Alice, eyeing Porter's suit, "*that* explains the costume."

"As a boy," Sam continued, "I accidentally bumped into The Sage and have been helping them ever since in their battle against a race of evil beings known as The Fen. There's a lot more, too, but that's as much as I dare tell you for now. You've caught us at a moment of such calamity that any further explanations will have to wait. Something horrible has happened and—"

The sound of soft crying distracted Sam. Reminded of the fate of his little nephews and Beatrice and Jasper, Porter had begun to weep again.

"Please, Porter," Sam pleaded, "try to hold on, if you can."

But the sound of Porter in anguish was more than Sam himself could bear. He felt the tears flooding back to his own eyes, too. He covered his face with his old and wrinkled hands and began to tremble.

"What is it, Grandad? What's happened?"

"Oh, Alice," Sam groaned. "They're gone and it's all my fault."

When Sam took his hands away from his eyes there was a look of such despair in them that Alice felt her own heart sink. She had never seen him like this before.

"Who's gone? "she asked fearfully.

"I promised Edgar that I would guard his children with my life and I've let them slip through my fingers to a fate that is probably too horrible to imagine," Sam's voice rasped.

"Edgar?" Alice asked.

"My friend," Sam replied quietly. "A Sage I shared a great bond with. I'm not even sure right now that Edgar is still alive, but if the poor soul is, it will kill him anyway to learn that his sons have been taken by The Fen."

"So we'll just have to find them, then, won't we? And take them back," Alice declared with as much confidence as she could muster. She grabbed hold of one of Sam's hands, and pulled him toward the door. But Sam stood fast.

"Listen to me, Alice Hannah," he said, gently taking his granddaughter by the shoulders. "We haven't a single clue where to begin. They'll be off the island by now, I expect. Maybe even out to sea. The trail will be dead cold. We could set off in the wrong direction and end up farther away from them than we already are—"

"But shouldn't we at least try?" asked Alice.

Sam took a deep, calming breath. "I've been thinking," he replied. "The rest of The Sage were lured away from here. When they discover the trick, if they haven't already, they'll be back as soon as they can. I think we should wait."

"But it may be too late by then," Alice said quietly.

Sam groaned again, then started to rub at his temples as if he was in great pain.

"I hadn't even thought about it until now," he murmured, looking helplessly at Porter. "What on earth am I going to say to Charlotte?"

Porter just sniffled and shook his head.

"Or Mr. Goodfellow . . . ?" Sam continued, his voice trailing off into a dry whisper. "Beatrice means the world to him."

When it appeared as if the situation couldn't possibly get any more desperate, Porter suddenly cocked a mouse ear to one side and held a paw up to his lips.

"Ssshhh!" he whispered. "Did you hear something?"

13

WHERE THERE IS LIFE
THERE IS HOPE

At about the same time that Alice was stumbling upon Sam and Porter in the lighthouse, another drama was unfolding on the open sea, little more than half a mile away. In a tiny boat, barely visible as it tossed up and down on the dark waves, Shrike Fen maneuvered his robotic leg into position and pressed the button at his hip. The mouse with the diamond patch at his throat was propelled forward violently as Shrike delivered a swift kick to the middle of its back.

"Faster, you useless bag of wires!" The Fen shrieked.

The mouse, rowing with slow, mechanical precision, started to pick up the pace. Despite the harsh blow it had just endured, the macabre grin on its face had not slipped at all.

"That's better," Shrike sneered, turning around to speak to the figure seated at the back of the boat. "I trust you can keep this one running smoothly, nephew, until you're able to find another suitable subject. I still don't understand the delay. You've had plenty of time!"

Bogg looked down at his feet and mumbled.

"I expect more from you than sorry excuses!" Shrike

complained bitterly. "You've been shirking your duties far too long, Bogg! You will take care of this before the day is done. Is that clear?"

Bogg nodded his head. He was clenching his fists together so tightly that the tips of his jagged nails had started to pierce his own flesh. Being admonished by Shrike in this manner and in the company of the enemy was an unbearable humiliation.

Shrike sat back and rubbed his bony hands together in glee. Apart from his obvious disappointment with Bogg, everything else was going according to plan. The only real fly in the ointment, so far, had been the unexpected arrival of the Sage female. He had come very close to doing away with her in the rodent tunnels when she'd interrupted the kidnapping, but he complimented himself now on his restraint. She had actually proven to be quite useful in the handling of the two brats. He hadn't realized until now what a tiresome burden infants could be with their constant demands for food and dry clothing and their endless whining. He couldn't wait to get as far away from the little pests as he could, but first he would have to complete his mission and deliver them into the appropriate hands. He was, of course, expecting the highest accolades for this achievement. If he succeeded, he might become the most revered Fen of all time, perhaps even surpassing the reputation of his dearly departed brother. Despite the passage of years, revenge for Feral's death at the hands of The Sage would still taste sweet. It was poetic justice to Shrike that his ticket to adulation might now depend on the famous Edgar Goodfellow's offspring. He had been overjoyed when he'd read that intercepted note of his, too. What a stroke of luck, he mused, for Bogg to have stumbled onto *that* particular mouse courier with *that* particular note. Infiltrating the world of their enemies with the first furry little spy they'd planted had proven to be a most fruitful endeavor, but this new development was just too good to be true. Shrike and Bogg had learned about The Book of The Sage from their mechanical diamond-patched mouse not long after The Sage themselves had discovered its existence. The Fen had also been informed of the location of the Martian scrolls by the same means and had actually been hatching a plot to steal them, but then that wonderful little note had come along and changed everything. The scrolls could wait. There would be time enough to take over the world and rule its human masses another day. Apprehending the Goodfellow twins first and putting an end to those interfering Sage once and for all was more appealing to Shrike than anything else he could possibly imagine.

Sitting on the bench next to Shrike, Beatrice had spent the last few moments shuffling her feet as close as she could to the sharp-edged anchor that lay in the bottom of the boat. One good swing with something like that, she'd calculated, would cause considerable damage to one of those sickly white Fen heads. She slipped a foot into a loop in the anchor rope and started to pull it slowly toward her.

The nasty smirk on Shrike Fen's face suddenly turned sour. He thrust his bony hand in Beatrice's direction. She winced as the jagged edge of one of his nails caught her just below her eye.

"Try something like that again, Madam," Shrike hissed, "and I'll drown one of those brats right now! I need only one for my purposes, you know. That, very conveniently, leaves a throwaway, doesn't it?"

Shrike Fen lashed out with a handful of sharp nails again, this time hooking Little Jolly by the collar of his blue terry-cloth sleeper and wrenching him from Beatrice's arms. Shrike swung the baby far out in front of him, as if he couldn't bear to be any closer to it, then dangled the struggling infant over the side of the boat, just above the waves. The cold, dark swells of water licked at the tips of Little Jolly's toes. Shrike let out a cruel cackle as the baby began to cry.

Beatrice struggled to stand up, but Shrike held her back with his other arm.

"Remember this, Madam!" he shrieked, just before he swung the baby back at her. "Etch this picture in your foolish head! The next time I will not be so generous!"

Beatrice fell backward onto the bench, clutching both of the babies close to her. A thin line of blood trickled down her cheek. She tilted her head sideways and tried to rub the stickiness away with her shoulder. She had almost managed to soothe Little Jolly to sleep when Winston started to fuss.

"Keep those squawking brats quiet!" Shrike screamed at her.

Beatrice was angry with herself. Imagining that she could have overpowered all three of her captors had been a foolish thought. If something had happened to her, all hope for the twins might have vanished, too. She would have to think of something else; a way to leave a clue or a trail. But she was running out of time. She propped her feet awkwardly on the knapsack beneath her, the one she had grabbed from a hook and filled with a few baby needs before The Fen had pushed her through the tunnels and out into the chill of dawn. Beatrice hadn't thought much about it until just now. It was Porter's knapsack, she slowly recalled. *That* realization caused her to catch her breath. She looked up at Shrike Fen. His piercing eyes were staring right at her. She quickly averted her gaze from him and tried very hard not to look down at the

knapsack again. She could only pray that she hadn't squished or suffocated Porter's pet with all the diapers and formula bottles she had stuffed in on top of him. She gave both of the sniffling babies a tender kiss on the forehead then hugged them tight. She stared straight past Shrike and out to sea, her mind racing now with fear and hope and the realization that poor old Jasper, in whatever condition he was in, might be their only means of rescue.

"We'll circle around one more time, Bogg, then head in to shore!" Shrike bellowed, as he gave their grinning mouse rower another brutal kick in the back. "That should be enough to throw anyone off our trail, wouldn't you say?"

Bogg, whose eyes had been glued to the bottom of the boat until then, his mind occupied with what he considered more pressing thoughts, slowly looked up at Shrike and gave him a hollow stare.

"BOGG!" Shrike screamed. "Did you hear me? What's the matter with *you*? Seasick or something?"

Bogg did not answer his uncle directly, choosing to shrug his shoulders instead. Then he stood up in the boat, leaned toward the mouse and shouted some instructions.

Beside her, Beatrice could feel Shrike's body bristle with anger. He threw the black cowl back from his head and thrust his white, pointed chin in Bogg's direction.

"I hope for your sake, nephew, that your lack of enthusiasm is nothing more than a sickly stomach," Shrike hissed. "I will not tolerate insolence!"

Bogg slumped back down on the small seat in the stern of the boat, wrapped his long black cloak around himself and stared off into space.

Concerned that The Fen might be moved to direct their growing wrath at her and the twins, Beatrice didn't dare glance at Shrike or Bogg. She didn't want to risk looking down at her feet again, either, for fear of drawing attention to Porter's knapsack. She was almost certain that she had detected a slight rippling movement through the soles of her mouse shoes. She prayed that if Jasper was indeed alive and well, he would choose another, more appropriate time to tune up the vibrating membranes on his tummy. Gently rocking Winston and Little Jolly in her arms, Beatrice decided it might be prudent just to close her eyes. When a steady drizzle began to fall, she tilted her head upward. The cold droplets of water felt harsh on her face, but they washed away the streaks of blood that had started to dry on her cheek. Feeling the fear rising within her, Beatrice fought to push it back down, concentrating instead on the rhythmic sound of the wooden oars as they slapped against the waves. After all, she reasoned to herself, she had countless years of experience to draw upon and she had been in a few tight spots before. But she was also painfully aware of how very different this spot was from any other she had encountered. This time the future of The Sage, and of humankind, too, lay wriggling in her arms, clothed in soft, blue terry cloth, pure and innocent and oblivious to the magnitude of everything that was transpiring.

Beatrice still had her eyes closed when the mechanical mouse rowed them up onto the beach. The boat suddenly lurched forward with a jolt, catching Beatrice off guard and knocking her right into Shrike Fen. When little Winston fell from Beatrice's arms and rolled onto his lap, Shrike let out a disgusted cry. He quickly slid sideways, then staggered to his feet, sending the baby tumbling to the bottom of the boat where his fall was broken by the knapsack. Beatrice let out a gasp as Winston, screaming heartily now, rolled off the sack and then along the hard bottom of the boat, finally coming to rest somewhere beneath the small wooden bench in the bow of the boat. Struggling to find the baby in the half-light, Beatrice fell to her knees, but Shrike, clasping one bony hand against his throbbing ear, grabbed her with his free arm and pulled her from the boat.

"You should have had a better hold on him, Madam!" Shrike sneered. "You only have yourself to blame, don't you? Now you'll just have to leave the squawking brat behind! He's giving me a headache, and I warned you before that we need only one of them."

"No!" Beatrice cried. "You can't!"

Holding on to Little Jolly as tightly as she could, Beatrice struggled to free herself, but Shrike's grip was ironclad. He dragged her up and out of the boat, then threw her down onto the sand.

Before he exited the boat himself, Bogg pushed the mechanical mouse out in front of him, then quickly reached under the bench and scooped Winston up with one sweep of his long, sharp nails. He lifted the baby high and proceeded to swing him across to Beatrice, but suddenly stopped and froze as Shrike, eyes flashing wildly, spun toward him.

"What do think you're doing?" he hissed. "Leave that wretched, howling thing where it is, Bogg! I've grown tired of all this endless squealing. It will be a relief to get rid of one of them, at least. And it's time we taught this stupid Sage a lesson."

"I was just m-moving it aside," Bogg stammered. "It was in my way."

Bogg slowly lowered the baby into the bottom of the boat and started to climb out.

"Wait, Bogg!" Shrike shouted. "What *am* I thinking?"

Beatrice, praying that he had reconsidered, held her breath.

"We'll be needing that bag of supplies to keep the other brat quiet," Shrike sneered. He looked over at Beatrice and smiled. "Bring it with you, Bogg."

Bogg reached down and hooked a nail into one of the knapsack's straps, pulling the bag along with him as he jumped out of the boat.

"You monster!" Beatrice screamed. "You can't just leave him there!"

"I can, Madam," Shrike snarled, "and I will."

Bogg dropped the knapsack from his hand and kicked it across to Beatrice. The strange buzzing sounds that immediately followed caused Shrike to stiffen for a moment. His eyes darted back and forth along the beach.

"On second thought," he slowly growled. "I have a much better idea." He circled about the little boat, sweeping his black cloak around him with a flourish. "Yes," he chuckled, "a much better idea, indeed." He paused and made a motion with his leg to board the boat again. He turned his face to Beatrice and flashed her another smile. "We can't *really* leave the brat here, I suppose, can we? That incessant howling of his will lead everyone and his dog here."

"Thank goodness," Beatrice whispered under her breath.

She let her head fall to her chest and breathed a sigh of relief. But then the sudden, sickening sound of splintering wood filled her ears. She looked up in horror to see the end of Shrike Fen's robotic leg piercing the side of the boat.

"Send that stupid mouse contraption over here, Bogg!" Shrike shouted. "I need help!" He was struggling to push the boat back down the sand and into the sea.

"No!" Beatrice screamed, as she watched the seawater trickling through the hole in the hull. "He'll drown!"

"Is that so, Madam?" Shrike sneered. "How unfortunate!"

Leaving Little Jolly lying on the sand, Beatrice raced down to the surf and began pummeling Shrike's back with her fists. She was hitting him so hard that she could feel the jagged points of his bony shoulder-knobs through both her mouse paws and The Fen's thick black cloak. A feeling of revulsion rushed through her. Shrike Fen shrieked and reeled around, his razor-sharp nails drawn to strike her down. But Bogg pulled her out of the way from behind, before Shrike could find his mark.

"We need her, Uncle!" Bogg reminded him. "For the other one."

Shrike snarled angrily, then pulled his nailed hand back inside his cloak, but not before directing a foul hiss at Beatrice. The cold, slimy spray of Fen mingled with the warm tears that were trickling down her face.

"*Never* touch me again, Sage!" Shrike snarled. "I need you now, but that may not always be so!"

The grinning mouse, meanwhile, had almost completed its appointed task, pushing with all its mechanical might on the stern of the boat until it was well into the water. The boat bobbed up and down like a little cork for a few moments until the current captured it and swept it out to sea. There was nothing more that Beatrice could do. She slowly walked back along the beach, picked Little Jolly up from the sand, then sank to her knees in horror and grief as the sound of Winston's cries grew fainter and fainter. The boat was visible on the horizon for just a few seconds more until it vanished from her sight. After that, the swirling current would draw it farther and farther out, Beatrice imagined, while the weight of the seawater that was sloshing through the jagged hole in the hull began to pull it and its little passenger beneath the waves.

Beatrice barely had time to shed another tear for Winston before Shrike savagely grabbed her by the arm and pulled her to her feet. She reached down for the knapsack and quickly slung it over her shoulder. Thankfully, there were no suspicious sounds emanating from it this time.

Shrike, however, was still clearly agitated.

"Hurry up, Madam!" he snapped. "We have no time to dawdle here! We have an appointment to keep!" He twisted his head about. "BOGG! Where are you?"

Scanning up and down the beach, Shrike noticed that the mechanical mouse, grinning even more grotesquely than before, and up to its armpits in seawater, had not moved from its last position. The steadily rising tide, creeping ever closer to its face, seemed to be having no effect on the mouse's demeanor at all. Bogg, desperately fiddling with the wiring behind its left eye, was not having any luck either.

"Bogg!" Shrike bellowed. "What's the matter *now*?"

"Too much water," Bogg shouted back. "Electrical short."

"Well, fix it immediately," Shrike snarled, "or leave the useless thing where it is! We don't have all day!"

Bogg spent a few more moments poking about in the robot's central circuitry, then announced that they were ready to leave. He took the staggering mouse firmly by the paw and slowly steered it out of the water and back up the beach. Shrike eyed both of them suspiciously as they approached.

"Are you quite sure it's fully operational?"

"Um...more or less," Bogg answered hesitantly.

"See to it that it stays that way, then!" Shrike growled impatiently. "We can't be playing nursemaid to this-this-*thing* on top of the Goodfellow brat, too! Let's just get on with the assignment and be done with it! We're wasting time here and it's going to take us most of the day to get there as it is!"

"Get where?" asked Beatrice as forcefully as she dared, while Shrike dragged her through the dune grasses toward the edge of the forest. Beatrice swallowed hard. "I demand to know where you're taking us!" she blurted out.

Shrike stopped short and spun around to face her.

"Ahhh, do you now?" he slowly hissed, pushing his white, pointed chin closer to Beatrice than she would have liked. "How can I aptly describe it for you, then? It's a lovely place, Madam... if you're a FEN!" he screamed. He slowly poked one of his nails against her cheek. "Do not demand anything from me, Sage!" he warned. "I am not about to answer any of your ridiculous questions!" Then he smirked. "Where did you think we might be taking you, anyway? A holiday resort?"

Beatrice tightened her embrace on Little Jolly and stared Shrike in the face.

"You will not win this battle, Fen," she spoke firmly. "Our kind will prevail in the end."

Shrike began to chuckle.

"Win this *battle*, you say, Madam?" He took his nail away from Beatrice's cheek and gave Little Jolly's tiny chin a scratch. "Why, I have almost won the war. Haven't I, Sageling?"

Little Jolly flailed his fists at Shrike and started screaming, sending The Fen into another rage.

"Rotten little creature!" he snarled at Beatrice. "Keep it quiet!"

Grabbing her arm, Shrike began dragging Beatrice across the forest floor. Another sound, even more piercing than Little Jolly's screams, filled the air. Shrike stopped dead in his tracks again.

"What the devil was *that*!" he growled. His eyes darted back and forth, then upward through the huge canopy of hanging tree branches. "I've heard that sound before! Back on the beach!" He shouted down to the figure at the end of the line. "BOGG! Find out what that other racket is and put an end to it! If it's that stupid mouse machine, then sever the rest of its circuits immediately! We don't need it any longer, anyway."

While Bogg proceeded to examine the mouse for any unusual sound emanations, Beatrice swayed back and forth in an effort to soothe the baby and the stirring cicada, still hidden in Porter's backpack.

"I warned you, Madam," Shrike barked. "I cannot tolerate that incessant squealing much longer! Clean the creature or feed it if you must! Just do something!"

"If you insist," Beatrice replied as calmly as she could. It was the opportunity she had been praying for. "I'll need a quiet spot, though. He's very upset, you know."

"I can see *that*!" Shrike grimaced, thrusting his bony hands under his hood to cover his ears. He nodded toward a small clearing. "Over there, on that rock," he snarled. "And don't try anything foolish. I'll be keeping my eyes on you."

Beatrice moved over to the spot that Shrike had indicated, gently laying Little Jolly on the flat surface of the rock and lowering the knapsack onto the ground behind it. She walked around to the back of the rock, then knelt down, carefully unzipped the sack and pulled out a bottle of baby formula and a few squares of white folded cloth. She wished now that she had been able to reach her things back at the lighthouse and stuff her Scandinavian Sea Mouse knife in the knapsack, too, but there had been neither the time nor the opportunity. Groping deeper inside the bag, Beatrice rummaged about with her paws until she found the metal clip that attached the cicada's collar to his tether leash. With one quick snap, Jasper was free. Beatrice leaned over Little Jolly and fed him his bottle, whispering soft, comforting sounds in between her important instructions to Jasper. Every now and then, Shrike would turn to stare at her with an expression so cold and wicked it made her shiver. Beatrice dared not react, though, even when Jasper tumbled out of the bag with a thud, then scurried frantically across her legs, heading for the freedom of the deep forest. When she had finished feeding and changing Little Jolly, Beatrice lifted him up and cradled him in her arms, then returned reluctantly to Shrike, hoping that Jasper had understood her instructions. She hadn't had much personal experience with cicadas, but if Jasper was anything like Porter's other pets (most notably Duncan, the now legendary worm), they might have a fighting chance. Especially if he could manage to follow them far enough back to avoid capture, but close enough to lead any would-be rescuers to them.

"Nothing wrong here," Bogg shouted, as he tried to force the grinning mouse's eyeball back into a socket that suddenly seemed too small. "Well, nothing of an acoustic nature, anyway. The water shrinkage is another issue, however—"

"Spare me your tiresome technical details, Bogg!" Shrike snapped. "If the rodent isn't the source of that grating noise, then I don't want to hear about it!"

"It's stopped now, anyway." Bogg sighed with frustration. He had pulled the crooked eyeball out of the mouse again and was attempting to reinsert it. "You made me take him apart for nothing, you old snake," he growled under his breath.

"What did you say, Bogg?" Shrike slowly pulled his hands away from his head. "Ahhh, it's finally gone!" he announced with relief. "What was it, anyway? A machine of some sort?"

"More like an animal, I'd say," Bogg replied. "Or an insect, maybe."

Beatrice felt the blood rush to her face. She quickly dropped her head and stared at the ground, unwilling to risk eye contact with either of The Fen.

"Is that so, Bogg?" Shrike replied. "How fascinating."

Beatrice could feel Shrike's steely eyes boring into the back of her neck.

"That would explain why the sound is so especially unsettling to me, wouldn't it, Madam?" Shrike continued, directing his words right at Beatrice now. "Like all my kin, I despise animals. But I have had so many personally unpleasant encounters with them, that I've reserved a special feeling of revulsion for them. And an insect, too? Curiously, that sounds familiar to me. There was a Sage youngster in your little group who had a passionate interest in them. Isn't that right?"

Beatrice, continuing to stare down at the ground, did not reply.

"Is there something you would like to get off your chest, Madam?" asked Shrike, his voice rising in anger.

"No, of course not." Pushing down her fear again, Beatrice looked up and stared straight into The Fen's eyes. "I don't know what you're talking about."

"Let's hope for your sake and the child's that you speak the truth, Sage!" Shrike snarled.

Holding in her breath, Beatrice continued to stare unflinchingly at Shrike, until he finally turned away. As soon as he did, she released all the air from her lungs and began to tremble.

A short distance behind them, at the very top of a massive pine tree, Jasper the cicada shook himself from top to bottom. He smoothed out his slightly crumpled wings, flexed the vibrating membranes on his abdomen and prepared to perform.

Back at the lighthouse, no one had moved an inch since Porter's last announcement. The boy swore that he'd heard something—something very familiar—and now they strained to hear it, too.

"There it is again!" whispered Porter. "It's kind of faint, but it sounds like...like a cicada!"

"It does?" asked Sam, a little unsure. "Not at this time of the day, Porter. On a really hot, midsummer afternoon, maybe, but—"

"No...wait!" Porter whispered again, listening very carefully this time. "It *is*, I'm sure of it!" He looked at Sam "Do you think..."

Sam raised his eyebrows.

"You think it's Jasper, don't you?"

Porter nodded his head. "Maybe—"

"Wait a minute. There's a cicada out there somewhere... and it-it has a name?" Alice interrupted, blinking her eyes.

"Of course he has a name," answered Porter a little indignantly.

"He's with Beatrice and the twins, or so we assume," Sam replied. "And if Porter is thinking what I'm thinking, then we may have just had our first clue. We'd better get going." Sam bent down on one knee and pulled open the large pocket in his bathrobe. "Come on, Porter, hop in." He turned to Alice. "When Nana wakes up, tell her that I've gone into town for something."

"You're not going by yourself, are you?" Alice protested.

"No, I'm taking Porter along. I'll be perfectly fine, Alice. Quit worrying. I've been doing this for seventy-five years. And Porter's been at it for a lot longer than me."

"Forget it, Grandad," Alice replied sternly. "There's no way I'm letting you go alone. Then she smiled at him. "And there's no way that I'm *not* going, either."

"But your algebra—" Sam began.

"Can wait until the makeup test next week," Alice finished. "And don't try to talk me out of it, either. I know all about this secret stuff now. Remember? I can help you. We'll leave Nana a note that you've gone to town to run a few errands. And she won't miss me until after school. Maybe we'll have this whole baby Sage thing settled by then."

"You don't know much about The Fen, do you?" said Porter dryly from the top of Sam's pocket.

Alice gave him a tired look.

"These Fen things are about the same size as you, right?" she asked.

"Well, yes," Porter replied, "but—"

"So?" Alice declared. "Big deal. Let's get going."

Porter stared at Alice in horror. Sam took her gently by the arm.

"Listen to me very carefully, Alice Hannah," he spoke sternly. "You don't understand yet what they are capable of. They may be small, but don't be fooled. You must never, *ever*, underestimate the power of a Fen. They are pure evil and, as I have seen on many occasions throughout my life, masters at using every kind of deceit and trickery to get what they want." He stared deep into her eyes. "Do you understand?"

Alice nodded her head very slowly. She wished he would stop talking like that. It was beginning to make her feel uncomfortable.

"Now that we have all of that straightened out," Sam announced, "we'd better get moving." He glanced over at Alice and then back down at himself with frustration. "As soon as we change out of our pajamas, that is."

14

THEY CONQUER WHO
BELIEVE THEY CAN

Back in the forest, as the sounds of high-pitched buzzing floated through the canopy of towering white pines, Shrike looked up through the lower layers of striped maple and mountain ash in an attempt to spot the source of the irritating noise. Jasper, however, was far too crafty to expose himself needlessly to the eye of a Fen. Porter's cicada was a particularly agile and talented fellow, hiding himself behind clusters of leaves at just the appropriate moment and practicing the unusual ability he had for throwing his voice. If she had not been so aggrieved at Winston's horrific fate and fearful of what awaited Little Jolly, Beatrice might have found Jasper's antics quite amusing. But she stared straight ahead as she plodded along, determined to display no emotion whatsoever. It was rather satisfying, though, to see Shrike becoming more and more agitated as the journey progressed. Not only was Jasper's racket grating on his nerves, but the distrust between himself and his nephew had festered to the point where neither seemed to be able to control it any longer. Beatrice lived in hope that she could in some way exploit the situation.

As the thick trees of the deep forest gave way to sparser vegetation, Beatrice began to wonder about the nature of their destination, especially when the ground beneath her mouse feet turned soft and squishy. When they started to pass the patches of sphagnum moss and leather leaf, Beatrice realized that they might be heading into a fair-sized peat bog. But it wasn't until Shrike's foul mood suddenly started to improve that she became convinced of it. He actually seemed to brighten up, even ignoring the buzzing sounds for a moment, as the wet ground oozed up between his long toenails.

"Ahhh...how I've missed this," he trilled. "What a simply wonderful feeling."

Beatrice thought she'd try her question again.

"Where exactly are you taking us?" she inquired with trepidation.

Instead of snarling at her, Shrike just rolled his eyes.

"Come, come now, Madam," he replied. "As I'm quite sure an intelligent Sage like you has already guessed, we are entering a place that is very dear to my heart; dear to the hearts of all Fen, in fact. Isn't that true, Bogg?"

Bogg simply nodded his head. Shrike sniffed at him with growing impatience, then turned back to Beatrice.

"As a matter of fact, there is going to be quite a little event here soon," he crowed. "And since I doubt that you'll see the light of another day, I don't suppose it matters whether you know about it or not."

Beatrice didn't even flinch.

"How fascinating," she commented brightly. "What kind of event?"

"One of the best kind, Madam," Shrike continued. "The highest order of Fen are having their annual gathering on this very ground at sunset tonight. And for those without official status, it is by invitation only. Since I have informed them that I have a matter of great importance to bring to the table, Bogg and I have been deemed honored guests." Shrike glanced over at his nephew. "It will be Bogg's first gathering of this kind and an exceptional opportunity for him to meet the most powerful and influential of The Fen. Isn't that right, Bogg?"

When Bogg looked up and just shrugged his shoulders, it looked to Beatrice as if his uncle might rush over to strike him, but Shrike, eyes flashing, held himself back. He paused and took a deep breath instead.

"My only regret," said Shrike, through sharp, clenched teeth, "is that Bogg's father cannot be here to share this moment." He glared straight at Beatrice then. "But as you well know, Madam, my dear brother, Feral, was cruelly cut down by Edgar Goodfellow before Bogg had a chance to really know him. And then it fell to me to provide guidance to the boy." Shrike's expression turned particularly sour then. "Of course, our younger brother, Sorrel," he seethed under his breath, "was *far* too busy and important to be saddled with that kind of responsibility."

Beatrice tried not to act too surprised. She wondered if she had heard correctly. There had never been any talk, as far as she knew, of another brother.

"Sorrel?" she inquired hesitantly.

"Thought he was above the rest of us," Shrike snarled, "with his special little assignments. Always trying to make a big splash somewhere while the rest of us did the real work. But when he tired of all that nuclear and biochemical business, he drifted off into something else, as was his way. I've heard now that he fancies himself a bit of a space traveler," Shrike snickered. "Idiot!"

"Space traveler?" Beatrice asked nervously.

"Something like that," Shrike sneered. "Years ago, I heard he'd latched himself onto a human in that line of work, called Slocumb."

Beatrice felt faint. Slocumb, she thought anxiously. Eustace Slocumb? The very same one whom Jolly had told them about before he'd left for Cornwall?

"But enough of Sorrel," Shrike suddenly announced with a dramatic wave of his long and bony hand. "Speaking of him is tiresome. I would much rather think on what is going to transpire this evening when I present my little prize to the gathering of The Fen. Sorrel would never be able to top *that*, would he?" Shrike looked down at Little Jolly, nestled in Beatrice's arms, and smiled wickedly. "Won't they be surprised when I explain to them exactly what it is that I have discovered about *you*, young Sage? Why, I'll have them all bowing at my feet, as well they should."

"I'm sure they'll be most impressed," offered Beatrice, smiling sweetly to hide the fact that she was feeling physically ill at the thought of the dozens and dozens of Fen who were shortly to arrive.

"They will be impressed enough, I trust," Shrike bellowed (loudly enough to catch Bogg's attention), "to consider something else that I have been planning for some time now."

"Really?" Beatrice remarked with feigned interest. "And what would that be?"

"A union of two proud families," Shrike crowed. "Ours and that of the Great High Fen. He has three daughters, the oldest of whom has just reached marriageable age. After I present them with the exceptional gift of your Sage child here, I have little doubt that my suggestion of a union between this girl and my nephew will meet with their wholehearted approval. It will be quite a coup for me."

"What?" cried Bogg, looking at his uncle in horror.

"Be quiet, Bogg!" Shrike growled. "This has nothing to do with you!"

"Nothing to do with me?" Bogg screeched. "You're about to marry me off and—"

"Silence, Bogg! I've had enough of your insolence for one day!" The blue veins on Shrike's temples were pulsating. The muscles in his hollowed white cheeks twitched wildly. "I do not understand young people these days," he growled. "They are spoiled and ungrateful little wretches."

"Indeed," Beatrice replied.

When Shrike looked at her again, his expression had changed dramatically.

"Do not try to befriend me, Madam!" he scowled. "I'm well aware of your little tricks." He pushed her down onto a patch of wet moss. "It must be time to tend to the infant now. Get on with it!"

While Beatrice changed Little Jolly and prepared his food, she continued to watch Shrike out of the corner of her eye. He was too busy glaring at Bogg now to notice her. And Bogg, clearly upset at everything Shrike had just said, was fiddling absently with the mouse robot and trying to look anywhere but at his uncle. The air was thick with tension.

Beatrice began to worry more than ever. Her attempts to flatter Shrike had backfired miserably. She was no further ahead and probably much worse off, considering Shrike's incredibly foul mood and the fact that she was about to be sur-rounded by an entire troupe of Fen. All of these things preyed on her mind, as did Shrike's revelations about Sorrel Fen and Eustace Slocumb. Beatrice could not get Fletcher Jaffrey and Winchester Redwood out of her thoughts. What must they have encountered on that lost journey? Her only glimmer of hope was the rapidly disintegrating relationship between Shrike and Bogg. Shivering, Beatrice crouched on the mound of wet moss, cuddling Little Jolly as he sucked hungrily on his bottle, and wondering how all of these things would play out, and whether anyone had heard Jasper's calls for help.

After rowing across the channel, Sam, Alice and Porter made their way due west, past the bustling village shops and then along the meandering riverbank that led into the forest. The faint sound of buzzing grew steadily louder after they'd entered the thick swath of trees on the outskirts of town. Every now and then, they could make out Jasper's trademark song as it reverberated off the hardwood branches, leading them (they hoped) closer to Beatrice and the twins. Anyone else who was listening would have puzzled over the sound of a cicada so early in the morning and on such a cool day. It was quite out of the ordinary and most people would have been annoyed to be woken up in this manner, but for Sam and Alice and Porter, it was music to their ears.

Alice pulled her wool sweater tighter around her chest as the damp air of the deep forest burrowed beneath her skin. Just steps ahead, Sam had already established a steady pace, crunching across the bed of leaves and twigs that littered the forest floor with an expression of grim determination. His eyes darted through the trees every now and then, as if he fully expected to run into something unpleasant at any turn. He stopped only once to pick up a thick, straight maple branch, about four feet in length. An excellent walking stick, he announced to Alice, as he pulled off some smaller twigs and leaves that were still clinging to one end. They continued on their way, with Sam occasionally lifting the stick up to poke at any suspicious mounds. Alice didn't want to think too much about what he might be looking for. She concentrated instead on putting her own feet directly into her grandfather's footprints and counting off the paces. Porter, leaning out of the large breast pocket of Sam's jacket, was busily interpreting the direction from which Jasper's signals were coming. He would frequently nudge Sam in the chest to suggest they make a slight navigation adjustment. And each time they did, the noise of the cicada grew just a little bit louder than before.

The tall trees soon gave way to shorter ones as Sam and Alice followed Jasper's route. It would eventually lead them into the same sphagnum moss and leather-leafed area that The Fen and their prisoners had entered just a short time before. The deeper they ventured into the bog, the more intense Sam's anxiety grew. At first, it was a feeling that he could not explain. Perhaps it was the old superstitions about heaths and bogs—stories that had given birth to words like "heathen" and "boogeyman." Sam even remembered looking up the word "fen" in the dictionary as a boy and finding all the appropriate references; a bog, a swamp, a quagmire. Even knowing all of these things, Sam couldn't help but suspect that the reason for his overpowering sense of foreboding was the close presence of a much more villainous type of "fen" than any dictionary could define.

"Where exactly do you think *you* are going, Madam?" Shrike bellowed.

Crawling on her hands and knees, with the sleeping baby tucked into the front of her mouse suit, Beatrice had almost made it past the mossy clearing and back into the dark sanctuary of the forest. She really thought that she might have had a chance while Shrike and Bogg were engaged in another noisy disagreement over the condition of the mechanical mouse. Her heart sank at the sound of Shrike's grating voice, and what he said next made her wish that she hadn't attempted another escape.

"The time has finally come to put an end to this nonsense!" he announced angrily. "I was reluctant to strike you down before, Sage, but only while I needed you to look after that squawking brat. Now that we have reached our destination, I no longer require your assistance."

Shrike moved toward her then, rolling the sleeve of his black cloak up past his elbow. When he flexed his hand, five razor-sharp nails sprung out from the ends of his fingers. Beatrice closed her eyes and prepared for the end. She was not expecting, at that moment, to hear Bogg's quivering voice in her ears.

"Wait, Uncle!" he called out nervously. "The rest will not be here for awhile. He gestured upward toward the thin shafts of sunlight filtering down through the trees. "See? The angle is still too high. If that baby needs changing or something, I'm not doing it!"

Shrike stared down at Beatrice and Little Jolly and grimaced. "Nor I," he growled with disgust. He pointed one of his sharp nails at Beatrice. "You have been spared, Madam, at least for the moment. Unless, that is, you attempt something foolish again. Then I will be forced to take action, regardless of how unpleasant the consequences may be." He looked at the top of Little Jolly's head, poking out from the neck of Beatrice's mouse suit and shuddered. "Is that perfectly clear?"

"Perfectly," Beatrice replied hoarsely.

"And just to make it a little harder for you to give in to your temptation to flee, I believe I will restrain you whenever you are not tending to the child."

Beatrice hung her head. Well, that decided it. There would be no more chances to escape now.

"BOGG!" Shrike shouted. "Bring something to tie this Sage up with."

While Bogg was winding a long length of string through Beatrice's wrists and then around the rock that Shrike had sat her in front of, she kept glancing furtively into his eyes. She cleared her throat to speak once, but changed her mind. Bogg seemed relieved that she had stayed silent. She wanted to thank him, though. It was, after all, the second time that he had saved her from Shrike's violent hand. But it didn't seem appropriate or safe. She certainly didn't want Shrike to overhear. That would probably put both her and Bogg in grave peril. The young Fen, more distracted and fidgety than ever, had a secret, she suspected. He kept looking past Shrike through the trees, as if there was someplace else he desperately wanted to be.

It had not been Sam's intention to stumble onto Shrike Fen's little outpost without first sizing up the situation, but it all happened so quickly that there was no time to prepare. Sam's first indication that they had indeed found what they were looking for was the sharp pain in his ankle. He stumbled forward onto his knees. His maple walking stick flew out of his hands and rolled away. There was blood on the tips of his fingers when he took them away from his aching leg and a deep gash in the flesh just above his anklebone.

"Grandad," Alice cried, as she rushed forward to help him. "What is it? Are you alright?"

Sam nodded his head. "Just a cut." But Sam was already beginning to suspect that it was more serious than that. The wound on his ankle was throbbing with greater ferocity than any normal injury. And when he spied, out of the corner of his eye, the small figure of a Sage lashed to a rock, his worst suspicions were confirmed.

15

A Day of Sorrow Is Longer than a Month of Joy

"Well, well, well!" Shrike gurgled as he crept out of the shadows. "How absolutely smashing! Not only do I have a Sage child to offer up tonight, but it seems I have the famous Sam Middleton, too; keeper of the precious scrolls and thorn in my side for 75 years. What luck! Funny thing, isn't it?" he announced with a wave of his hand, as Sam's blood still dripped from the sharp edge of his nail. "After all this time, I find that I don't even want those scrolls of yours anymore, Middleton." He slithered over to Beatrice. "I have something so much more impressive now, don't I, Madam?" Shrike snickered. He tapped the top of Little Jolly's tiny head with his bloody nail, then sidled closer to Alice. "And who's this young lady?" he chuckled with glee, giving her a long and steely stare. "It couldn't be another Middleton, could it? Why, things are getting more interesting by the minute, aren't they?"

"Keep away from her, Fen," Sam warned, as he rubbed at his ankle. The throbbing wound was already making him feel faint.

Without fear, Alice looked down at Shrike dead in the eye. But as she did, a strange feeling of dread began to pass through her. She tried repeatedly to shake it off. It seemed that she could push Shrike's creeping thoughts away for a moment, only to have them slither back into her head a second or two later with even greater force than before.

"Oooo!" Shrike swooned, clutching his bony hands against his head in mock surprise. "This one's feisty, isn't she? She must be one of yours, after all, Middleton!" he sneered at Sam. "The family resemblance is quite sickening." He turned to Alice again. "Has the old man told you about our little encounters over the years, my dear? I would have had him for my very own by now, you know, if it hadn't been for those interfering Sage. This time, it seems, the best that they can offer is a trembling boy, a tired old lady and a babe in arms. It's almost *too* easy! And better yet," he snarled, "there's not a blasted *dog* in sight!"

The longer Shrike spoke, the more Alice's temples began to pound. Whenever his eyes locked onto hers, she felt as if something had crept inside her head and was busy picking away at her thoughts.

"Let me see now," Shrike muttered. "I need to find the most amusing way to do this. If I can search those primitive brain cells of yours long enough, I should be able to find something I can use; a tidbit of personal information that will be your undoing. Everyone has something to hide, my dear girl, some revolting weakness or delicious little temptation. Or I could toy with these pitiful Sage for a while I suppose, just to make sure that I command your full attention." He tapped his long nails against his chin. "Hmmm...that might be fun. What do you think, Bogg?"

Bogg stared back blankly. Shrike had caught him daydreaming again.

"Pay attention, Bogg!" Shrike snapped. "Surely that's not too difficult! Even for you!"

Finding himself humiliated in front of the enemy again, Bogg felt the anger rising in his body. Shrike gave him another disgusted look before he turned back to Alice.

"Come on now, my girl. Give me something to work with," he snickered. "It will be easier for you in the long run."

"Push him back, Alice," Sam whispered into her ear. "Don't let his thoughts in, no matter what he says or does. Listen to *me* now. I've had a little practice dealing with the likes of Shrike Fen. Try to think of something you truly love instead, like—"

"Silence, old man!" Shrike snarled. "I wouldn't be giving out advice if I were you. You're next!" A nasty smile slid across Shrike's face. "You may have had a lifetime of experience in fending me off, but everyone has their breaking point. Perhaps a few more of my kind will help you to reconsider. In fact, I'm thinking now that I might just soften up the young one here, a bit, and leave the rest of the fun for when my associates arrive."

"Associates?" asked Sam nervously.

"Silence!" Shrike growled. "I've no time for questions!" He turned back to lock his cold, mesmerizing eyes onto Alice again and smiled. "After all, I'm busy. Isn't that so, my girl?"

Alice was finding it even harder to push Shrike's evil thoughts from her mind now. There were fleeting moments when she felt as if she was losing touch with the real world, falling instead into a deep pit of blackness and despair. When she found the strength to turn her head toward Sam, his features seemed blurred, his words distant and unclear. But just when Alice felt as if she was on the verge of losing herself completely, something intervened. For a split second, Alice felt herself coming back. She slipped into darkness once more, but returned again a few moments later. She could still hear Shrike's voice inside her head, but it was not having the same effect. His sly, slithering suggestions had been replaced with words that sounded loud and jarring.

"That hideous noise, Bogg!" Shrike screamed. "It's back again, and it's louder than ever! Get rid of it! It's ruining everything!"

Fearful of angering his uncle any more than he already had, Bogg quickly scurried into action, positioning himself under the tallest trees where the sound was coming from. He strained his neck and jumped up and down awkwardly in an effort to see what was causing all the disturbance.

"I can't see anything," Bogg whined.

"What do you mean?" Shrike growled. "There's clearly something up there! You must be blind!" He moved under the trees and shoved his nephew aside. "Do I have to do everything myself, Bogg?" He squinted into the sunlight, then pointed one of his long, bony fingers up through the tree's branches. "There, you idiot! What's *that*?"

Jasper, who for all this time had been watching everything unfold from his perch high atop a pine tree, was not at all satisfied with the way things were going. He had followed Beatrice's instructions to the letter, buzzing out his message as he pursued The Fen and their captives from a guarded distance. He had experienced a feeling of great accomplishment after alerting the potential rescuers to the area, but it now appeared as if everything had dissolved into total chaos. And so, in a testament to the courageous heights to which one of God's smallest creatures can ascend, Jasper had decided to take on Shrike Fen all by himself. He began creeping down the trunk of the pine tree until he had settled onto a lower

branch. The closer he got, Jasper noticed, and the louder the noises he made, the more enraged The Fen became. Even the stranglehold he had on the human girl seemed to be slowly lessening. With Shrike distracted, Porter had managed to crawl, unseen, over to Beatrice's rock, where he was now attempting to loosen the ropes on her wrists. Encouraged by these events, Jasper moved even closer, until he finally alighted on the lowest branch, directly above Shrike Fen's snarling head. It was, however, just a fraction of an inch *too* close. Without warning, Shrike suddenly reached upward, lashing out at Jasper with his nails and sending the buzzing cicada tumbling to the forest floor. Jasper landed on his back a short distance away, unable to right himself, the membranes on his abdomen still vibrating. Shrike, chuckling triumphantly, moved in for the kill. Porter cried out in anguish as Beatrice gasped and covered her eyes. But when Shrike was almost upon him, Jasper quickly rolled out of the way, then flittered back into the trees. Shrike growled. He had been looking forward to tearing the annoying bug apart.

"Get over here, Bogg!" Shrike snarled impatiently. "Make yourself useful! I've got work to do and I've wasted enough time with this wretched creature. I've made a good dent in the job, but I need you to complete the elimination of that bug now! If you think you can, that is. Redeem yourself, Bogg, while I have a bit of fun with old Sam, here. It's something I've been dreaming about for years. Watch and learn, nephew."

Bogg, however, did not answer.

"Bogg?" Shrike shouted in confusion, as his eyes darted in every direction. "Bogg? Where in the blazes are you? Messing with that ridiculous mouse contraption, no doubt!" His eyes shifted to the base of a tree where the mouse robot sat alone.

After a few moments, when it dawned on Shrike that he had been made a fool of, those same eyes began to smolder with anger. "BOGG!" he screamed at the top of his lungs. "This is an outrage! Get back here at once and assist me! I'm not finished with these humans yet!" He pressed his hands against his ears as Jasper started up again and shrieked with rage. "When I get my hands on you, Bogg, you will wish that you had never dared defy me!" Cursing Bogg's name, Shrike stormed off into the woods, stopping to grab the mouse robot by one limp arm.

His ankle throbbing painfully, Sam crawled over to his granddaughter and lifted her head from the damp ground.

"Alice?" he whispered, gently cradling her in his arms. "Can you hear me?" When there was no response, tears welled up in Sam's eyes. "What has he done to you, Alice Hannah? What have I gotten you into?"

At the sound of her grandfather's voice and the gentle fall of his tear on her cheek, Alice's eyes flickered twice and then slowly opened.

"Grandad?" she whispered back.

Sam's heart skipped a beat. "Alice!" he exclaimed. "How do you feel?"

"Well, I did have a *splitting* headache," she mumbled, trying to sit up, "and these really horrible thoughts, too, but I think I'm starting to feel better now."

The farther away that Shrike slithered, the faster Alice began to recover. Sam helped her to her feet. Although she was still feeling a bit groggy, Sam insisted that they had little time to lose.

"Come on, Alice. We've got to get out of here!" he pleaded, putting weight on his injured ankle with hesitation. "Before Shrike gets back with Bogg!"

"I doubt that Bogg or Shrike will be returning too soon, Sam," Beatrice explained, as Porter finished untying her. She quickly gathered Little Jolly's supplies and shoved them back into Porter's knapsack. "There's been a problem brewing with those two. Something's been troubling the boy all day and I'd venture to say he's made good his escape." She paused just then, listening to the wind as it rustled strangely through the trees. "What concerns me more than either of those scoundrels, however, is the thought of the impending arrival of a hundred or so Fen."

"What?" Sam cried in shock.

"I'll explain later," Beatrice remarked hastily, as she slung the backpack over the shoulder of her mouse suit and repositioned Little Jolly more comfortably in her arms. "There now, we're all set, I think." Beatrice looked up at Sam. She had been operating in survival mode for the last few hours, and hadn't been able to think of much else. But now, the expression on Sam's face made her heart ache all over again. He was staring down into her arms, too frightened it seemed to ask the obvious question.

"Winston's gone, Sam," Beatrice answered for him, choking back her tears. "Shrike set him adrift to drown."

Sam felt himself go numb. Alice gasped.

"We have to get Little Jolly to safety as quickly as possible," Beatrice continued.

Sam nodded his head and took Alice's arm.

"Where's Porter?" Beatrice asked with concern.

Sam looked anxiously about on the ground, then cupped his hands to his mouth.

"Porter!" he cried into the air. "Porterrrr!"

Porter, in the process of scrambling down a tree trunk with Jasper in his arms, called back to him.

"I'm...coming!" he panted breathlessly. "I...had to find...Jasper. I...don't think he's feeling very well."

"We're going to have to tend to him later, I'm afraid," Sam replied. "We've no time now."

"He's been buzzing about all morning, Porter," Beatrice interjected, opening the knapsack again. "He's probably just exhausted, dear. Pop him back in here and he can have a nice rest."

After Porter had obliged, Sam quickly picked up all three Sage and the knapsack, and deposited them in his jacket pocket.

Sam and Alice made their way through the forest then, with barely enough time to catch their breaths. Alice was still a little unsteady on her feet and Sam's ankle gash reduced their speed to little more than a moderate limp. With each jarring step, Beatrice, clinging to Little Jolly in Sam's pocket, kept tumbling into Porter as he clung to his knapsack.

"What's that?" Alice shouted, pointing to a swirling black cloud in the trees ahead. It was floating just above the ground, arcing and sweeping its way through the air toward them.

"Bats...I think," panted Sam, trying to peer through the branches. He grimaced as a high-pitched squealing reached his ears. "Sounds like it, anyway."

Hearing the noise, Beatrice scrambled to the top of Sam's pocket and poked her head out. There was a look of horror on her face.

"It's not bats!" she cried. "It's Fen! Hundreds of them! Cover yourselves!"

Sam immediately turned around and grabbed hold of Alice, pushing her as gently as he could to the ground and covering her head with one side of his jacket. He jammed his hands against his own ears in an effort to block out the unearthly squeals and the loud rustling of black cloaks. With his nose pushed into the damp ground, the revolting smell of rotting things crept into Sam's nostrils. He could feel the creatures scurrying across his back by the hundreds. The icy-cold touch of their bony feet and the tips of their sharp nails penetrated his thick jacket and shirt. Far worse than that, though, were the drops of Fen drool splattering around him like slimy rain. Sam could not understand why none of the creatures had stopped yet to quarry such an easy prey, but it was as if they had been whipped into a state of such frenzy that they did not seem conscious at all of the humans or Sage beneath their feet. Alice was trembling so violently on the ground next to him that even when the last of The Fen had passed over and scurried off into the shadows, Sam continued to hold her tight. He could feel Beatrice stirring about in his jacket pocket. She slowly emerged on all fours, holding on to Little Jolly almost as tightly as Sam was clutching Alice, with Porter and his knapsack tumbling out at her heels.

"Well..." Beatrice mumbled breathlessly, tiptoeing through the puddles of Fen drool that had settled on the ground. "A fascinating experience, but one that I'm not eager to repeat too soon."

Sam, unable to speak, nodded his head.

"We should be very thankful, I imagine," Beatrice continued, "that we encountered that little group while they were all in a trance. During these types of gatherings, The Fen have a tendency to slip into a form of mass hysteria until they reach their appointed destination. I've heard rumors about this sort of thing before, but I have never actually seen it firsthand." Beatrice gave a great shudder. "And seeing it once, I am sure you'll all agree, is quite enough!"

Sam slowly pulled himself up from the ground. "What

worries me now is that their appointed destination is not far from here," he remarked.

"Point well taken, Sam," Beatrice replied, picking up herself and Little Jolly, too. "We shouldn't dally here for long. Shrike, after all, is still out there somewhere and he has a very interesting story to tell them." She gave one of the knapsack straps a gentle tug. "Come on, Porter, dear. We really should be—"

Beatrice stopped speaking as the leaves in the stand of trees ahead of them began to rustle.

"The Fen?" Alice asked Sam nervously. She had turned pale and was beginning to tremble again. "They've circled around and come back for us, haven't they?"

Sam gripped her hand and shook his head.

"It's too quiet for that, Alice," he replied. "It could be Shrike, I suppose—"

"Sshh!" Beatrice whispered, holding her paw to her lips. She motioned for them to back into the bushes and wait. No one dared moved an inch as the leaves continued to rustle and then the branches closest to the ground slowly parted.

16

THE LONGEST DAY MUST
HAVE AN END

"Jolly!" Beatrice cried. She rushed out from the shadows and embraced her husband with such exuberant relief that she almost knocked him off his feet.

He hugged her tightly, then looked deep into her eyes. "I thought I might never see you again, my love! Are you alright?" He strained his neck to see behind her. "Sam, is that you? And Alice, and Porter, too? I can't believe that you're all safe!" he continued with excitement. "When we encountered that hideous swarm of Fen back there I must admit that I feared the worst."

"Jolly..." Beatrice began, as tears welled in her eyes. "There is something I must tell you."

"No, wait! The others are right behind me! They'll want to hear everything, too! And you're not going to believe who's with us! Edgar and Cyrus are alive, Beatrice! We've brought them back home! Isn't that wonderful? The message about the accident at the cliffs was just an evil lie and—"

"But Jolly—" Beatrice tried to interrupt again.

"No need to explain, dearest," Mr. Goodfellow prattled on. "When we returned to the lighthouse, Lydia told us everything—how The Fen intercepted Edgar's note, the twins' kidnapping...all of it!" Mr. Goodfellow lifted up his paw then and slapped it against his forehead. "Good gracious, Beatrice!" he exclaimed. "In all of the excitement, I've forgotten to tell you that Delphinia Shipton has come back with us, too! A bit of an historic event, as you might imagine! She's not been away from that cave of hers for at least 500 years!" He peered anxiously into the bushes. "I'm afraid it's a bit of an effort for her and Cyrus to keep up with the rest of us. They'll be here presently though, I'm sure. Then we'll all be reunited."

"But Jolly," Beatrice whispered again, dropping her head to her chest, "you don't understand." The tears that had pooled in her eyes were now streaming down her face.

Mr. Goodfellow seemed confused for a moment, until he glanced down at the single baby in Beatrice's arms. His searching eyes flashed all around, first at Porter clutching his knapsack and then up at Sam and Alice, both empty-handed. When he paused to stare into Sam's eyes, the look in them was so profoundly sad that Mr. Goodfellow knew in an instant that something dreadful had happened.

"The other child?" he asked in a slow, dry whisper. "Is he...dead?" Beatrice, quietly weeping, nodded her head.

"We think so," Sam explained. "It doesn't seem very hopeful."

"No, it can't be," Mr. Goodfellow groaned in pain. "When I saw you all here just now, I thought that everything was going to be alright."

"I tried to save him, Jolly, I really did," Beatrice sobbed. "But Shrike was too—"

"Please, my dear," Mr. Goodfellow interrupted, gently stroking her hair. "Don't torment yourself like this."

"If anyone is to blame, then it's me!" Sam cried out. "I

promised Edgar that I would guard his children with my life and I've failed him!"

"If that's true, Sam, then what of me?" Mr. Goodfellow lamented. "What of my part in all of this? A Sage of my experience being duped so easily by a stupid Fennish trick is not something to be proud of. If we hadn't rushed off to Cornwall like that without taking the time to check the validity of the story, none of this would have happened!"

"But you thought that Edgar was dying, Jolly," Beatrice offered through her sobs. "There was no time. You had no choice—"

"No, my dear," Mr. Goodfellow interjected. "I must take full responsibility for this whole horrible mess—"

"The children were left in *my* care, Jolly," said Beatrice sternly. "It's as simple as that."

They all stopped speaking as the shrubbery branches parted again and Edgar and Charlotte emerged. It was clear by the looks of devastation on their faces that they had heard and understood everything. Filbert and Hazel, clutching each other's hands, stood quietly at their sides, as Great-Uncle Cyrus and Delphinia Shipton shuffled into position behind them. Without a word, Charlotte walked up to Beatrice and embraced her.

"Thank you for saving my Little Jolly," Charlotte finally murmured, the tears flowing down her cheeks.

"If it hadn't been for you," Edgar added, putting his arm around Beatrice's shoulders, "then we may very well have lost them both."

Even though she was terribly exhausted and grimy after her ordeal, the very first thing that Beatrice did when she reached home was to find her Scandinavian Sea Mouse Knife and pin it firmly to the inside lining of her mouse suit. She was determined that she would never again be caught without it.

The very first thing that Mr. Goodfellow did was to insist that Sam's ankle injury be attended to immediately. He'd had enough experience with such things in the past to know that leaving Fen wounds too long could result in a most unpleasant and lingering infection. Never one to enjoy being fussed over in this manner, Sam had to admit that when Mr. Goodfellow finished applying herbal remedies and bound his ankle in a tight, clean bandage, he felt much better.

It had been rather awkward for both Sam and Alice upon returning home past suppertime, much later than either of them had expected. Alice rushed into the house first, shouting something out to India about an after-school choir practice, before bolting into her bedroom. Sam entered a few minutes after that, trying not to hobble too noticeably on his injured leg. He found India at the dining room table, sorting through the household accounts.

"I've kept supper warm for you," she announced, without looking up.

Sam wasn't sure if he should apologize for his tardiness or not. Even after knowing her for so many years, it was still difficult sometimes for Sam to read India's moods. Well, perhaps it wouldn't hurt to offer a word or two.

"I'm sorry, love," he said, sitting down at the table opposite her. "I suppose I should have called."

India looked up at him. "It's alright. I'm not angry. I do worry about you, though. A lot. And everything you must have on your mind, too."

Sam chuckled. "On *my* mind? Like what? Sailboats and seagulls?"

India smiled.

"I *do* remember that word game we played when we were kids, you know."

Sam felt the hair stand up on the back of his neck. "You do?" He swallowed nervously. "I don't actually remember asking you about—"

"You talk in your sleep, Sam."

"Oh," he whispered. "Um...what else have I said?"

"Some very strange things over the years," India replied. "But not much that I can make sense of. It's not what you say in your sleep, anyway, Sam. It's you. I know there's something different about you. I've always known it. Something special. Something profoundly good. I sensed it the very first time we met. It drew me to you and it made me love you. And that's all that really matters. I don't ever have to know any more than that."

Sam took India's hand in his and gave it an affectionate squeeze. "Funny thing is, India," he said, "I've always thought of you as one of the special ones. Fletcher, too." Sam gazed off into space. "Do you miss him a lot?"

India squeezed Sam's hand back. "More than I can say," she replied.

The following twenty-four hours proved to be an emotional roller-coaster ride for all of The Sage, but particularly for Charlotte. Only a short time before, she had set out on the most difficult journey of her life, expecting to encounter her young husband either dead or dying. Finding him alive and well had been an indescribable joy. But now she had fallen once again into a pit of anguish and uncertainty, torn between the grief of losing one son and the overwhelming desire to love and protect the one who remained. Upon returning home, it became increasingly painful for her to let Little Jolly out of her sight even for a second, for fear that she would lose him, too.

Struggling with his own feelings of grief, it was doubly heartbreaking for Edgar to see Charlotte this way. Even though there was little chance that young Winston had survived being set adrift on the ocean in a leaky boat, there was no question in Edgar's mind that a rescue mission should be undertaken as quickly as possible. Everyone else heartily agreed. At first light, according to the plan, Mr. Goodfellow, Edgar, Filbert and Porter would go out in the sailboat with Sam and Alice into the area where Beatrice last remembered seeing the drifting Fen boat. A number of preliminary inquiries had already been made amongst the local seabird population. Lydia had even heard from a mouse acquaintance of hers who claimed to have some information about a Scandinavian Sea Mouse sighting, but this was later determined to be unfounded. Charlotte tried to be brave through it all, clinging to the hope that by some miracle her little son would be found alive. But she was clearly overcome with feelings of dread. Along with Hazel's assistance, Beatrice (more or less recovered from her encounter with Shrike and Bogg) would be able to help the distracted Charlotte tend to Little Jolly's needs while everyone else was away. Delphinia and Great-Uncle Cyrus remained preoccupied with their ongoing analysis of the sacred antiquity that they had carefully transported back with them across the Atlantic.

As they made last-minute preparations for the mission, it suddenly became apparent to Mr. Goodfellow and Filbert that they had not seen Porter (or Jasper for that matter) since everyone had been reunited in the forest. They searched high and low, finally finding the boy down by the island dock, staring out to sea. He was clutching Jasper tightly in his arms and sobbing his heart out.

"Good heavens, what is it, Porter? Tell me what's wrong," Mr. Goodfellow inquired as he walked over.

Between sobs, the boy managed to spit out a few words. Mr. Goodfellow tried his best to interpret them, but it was hopeless.

"Here," said Mr. Goodfellow, gently prying the boy's paws away from his pet. "Let's have a look."

Still sobbing, Porter leaned forward, releasing his grip on Jasper.

"Oh dear...well...I understand now," said Mr. Goodfellow quietly, as he carefully examined the cicada. "You've had a rough time of it, haven't you, old boy?" he whispered, giving Jasper a friendly pat before he returned him to Porter's arms.

Mr. Goodfellow walked back to Filbert with a grimace on his face.

"It looks bad. His wings are slashed beyond repair, I'd say. One of them is just hanging by a thread and his abdomen is damaged, too. I suspect some infection may have already set in." Mr. Goodfellow sighed. "Fen wounds can be a nasty business. He may survive with the proper care, but without it I doubt he'll make it through the week. And even if he does, his buzzing days are clearly over."

"Poor Jasper," Filbert replied. "And poor Porter, too."

"I don't quite know what to say to the boy," said Mr. Goodfellow with concern. "He won't be able to adequately care for the creature now. Not in this condition, at least. We need an expert, Filbert."

Mr. Goodfellow started drumming the tips of his paws together, as if he was desperately trying to summon a solution. It was Filbert, however, who spoke first. When

Mr. Goodfellow looked up, there was an expression of triumph on his older brother's face.

"I can't believe that you didn't think of it before me, Jolly!"

"What?" Mr. Goodfellow asked blankly. He was still struggling for an answer to the problem (and a little annoyed at Filbert's smug expression, too).

"Come on, Jolly, old man! Think!" Filbert smiled. "If *you* were an incapacitated cicada, where would you want to go?"

Mr. Goodfellow continued to stare straight ahead, until a slow smile began to creep across his face.

"A retirement villa in Florida!" he suddenly shouted out. "Of course, Filbert! Cornelius Mango's! It's absolutely brilliant!"

He gave his brother a hearty slap on the back and chuckled.

"I really don't know how I'd manage without you, Filbert."

"Oh, you'd have thought of it eventually, Jolly. You did without me for 120 years, once. Remember?" Filbert smiled.

Puzzled by their odd behavior, Porter looked up and sniffled. It didn't seem appropriate, under the sad circumstances, for them to be acting this way.

"Do you think the boy will go for it, Jolly?" Filbert whispered.

"It won't be easy, but if he truly cares about his pet, he will." Mr. Goodfellow rubbed his paws together with satisfaction. "We're going to have to find a suitable way to get Jasper down south, though. A carry sling of some sort and a couple of mouse porters might do the job."

"I'm inclined to think that the boy should go to Mango's, too, Jolly," Filbert suggested. "It will make the decision to leave Jasper easier, if Porter can help get him settled. I'd be honored to take them both there myself. I know exactly where to find Cornelius, after all, and I have a much better rapport with the old soul than you do. If you think you can all manage without me, that is." A look of sadness and concern swept across Filbert's face.

"I'm sure Charlotte and Edgar will understand, Filbert," said Mr. Goodfellow kindly. "We owe that bug a rather large debt of gratitude. If it hadn't been for him, we might never have found our way to Beatrice and Little Jolly, right?"

Filbert smiled faintly and nodded his head.

"Very well then," Mr. Goodfellow answered with a great sigh. "All we have to do now is to convince the boy."

As Mr. Goodfellow had suspected, Porter was reluctant at first to even entertain the idea of taking Jasper that far away and leaving him. But when Mr Goodfellow and Filbert urged him to remember Mango's palm-tree home and the peaceful haven it afforded aged and injured insects, Porter finally agreed. Just a couple of hours later (with the mission to search for Winston already under way), Porter set off with Filbert on a high-speed magnet train to Miami, clutching the sleeping cicada in his arms.

17

A HOUSE DIVIDED AGAINST ITSELF CANNOT STAND

Standing in the hallway of Rook's rotting tree-trunk home, Bogg heard the creak of the door behind him. He held his breath and slowly turned around. Shrike, holding the limp mouse robot under one arm, was standing in front of him.

"Ahhh...so this is what's been distracting you all these months, is it, Bogg?"

Shocked, Bogg quickly stepped away from his uncle and swallowed hard. He had taken every precaution not to be tracked when he'd slipped away from Shrike's encampment.

"You've been busy keeping nasty little secrets from me, haven't you?" Shrike snarled. "Too busy to do your work properly. And I suppose you don't care how much this negligence of yours has cost me!" Shrike let the robot fall to the floor with a thump. He moved closer then and poked a bony finger into Bogg's chest. "You abandoned me at a most critical time, nephew. Those stupid Sage and their humans will be well gone by now, I've no doubt. And now I'm going to have to go through another messy procedure to catch up with them again. And it's all your fault!"

"But Uncle Shrike-I-I—" Bogg stammered.

"You stupid, ungrateful boy!" Shrike hissed. "After everything I've done for you! I took you in after the death of your father and treated you like my own son. I had one of the best Fen families eager to bestow one of their lovely daughters on you." He turned and glared maliciously at Rook. "And how do you choose to repay me now? With a union that you knew I could never allow!"

The sound of a baby crying caused Shrike's eyes to widen and glow with rage. Bogg gulped in fear. Rook scuttled into the back room and brought the crying child back in her arms.

"A child?" Shrike screamed. "*Your* child?" Tell me that this is not so, Bogg!"

When Bogg did not answer him, Shrike flashed his eyes at Rook again.

"This inferior creature is no match for someone with your pedigree, Bogg!" he growled. "It is an offense to me, as it would be to any Fen of our standing. But to have a child with her is no less than an abomination! A stain on the family! I cannot bear to lay my eyes on the thing!" He lifted his arm and roughly pushed Rook and the baby aside. "Get it out of my sight!"

His words were too much for Bogg. He clenched his fists and walked right up to Shrike, placing himself between his uncle and Rook and the baby.

"Don't be foolish, Bogg," Shrike warned. "They're not worth it."

Rook, meanwhile, was backing a little farther away from them, but not out of fear. She slid closer to the wall where she'd spied a stone that had been kicked into the corner. Holding the baby under her arm, she slowly stooped down, took the stone in her empty hand, rose again and moved forward. As Shrike continued to vent his wrath at Bogg, Rook raised her arm and hurled the stone as hard as she could at Shrike's head. It struck the side of his bony cheek with considerable force. Shrike growled in pain, then lifted his hand up to where the sickly, translucent skin had split open. It wasn't a serious injury, but it was enough to send Shrike into one of his furious rages. Screeching with anger, he lunged past Bogg, clasping his white knuckles around Rook's neck. The baby began to scream. Gasping for air, Rook fell to her knees, letting the child slide from her arms and onto the floor. Bogg jumped forward to help, but his attempts to pry his uncle's hands away were in vain. When Bogg began to beat on his head instead, Shrike loosened his grip and when he did, Rook broke free and raced for the door. Shrike threw himself across the floor, catching the torn hem of Rook's grubby cloak with his nail. Rook slid backward an inch or two, then tumbled sideways, striking her head against the sharp edge of a rock table as she fell. She rolled over just once, then lay very still.

While Bogg picked the screaming baby up from the floor, Shrike crawled over to Rook's motionless body and gave it a prod.

"Stone cold," he remarked dryly.

Trembling, Bogg began to whimper.

"She's-she's gone?"

"Stop sniveling, Bogg! It's just as well," Shrike snarled. "She'd have brought you nothing but grief!"

"But she was...my-my wife! You've killed her!"

"I did nothing of the sort!" Shrike snapped. "The stupid thing brought it on herself. I was just defending myself."

Bogg looked down at the little baby in his arms and began to feel very frightened. Shrike had already pulled himself to his feet and was sliding toward them. Grakul's cries grew louder.

"Don't come any closer!" Bogg warned.

"It's not for you to be giving *me* orders, nephew!" Shrike growled at him. "You're barely grown, foolish boy! You know nothing about these things! The family line cannot be sullied in this way, Bogg! You will realize that one day. Give the child to me!"

"No!" Bogg screamed. "She's mine! I'm all that she has now and I won't let you take her!"

Bogg turned on his heel and ran for the entranceway, stumbling over the mounds of garbage on the floor and Rook's lifeless body as he scrambled to get out.

"You'll never get away from me now," Shrike chuckled. "Not with that whining brat in your arms. Come on, let me lighten your load, Bogg. Hand the child over."

With his nails bared, Shrike lunged forward as Bogg tried desperately to squeeze himself and Grakul through the half-open door. When they finally popped out into the daylight, Bogg began to sprint through the forest in the direction of the sea. With no idea as to where he might find sanctuary, Bogg ran on anyway, hoping that something brilliant might come to him along the way. But the only thought that was filling his mind now brought with it a strange feeling he had never experienced before. The desire to save the child in his arms was so powerful and so overwhelming and so all consuming that it suddenly spilled out of his brain and into his heart, spurring him on. Bogg raced through the forest, navigating his way past layers of thick moss and rows of towering ferns until the stalks began to thin out in front of him. He darted through the outcroppings of juniper, bayberry and bunch-berry, past plants that had been battered and misshapen by years of salt spray and sea winds, until he reached the world of black lichen and algae, on the band of bare rock that separated the forest edge from the seashore. He stopped to rest for a moment and to check on little Grakul, wrapped in a tight cocoon of dirty, gray cloth. He dared not pause for too long, though. Shrike, he feared, would not be far behind. When Bogg looked down the slope of sand that led to the edge of the water, past the rows of periwinkles and barnacles, seaweed and Irish moss, his heart sank. There was nowhere left to run, save for a thin spit of sand and rocks that ran down one side of the beach and into the churning sea. As a twig snapped at the edge of the forest behind him, Bogg gasped and spun around. Shrike, dragging the mechanical mouse by his side again, emerged from the dark shadows and began to cackle.

"Well, I have you now, haven't I?" he sneered. "You might as well admit it, Bogg. This ridiculous chase is over."

Bogg scurried across the sand toward the rocks, clutching Grakul to his chest. He climbed awkwardly onto the first uneven boulder, and then the next one. He turned his back to the sea, not daring to take his eyes off Shrike for a second. He shuffled backward along the rocks, feeling his way with the heels of his feet until he had almost reached the edge of the water. The sound of Shrike's cruel laughter filled his ears.

"Don't be stupid, nephew. Get back here!"

"No!" Bogg cried. "I won't."

As Shrike inched his way closer, Bogg turned to face the sea. He stared into the swirling surf for a moment, then lifted his eyes to the horizon. Streaks of sunlight had started to burn through the thick fog. A wooden boat appeared on the horizon, its bright white sail gleaming in the sun.

"What are you staring at, fool!" Shrike demanded. "I'm growing impatient with you, Bogg. Give me the child! NOW!"

Bogg turned to face his uncle one last time. There was a strange look on his face, as if something had suddenly twigged in his mind. He took his daughter under one arm and gave her a kiss on the top of her head. Then he threw himself and the child into the sea.

Screeching with rage, Shrike clambered over the rocks, dragging the mouse behind him.

"Come back here at once, Bogg!"

"Never!" Bogg shouted breathlessly, trying to swim farther away.

"Insolent ingrate!" Shrike whispered under his breath. He shoved the grinning mouse into the water and awkwardly climbed on top of it.

"I had a feeling this stupid ball of wires might come in useful one day!" he growled.

Moving himself into a comfortable position, Shrike straddled the mouse's furry body, trailing his black cloak and legs in the water. "Look at me!" he complained bitterly. "I cannot believe that your idiocy has reduced me to this, Bogg!" He gave the mouse a kick in the side to get it moving. "Start paddling, rodent!" he snarled.

Bogg struggled even harder to escape. Determined not to be defeated, Shrike decided to try a more conciliatory approach, as he and the mouse drifted closer.

"You know, Bogg," he offered in a slow, syrupy voice, "perhaps I might be persuaded to reconsider my position about the child. I have the power to save her."

"I don't believe you!" Bogg shouted back. "It's all lies! You forget, Uncle. I know you too well!"

"You'll regret this, Bogg!" Shrike snapped in anger. "It's gone too far now, and if I must get past you to take the child, then so be it! Prepare to be sacrificed for the honor of your family!"

With those words, Shrike rose up from his perch atop the

soggy mouse and reached forward as far as he could, dragging a handful of sharp Fen nails across the top of Bogg's head and slashing him viciously.

Sam's sailboat, bobbing up and down on the waves, was sweeping closer to the shoreline now. Noticing an unusual commotion in the water, Edgar directed Sam to sail the boat toward the rocks, while he quickly donned his harness and tethered himself to the boat's side to get a better look.

"What is it, Edgar? Mr. Goodfellow inquired. "What can you see?"

"I'm not sure. Something is struggling by those rocks, I think," Edgar replied. "If we could just get a little closer..."

Exhausted and swooning under the sharp pain of Shrike's assault, Bogg was floundering in the water with his one free arm, fighting to stay conscious. Blood from a deep gash in his forehead had started trickling down his white, pointed nose and into his eyes. He cradled Grakul as tightly as he could, struggling to keep her head above the waves. With his dwindling strength, he pushed his body through the water toward Sam's approaching boat and the blurred figure of Edgar Goodfellow, dangling by his harness above the waves. Bogg suddenly reached up through the water, grabbed onto one of the harness straps and stared straight at Edgar. Gasping in surprise, Edgar swung himself away. The look in Bogg's eyes was one he had never seen on the face of a Fen before.

"Do not turn from me, Sage," Bogg groaned in exhaustion.

Mr. Goodfellow, Sam and Alice stared in disbelief as Bogg lifted a bundle high above his head and into Edgar's out-stretched arms.

This," he rasped, "is my child...Grakul."

"You fool!" screamed Shrike, who was now furiously

paddling along with the mouse. "Do you know what you are doing?"

Bogg ignored his uncle and continued to look up at Edgar. "Take her..." he whispered.

"You idiot!" Shrike screamed. "You have sacrificed all of us!"

But Bogg did not hear the rest of his uncle's angry words. The next wave to wash over his head sucked him under the water and carried him away.

Shrike quickly spun the robot mouse toward Sam's boat and gave it a great thump in its side.

"Get moving, you useless wretch!" Shrike growled. "It's not over yet! Just a little closer and I can seize control of those stupid humans again!"

When it didn't respond immediately, Shrike gave the mouse a more vigorous kick. But it was in vain. The robot had finally succumbed to the onslaught of saltwater into its circuits. The waves lapped victoriously over its insipid grin. Little puffs of foul-smelling smoke rose from behind its staring eyes.

"Useless piece of junk!" Shrike snarled, giving the unmoving mouse one final kick in the side. "But the great Shrike Fen is not done just yet, pitiful Sage!" he bellowed. "I still have something else up my sleeve!"

Shrike swept the black cloak up at his side to reveal his shiny robotic leg. With an evil grin, he pressed the button at his hip. The leg began to spin slowly at first, then faster and faster. Like a miniature outboard motor, the rotating leg pushed Shrike and the sinking mouse dangerously close to where Edgar and the baby were dangling above the sea. Just as he was about to grab for the child, Shrike suddenly gasped and clutched his hip. The leg flew out of the water and sailed through the air for a few feet before it reentered the waves with a majestic splash.

"Curse you, Bogg!" Shrike shrieked in frustration. "You swore to me that you had fixed that blasted thing! Even in death you mock me!" He turned and pointed a long, bony finger in Edgar's direction.

"I'll hunt all of you down, Goodfellow, and the Fen child, too! That's a promise!" he screamed angrily. "She may be of my own blood, Sage, but I swear that I will see her dead before I let you keep her!" Shrike's voice grew steadily fainter as a strong current caught him and the listing mouse and sent them floating off. "Not one of you who harbors her will be safe from me now," Shrike screeched through the last lingering remnants of fog. "Not one cursed one of you! And that's not all, either! I'll have that deliciously wicked Ramona Mandrake working overtime for me! No more of these ridiculous robotic contraptions! Let's see how well you can deal with a hundred genetically mutated little mouse friends in your midst!" he snickered. "You'll never know what hit you!"

Alice shuddered. Sam picked up the tiller and turned the boat toward the island. They could still hear Shrike Fen's vicious snarls behind them as he slowly disappeared into the mist.

"Is the Fen child alright, Edgar?" Mr. Goodfellow asked, as he reached over the side of the boat to retrieve the harness.

Edgar looked down at the squirming infant in his arms.

"I think so," he replied with hesitation, folding back the layers of filthy wet cloth. "It's a little skinny looking, and really pale, and its toenails are all sharp and curled under. It could probably use a good scrub, too." Edgar gave the end of Grakul's tiny vulture nose a gentle tickle. When she reciprocated with an ear-piercing shriek of delight, Edgar grimaced.

"That may not be all that unusual for a Fen youngster, I suppose," Mr. Goodfellow offered. "But we'd best get her back on dry land so we can discuss our next course of action." He looked at Edgar with a somber expression. "Although I suppose that's already been decided for us, hasn't it, my boy? As I'm quite sure you'll agree, we have no choice but to shelter the poor child now."

Edgar looked up at Mr. Goodfellow and nodded. Then he gave Grakul a tickle under her pointed chin. "She's all alone in the world, isn't she?" he murmured.

"I would be inclined to believe so, Edgar," Mr. Goodfellow remarked, "considering that her closest known relative seems hell-bent on doing her in."

"I'm a little worried, though, Uncle Jolly," Edgar sighed, "about how Charlotte will react to all of this..."

"If I know Charlotte as well as I think I do," Mr. Goodfellow suggested, "then she will rise admirably to the challenge. She has just lost one of her own precious children. The sight of another small, defenseless creature to protect will serve only to strengthen her resolve. Believe me, Edgar, Charlotte will take all of this in stride...and so, my boy, must you."

Edgar wiped away a tear that was welling in his eye.

"I'll try, Uncle Jolly," he sighed. "I'll try."

18

IT IS NOT PERMITTED TO
KNOW ALL THINGS

It was almost midday before Sam's boat appeared from behind the rocks on its final leg home. All of The Sage were waiting anxiously for its return, but none was as distraught as poor Charlotte. Clutching Little Jolly to her chest, she had been pacing back and forth the whole time that Sam, Alice, Mr. Goodfellow and Edgar had been out on the ocean. When she saw Edgar jump onto the dock with a baby-sized bundle in his arms, her heart leapt with joy, only to sink back into despair when she discovered that it was not Winston. Edgar's return to the lighthouse with a Fen child in his arms resulted in some serious misgivings and heightened emotions all around. But when Charlotte reluctantly picked up little Grakul for the first time and saw her thin, grimy body and soothed her sobbing, any doubts were washed away in seconds. When Filbert and Porter returned home the following day from their mission to Cornelius Mango's and laid their eyes on the new houseguest, the same emotions of initial horror and then growing sympathy played out again.

For many nights after that, The Sage, Sam and Alice gathered to try to understand all that was now unfolding.

Delphinia Shipton continued to scrutinize The Book of The Sage, its crystal map and the Martian scrolls, too, taking very little time to rest as she attempted to piece everything together.

"Ahhh," she finally whispered, late into the evening of the seventh night. "It's all starting to come to me now!" She clapped her hands together with excitement, then slowly lifted a finger and pointed it straight at Sam. "It has to do with *you*!"

"It does?" answered Sam timidly.

"At that fateful moment when you—a being of the physical world—discovered our existence," Delphinia whispered in awe, "then all of us, Sage and Fen and human alike, were instantly propelled onto a new course. Or more aptly, a collision course!"

"I'm sorry," Sam blurted out, looking at Delphinia with an expression of regret.

"No need to apologize," she replied, waving her hand about in the air. "It was entirely beyond your control, my dear. I am only thankful that when the time came, destiny chose *you* as the catalyst, Sam. I am quite sure that this fact has had great bearing on our salvation, so far. I do not believe that this would be so if destiny had chosen a human of ordinary qualities."

Mr. Goodfellow slapped his knee. "I knew there was something about the boy! Even then, all those years ago! Sam was special. There was something in the air!" Mr. Goodfellow continued with excitement. "I could feel it in my bones!" He turned to Delphinia. "I said then that I sensed the beginning of a convergence of some sort!"

"Indeed," Delphinia replied. "A phenomenon waiting for just the right moment—the right person, in fact—to set its wheels in motion. In the years since then, many mysteries have been revealed. From the discovery of our ancient book here, we now know that Sage and Fen have been bound together since the beginning of time. It has also been revealed that there exists a means for The Fen to overthrow us. If they were ever to succeed, we would cease to be who we are. We would lose our power to do good. We would be as dust in the wind." Delphinia looked across the room to where Grakul and Little Jolly were taking turns gurgling at each other. She whispered as she continued. "If we were once as one with them, then it only stands to reason that what is written for The Sage might very well be true for them, too. If a Fen child were to live with us, then freely choose our way at the time of its maturity, then what of this?"

Delphinia paused and looked at everyone in the room in turn. Her eyes were wild with discovery. "After murdering the mouse courier and intercepting Edgar's note, Shrike Fen must have realized all of this. But sharing such revelations with his compatriots was not in his own selfish interests. He planned to keep that knowledge to himself until he was able to deliver a Sage child into the hands of The Fen hierarchy. Imagine his triumph at that moment when he could announce that he, Shrike Fen, was holding the key to the destruction of The Sage. And that triumph would have been sweeter because the child he was delivering was a Goodfellow. Shrike Fen was unlikely to share the glory of that moment with anyone. He did, after all, quite conveniently do away with the only other Fen who knew of this." Delphinia wagged her finger. "We must be especially vigilant in the days ahead, my dears. Any mission that Shrike undertakes now will be twofold. He will use every evil trick in his arsenal to snatch Little Jolly away from us again and, by his own admission, he will not rest until Grakul is dead. Even if it were not too late, and the child could be spirited back into the fold of her own kind, I fear that he would not allow her to survive for long. I suspect he has a personal score to settle with her. She will never be safe while Shrike Fen is alive."

Charlotte shuddered. Delphinia's words had pierced her heart. She did not want to contemplate any of this. In the short time that Grakul had been with them, Charlotte had grown increasingly protective of her. Her overwhelming grief at the loss of Winston had combined with the arrival of this strange little creature, so pitifully alone and unwanted, to trigger the strongest parental instincts in her, just as Mr. Goodfellow had predicted. Grakul may have been alone in the world, but she had found, in Charlotte, a champion of enormous strength and determination.

"We may have learned much that troubles us about the relationship between Sage and Fen," Delphinia continued, "but that is not all. On our long journey through time and space we have been inextricably tied to the creatures called humans. It is a complex relationship. We may inspire these souls, encourage them, comfort them, even love them. But we must never forget that they are creatures of free will. We do not seek to control them as The Fen do. We can be there to offer guidance, but they must ultimately choose the course and direction of their own lives." Delphinia waved her arms about in the air. "I do not need to remind any of you about this. You all know it as well as I. When humankind discovered the meaning and origin of the Martian scrolls—and the messages that were left for them by their forefathers within the great crop circles—it served to solve another part of the greater puzzle. I do not believe in coincidences, and neither should you. This knowledge did not come to any of us by chance." Delphinia's eyes were flickering now with the fire of great excitement. "A cosmic convergence is indeed in play, but there is even more, and it points back, I believe, to something I have been studying here."

Delphinia opened up The Book of The Sage with reverence. The crystal map that had recently been hidden in a beetle's dung ball was now nestled in its rightful place within the back cover. Delphinia gently ran her finger over the sparkling surface.

"In order to trace the journey back to where it all began—to where human creatures first encountered Sage and Fen, and long before they dwelt on the planets of the Sun—we may need to look no further than here," she whispered, holding a trembling finger above a tiny round spot carved into the right-hand corner of the map. "A place, according to what I can decipher, that was so serene, so lush—a garden so indescribably beautiful—that it would be hard for mere mortals to even imagine now. And a place that by their own deeds was lost to them *forever*, from which they were cast out, and to which they are *forbidden* to return." Delphinia whispered some of her last words with particular emphasis.

Sam swallowed hard before he spoke. "Is it the place where Fletcher and Winchester Redwood were headed?"

"Perhaps," said Delphinia. "I cannot say for sure." She stopped speaking and stared into space for a moment. "But I must tell you now that there is something in all of this that troubles me greatly—so greatly, in fact, that I almost hesitate to speak of it."

Great-Uncle Cyrus, who had been quietly hanging on to Delphinia's every word, suddenly spoke up.

"What on earth is it, Delphinia? Here, take my hand, my dear. You look positively pale," he said. He looked over in Mr. Goodfellow's direction. "Perhaps we should make a spot of tea for her, Jolly?"

The other Sage tried not to appear too shocked at Cyrus's remarks. In the almost 1,000 years that they had known him, the crusty old bird had rarely spoken so many words in one sentence to another living soul before, and certainly never with that much affection. Mr. Goodfellow glanced over at Beatrice as he trotted toward the teakettle and very cautiously raised his eyebrows.

Delphinia smiled in Cyrus's direction and continued speaking. "The Book of The Sage, and its map in particular, were never meant to be seen by human eyes. There are warnings in the book that are most specific about this."

Sam and Alice both looked up with expressions of concern.

Delphinia shook her head at them and smiled. "*Certain* human eyes, my dears. You two have a rather special exemption, I believe. Nevertheless, The Book of The Sage is a testament of *our* history, *our* journeys and *our* link to humankind, and the information in it was meant to be protected for all time by The Sage alone. But the great flood on Mars tore it from our hands and buried it deep beneath the red Martian soil for ten thousand years. During all that time, however, it still belonged to *us*. Strangely, Sam, your friend Fletcher sensed that. He said as much in his letter to you, remember? He may not have understood the compulsion he had to give it to you, but he had an overpowering feeling that it belonged to someone else. He also believed that you would know what to do with it. Had you been able to return the book to us intact, then that would have been the end of it. But darker forces were at play, and the map, rather than finding a way directly back to its rightful place, took an unfortunate detour. It landed, as we all know, in the unsavory hands of Eustace Slocumb, and his dark muse. And as we have now learned from Beatrice's encounter with Shrike Fen, that would be—"

"Sorrel Fen!" exclaimed Edgar.

"As much of a force to be feared, I imagine, as his legendary brothers," Filbert interjected with a shudder.

"Thanks to Jolly and Filbert's expert investigations at Cornelius Mango's," Delphinia continued, "we know that Sir Percival Davenport tried his best to keep the information on the map from Slocumb. He paid for the attempt with his life, brave soul. But it was too late; the NASA mission went on as planned with the coordinates that Slocumb planted. As Jolly deduced, and as I am inclined to believe, too, Slocumb likely slipped aboard later with the true coordinates and a plan to take control of the ship when the time was right—and take for himself whatever powerful knowledge he presumed he might find at the end of the trip."

"But if what you say is true, Delphinia, and no human, especially one with a Fen at his side, was ever meant to return to that most reverent place," Mr. Goodfellow whispered, "then—"

"The journey would have been catastrophic," Delphinia whispered back. "I cannot even begin to imagine what dark forces might be unleashed as a result."

Sam wasn't the only one who felt a cold chill run down his spine. Everyone in the room fell suddenly silent.

Delphinia looked up at them all and sighed. "I do not want to plant false hope, but there may be one small glimmer still." She looked straight at Sam. "It rests, I believe, in the hands of your dear friend Fletcher. I have felt for some time now that there was more to him than any of us ever suspected. He is a person of unique insight and intuition, but also one, I now believe, who may possess a visionary gift. This may explain why you two were drawn to each other as children and have sustained a deep friendship that has lasted three-quarters of a century."

Sam nodded his head. "You know, now that you say that, I think it might be true. India has that same weird thing; as if she knows more than she lets on sometimes. And Alice..." Sam's words trailed off then as he stared at his granddaughter.

"Indeed," said Delphinia knowingly.

"This intuition thing of Fletcher's," Sam began again. "Is that why he stowed away on the ship?"

"Perhaps. I suppose only Fletcher would be able to answer that question for sure," Delphinia replied.

"I wish I could ask him," Sam lamented. "He would have been in terrible danger when Slocumb showed his hand, wouldn't he?"

"Fletcher may have sensed something dangerous before he even boarded the ship, Sam," Delphinia explained. "He was, after all, in the golden years of his life, surrounded by family and friends, still basking in the glory of a lifetime of honors and achievements. He did not *need* to accomplish anything more. But for some reason he *had* to go on that voyage."

"But why?" asked Sam.

"That is something that I, even after my long life, cannot answer for you," Delphinia sighed. "Except to explain that we Sage, like all creatures, are the creations of a higher power. And from time to time, this power intervenes in our lives. People call it many things: universal energy, the great spirit, a supreme being. It is something that we cannot fully understand or explain. This may be just the musings of an 1,800-year-old Sage, Sam, but I believe that your friend Fletcher was somehow *meant* to go on that voyage—to try and turn it back or stop it entirely—in an attempt to counter Eustace Slocumb and the forces of evil. It may be very difficult for us to face the possibility, but Fletcher may have found himself compelled to make the ultimate sacrifice for the greater good."

"Could it have ended any other way?" asked Sam.

"I sincerely hope so," said Delphinia. "But sadly, we may never know what transpired on that voyage. It is an information gap that we may just have to learn to live with, while we embrace the faith that Slocumb's plans did not succeed."

"It's really true, isn't it?" Beatrice observed. "You have been saying for so many years, Jolly, that history has an odd way of repeating itself."

"You're right, of course, my dear," replied Mr. Goodfellow soberly. "Fletcher and Redwood's journey was contaminated by unwanted passengers, just like our flight from the Martian flood ten thousand years ago was contaminated by The Fen. We can only hope that Fletcher and Redwood's journey concludes on a better note," he sighed. "Having Earth overrun with the likes of The Fen and their followers was ruinous. The plan for a benevolent world that the inhabitants from Mars carried in their scrolls is still just a dream. Instead of fleeing from a destructive and corrupt society, those poor Martian souls unwittingly transported to Earth some of its worst aspects."

"And, as far as those scrolls go, Jolly," Delphinia interjected, closing her eyes, "I fear that the world is still not ready for their release—even with all the progress that has been made. As long as The Fen can operate freely, as long as they have the power to destroy or undermine any creature who tries to do good, then the hope for a truly transformed world will always be out of reach. The great battles between Sage and Fen will continue on and on until one of us finally wins and the other loses."

When Delphinia opened her eyes again, everyone else in the room was completely transfixed on her. Some were barely breathing. "On a more hopeful note," she quickly added, "we must not despair, nor should we forget that even in the shadow of fear and uncertainty there are still many strange and wondrous things yet to be discovered." Delphinia tried to inspire her little group with an encouraging smile. "And on that concluding note," she continued, "I strongly recommend that The Book of The Sage and its map be returned to the safekeeping of The Sage Governing Council as soon as Cyrus and I have concluded our analysis."

"And the Martian scrolls, too?" asked Sam.

"No, Sam," Delphinia replied. "They belong to humankind, not Sage. They are your hope and legacy and they must remain in your faithful hands."

Sam rested his head on his chest and closed his eyes. Delphinia's words had made him uneasy. It was at moments like this that he missed Fletcher's friendship and company the most. For seventy-five years, Sam had carefully guarded the Martian scrolls, but now it seemed that the day they had all been waiting for was still very far away. And he was a very old man. He didn't have the luxury of time or the life span of a Sage. Who would carry on for him? He sighed and rubbed his tired eyes. When he finally looked up and those same eyes fell upon Alice, Sam felt a strange tingling sensation down his spine. It was a feeling too powerful to ignore. He sidled over to where his granddaughter was sitting.

"There is something important that I need to talk to you about," Sam began in a serious tone that Alice remembered hearing just a few times before in her life. She sat up respectfully and looked her grandfather straight in the eye.

"The Sage will come to you one day soon, to ask you a question," Sam continued. "It may be the hardest one that you will ever have to answer, and sadly, I can't help you with it. It's something that you alone must decide. That's why—"

"I think I know what it is," Alice interrupted. "They had to ask you the same question once, didn't they, Grandad?"

"Yes," Sam answered in surprise. "It was a very long time ago."

"And what was *your* answer?"

"Well, if you know what the question was, Alice, then you must know my answer!" Sam exclaimed. "After all, here I am, all these years later, with my lighthouse and my boats and—"

"And a lot more, too," said Alice.

"True enough."

"Have you ever wished that you hadn't chosen the way you did, Grandad?"

"Not for one single second."

"Then it will be the same for me, too."

"Don't be too hasty, Alice!" Sam implored. "There's a lot for you to consider. I suspect that there may be a Sage somewhere just waiting in the wings for you. You have already shown great promise and you come from a long line of accomplished individuals. Your Nana, for one, has had a remarkable career and made, with Charlotte's very able assistance, many great contributions to science. And so has your Great-Uncle Fletcher. Just think of all he has done, Alice! I know for a fact that Mr. Goodfellow considers him one of his most successful assignments. And Grandpa Sanjid..."

"But I come from *you*, too, don't I, Grandad?" Alice interjected.

"Well...yes...of course you do," Sam answered.

"And the real measure of a person should not be in what they accomplish, but in what they truly are, deep inside."

Sam sighed. "Those sentiments are very familiar to me, Alice. You've been taking heed of Mr. Goodfellow's words, haven't you?"

"And I probably don't have to remind you, Grandad, that we are *all* creatures of free will," she continued with a smile.

"And to Delphinia Shipton's words, too, I see," Sam sighed again. "Just listen to me, Alice. All I really want is for you to make the right decision for *you*."

"I know, Grandad," Alice replied. "And I promise that I will."

19

To Know the Road Ahead,
Ask Those Coming Back

Delphinia Shipton's revelations had given The Sage a great deal to ponder, especially considering that their concern for the life of one Fen child now appeared to be linked to their very survival. They had not planned for the future to unfold as it might. They had not sought the Fen child with the intention of fulfilling any prophecy or changing the course of the universe. They had reacted as any other creatures of courage and decency would have. They had rescued a helpless child from peril, and now they had no option but to continue to shelter her from what they believed would be certain death.

But further talk of these strange developments was forced to wait for another day. Something else just as remarkable—at least in the lives of Sam, Alice and the Goodfellows—was about to transpire. It began with a flurry of activity, deep within the tunnels in the lighthouse walls. Lydia popped out of the mouse hole first, wildly waving her arms, about to attract as much attention as possible, while an entourage of equally excited rodents spilled out behind her.

"What is it, Lydia?" Mr. Goodfellow inquired. "Slow down,

my dear! You're speaking far too fast for me to understand!"

Lydia repeated her lengthy stream of squeaks and whistles to no avail. In desperation, she finally grabbed Mr. Goodfellow by his mouse suit sleeve and dragged him toward the wall.

"Outside? Is that what you're trying to say?" Mr. Goodfellow turned to the others who were gathering round. "The poor thing is beside herself!" He turned to his older brother. "Filbert, you were always much better than I at these translations..."

"As far as I can tell," Filbert offered, struggling to make sense of Lydia's hastily delivered speech, "it's got something to do with a group of harbor seals in the southern channel."

"Oh dear," Mr. Goodfellow lamented. "I do hope they haven't tangled themselves up in some old fishing nets again. We had an absolutely dreadful time cutting them loose last year. It was a close call, but fortunately there were no fatalities."

"Harbor seals?" asked Sam with interest, looking down at Filbert. He had forgotten, until now, about his unusual seal encounter a few months earlier. "Lydia didn't happen to mention any of them in particular, did she? A smaller one, maybe, with stripes down his back?"

Filbert shook his head. "No details, I'm afraid."

"Wonderful creatures, seals," Mr. Goodfellow remarked as he readjusted his mouse mask and ears. "Highly inquisitive, though. And that curiosity has sometimes landed them in a scrape or two."

He pushed one furry leg through the mouse hole. "Come on, everyone!" he called. "I expect I may need help."

Filbert immediately followed his brother through the hole, with Porter, Charlotte and Little Jolly right behind him.

Beatrice and Hazel came next, supporting the much slower-moving team of Cyrus and Delphinia. Edgar brought up the rear, holding on, as best he could, to Grakul. It appeared that she actually had a better hold of *him*, though, grinning happily as she grasped the end of his nose with her recently trimmed nails. Edgar tried not to flinch too noticeably.

"We'll fetch the rowboat and meet you outside!" Sam shouted. As Edgar's tail disappeared through the mouse hole, Sam grabbed Alice's hand and they both raced for the walkway door.

By the time Sam rowed the boat around to the southernmost tip of the island, The Sage had already gathered on the rocks. A loud chorus of seal barks was drifting across the water toward them, but it was difficult to make out any shapes on the black surface of the sea. In an attempt to shed some light on the situation, Beatrice had extracted her Scandinavian Sea Mouse Knife from the inside of her suit and was now searching frantically for the flashlight feature. At the same time, Sam was pulling something from around his neck. He called out to The Sage, swinging the silver chain that held his own Sea Mouse Knife across the water and over the rocks to them, where it landed with a thud at Mr. Goodfellow's feet.

When the two flashlights had been finally switched on and their piercing beams directed at the offshore noise, it soon became apparent that this was no maritime emergency at all. The seal barking had not been a signal of alarm but a cry of excitement.

A large group of seals, diving and splashing through the waves, were circling around another seal as they steadily approached Sam's boat and The Sage onshore.

"I say," Mr. Goodfellow called out, "can anyone make out what's happening over there?"

"There's something in the water with them, Uncle Jolly," Edgar called back. "Can't you see? The smaller one with the stripes is balancing it on his snout."

Sam leaned forward in the boat with even greater interest then, straining his eyes to see.

"A new arrival, perhaps?" Filbert suggested.

"Well, it could be, I suppose," Mr. Goodfellow shouted. "It is the right season for it, but it's awfully puny for a seal pup, wouldn't you say?"

"Perhaps that's just it," Beatrice piped in. "They've come to show us that they've been blessed with an unusually tiny event this year and—"

But Beatrice's words were suddenly cut short by a loud cry from Charlotte's direction. Everyone stopped talking and turned to look at her. She was as white as a sheet and trembling from head to foot.

"Winston?" she whispered with hesitation, as if she dared not believe her eyes. And then, with growing confidence, she began shouting the name out louder and louder. "Winston! Winston! It's Winston!"

Sam almost fell off his bench. When he recovered, he struggled to maneuver the rowboat closer to the seals. Alice took one of the heavy wooden oars out of her grandfather's hands and began to row. Edgar had already rushed forward to the edge of the rocks. He shouted for a Sea Mouse Knife, and as soon as Mr. Goodfellow had tossed Sam's into his paw, Edgar pulled hard on the tiny ripcord that dangled from it. Just seconds after the bright yellow raft had inflated, Edgar hurled it into the sea, then clambered aboard and began paddling with all of his might. By the time he reached the seals, there was no doubt in his mind that the peanut-sized object bouncing about on the tip of the seal's nose was his own

beloved son. He swept the little boy up into his arms and hugged him tight before he spun the raft around and held the wiggling youngster up for everyone to see. To cheers of jubilation and tears of joy, Edgar brought Winston back to shore and to a reunion that just days before no one would have dared dream possible.

With all The Sage involved in welcoming Winston back, Sam took it upon himself to row out to the seals and to extend to them, as best he could, the gratitude of his friends. To Alice's delight, the entire group circled around the rowboat, splashing in and out of the waves with sheer exuberance. Sam reached over the side and gave each of their sleek gray heads a pat. The opportunity to get this close to the little striped seal was a bonus. When their eyes met *this* time, Sam knew for certain that fate had somehow intervened and allowed his old friend Figgy to find him again. And from that day on, whenever he went sailing or rowing, the little striped seal, like the loyal and faithful companion he had been so many years before, would always turn up at Sam's side.

The Sage were beside themselves with joy, and eternally grateful to the harbor seals for having rescued young Winston. Several seals, so the story went, had been following a school of fish offshore one day when they had found the almost submerged Fen boat with Winston still inside. Not quite sure what to do with the tiny creature, they took him back to the colony and cared for him, until the one with the stripes down his back suggested that they take him to the lighthouse. Winston seemed no worse for wear at having spent a bit of time in a seal colony. There was even one unexpected benefit, and it turned out to be of particular interest to Mr. Goodfellow. It had always irked him that he seemed to be the only member of the family who had never been able to tell one twin from the other. Even

242

Sam appeared to have no difficulty in this regard. But that, to Mr. Goodfellow's great relief, had all changed. From the day he was handed back into the arms of his loving family, Winston displayed an insatiable appetite for sea kelp and (to his mother's distress) the ability to hold his breath underwater for remarkably long periods of time. From that day forward, Mr. Goodfellow never had any reservations about volunteering to supervise the children at bath time, where he could often be found up to his elbows in soapy water, loudly and confidently calling out the names "Grakul," "Winston" and "Little Jolly" to the appropriate bathers.

Even young Porter, who was still very upset over the loss of Jasper, found something special to ease his pain. This had come in the form of a sea snail that he had conveniently stumbled upon on the night of Winston's return. Finding himself high and dry as the tide receded, the snail had all but given up hope until Porter plucked him off a rock, bestowed the name Triton on him and promptly deposited him in the children's bath. This arrangement caused some problems until a bathing schedule could be worked out, but even at that Mr. Goodfellow frequently found a suds-covered snail nestled in the bottom of the bath after he had finished draining the water.

With all of these significant happenings, Delphinia Shipton felt compelled to temporarily lay aside her reclusive way of life, announcing that she would like to stay on at the Goodfellows' to see firsthand what transpired next. Her mystical insights, she declared, seemed to be working overtime. There was such a high volume of metaphysical electricity floating about in the air that the last place she wanted to be was alone in a cave in Cornwall. And Great-Uncle Cyrus, who up until then had been quite happy to remain a remote and somewhat feared member of the Goodfellow clan, suddenly had a change of heart, as well. To everyone's surprise, Cyrus decided to stay on at the front lines with Delphinia, transforming himself from a crusty old disciplinarian into a beloved and patient playmate to all of the children. The former guest rooms at Blue Heron Cottage began to fill up again, but this time Mr. Goodfellow did not raise one word of protest. To have Sage of such high repute as houseguests was an honor he greatly cherished.

In regard to The Fen, Delphinia warned that Sage vigilance must neither weaken nor falter. Now that they found themselves solely responsible for little Grakul, The Sage felt it imperative to protect her from those who would do her harm. Danger would never be far enough away, they knew, as long as the murderous and vengeful Shrike Fen was lurking.

As for Sam, it came as a great comfort that he was no longer alone with his secrets. Now he had Alice, and he was confident that when the time came for her to make her important decision, she would think very carefully and responsibly about her answer. What Sam didn't know was that Alice had already made her decision. Mr. Goodfellow's words rang as true now to Alice as they had to her grandfather seventy-five years before: "Follow your heart, and it will never steer you wrong."

After the arrival of Grakul and the return of Winston, there were many evenings Sam and Alice and The Sage would gather together at the lighthouse. On one of those nights, at one of the small windows that faced the sea, Alice, balancing on a wooden chair, was staring into the night sky. Edgar, sitting on the window ledge next to her, was staring out in another direction, mesmerized by the eerie glow of a crescent moon that seemed to be rising straight out of the sea.

"Did you see that, Edgar!" cried Alice.

"See what?"

"Over there! That shooting star!"

"Rats!" Edgar exclaimed, spinning his head around. "I'm always missing those things. Did you make a wish?"

"Of course I did."

"So...what did you wish for?" Edgar asked. "No, wait!" he added quickly. "You're not supposed to tell me that, are you? It might not come true."

"Well..." Alice whispered. She glanced across the room to where Sam, Delphinia and Great-Uncle Cyrus were poring over The Book of The Sage again. "I think I probably *could* tell you, Edgar. I didn't wish it for me."

Edgar smiled. "For your grandad?"

Alice nodded her head. "I doubt it'll ever come true," she sighed, "but I figured it was worth a try. It's not every day you see a shooting star, right?"

"You wished that Fletcher would come back, didn't you?" Edgar asked, raising his eyebrows.

Alice nodded her head again. "Silly, huh?"

"Well, maybe not," replied Edgar. "Actually, I imagine that anyone unselfish enough to make a wish on someone else's behalf would have to be in line for a top spot on the shooting star list, if there is such a thing. If someone, somewhere, is taking note of good intentions, Alice, then you've got a favorable edge." Edgar smiled and shrugged his shoulders. "And anyway, even if it is just a silly superstition, I still think it was a very kind thing to do." Edgar paused and gave Alice a long and thoughtful look. He hadn't realized until then how much like Sam she really was.

In the days and years to come, as Winston and Little Jolly and Grakul grew up together and thrived, many more chapters in the Books of Sage and Fen and mortal man would be written. Many things both strange and wondrous would be revealed to Sam and Alice and the Goodfellows. They would learn that what transpires along a journey can be just as enlightening as reaching one's destination; that when the door to a mystery is finally opened it may simply reveal a path that leads to another and that the faith and courage of one single soul can alter the course of history. And Edgar Goodfellow would one day discover the answer to a question he had often pondered—that the good intentions of a kind and unselfish heart don't necessarily go unnoticed and that wishes on shooting stars sometimes do come true.